'A haunting, lyrical de [illegible] t *Jasmines* is an uncomp[illegible] r and the women whose [illegible] n takes the reader into the darkest depths of [illegible] d leads them back towards the faintest crack of light and hope. A brave, beautifully written novel.'
— Shahnaz Ahsan, author of *The Jackfruit Chronicles* and *Hashim & Family*

'Saima Begum's *The First Jasmines* is a brave and powerful novel about unspeakable wartime horrors. If the story does not break your heart, her prose will.'
— Sorayya Khan, author of *We Take Our Cities With Us, City of Spies, Five Queen's Road* and *Noor*

'Beyond a harrowing account of wartime violence and its gendered impacts, *The First Jasmines* is a tender and compassionate tale of love and family, of sisterhood and solidarity, of dreams and survival and all the ways in which they shift shapes in the face of pain and brutality. Heartbreaking and powerful. A wonderful read.'
— Silmy Abdullah, author of *Home of the Floating Lily*

'Lyrical and stunning in its prose, *The First Jasmines* gently yet powerfully leads us from the macro narratives of war and wartime sexual violence into its intimate terrain—relational fractures, quiet survival, and the lasting scars of the violence of 1971—making it a must-read.'
— Anam Zakaria, author of *1971: A People's History from Bangladesh, Pakistan and India*

THE FIRST JASMINES

First published in 2025
by Hajar Press C.I.C., London, United Kingdom
www.hajarpress.com
@hajarpress

ISBN 978-1-914221-24-8 Paperback
ISBN 978-1-914221-25-5 EPUB eBook

A Cataloguing-in-Publication data record for this book is available from the British Library.

Cover and interior art: Han Gunji Stephens
Cover design: Samara Jundi
Typesetting: Laura Jones-Rivera / lauraflojo.com

Printed and bound in the United Kingdom by
Clays Ltd, Elcograf S.p.A.

FSC www.fsc.org
MIX
Paper | Supporting responsible forestry
FSC® C018072

THE FIRST JASMINES

SAIMA BEGUM

This book includes descriptions of sexual violence, military violence and death by suicide.

For the women and girls who shared their stories,
wherever they may be

1. ANCIENT FABLES

Midnight was a vengeful orange. Its troubles began with a spark and its fires with a glance. Its flames hopped like hurried frogs away from monsoon rains, sheltered under veranda rooftops, until twilight's blaze dispersed like unsatisfied bees between budding spring leaves. It crawled into schools and down the throats of the young. It marched sideways with those in khaki, empty-eyed.

They marched from Karachi. Lahore. Faisalabad. Rawalpindi. Places that those fleeing had heard of only once or twice. Soldiers from another quarter come to restore order. In the dark, they were kin. Hair the same. Skin almost the same. But the ones who marched were marching from the corners of Gujranwala. From the creases of Peshawar. From the morasses of Multan. From the hinges of Hyderabad. From the innards of Islamabad. They marched a winding path down into Dhaka, casting a shadow that unfolded in three parts. Hair the same. Skin almost the same. Clay hearts rattling in their chests.

As children, when their hearts were still putty, years away from the kiln, they would fight-play. Play-fight. Count down to the kill. Sharpen skills in muddy pathways, high-jump into lakes, wrestle a mother's ice grip, sit firm and flush against her scrubbing hand that would polish mischievous faces until they shone medal-metallic. Poked at chickens and hatching chicks, and ran with putty hearts yearning to feel the fear of the enemy's chase. The first taste of war of the to-be-clay-hearted. Push a brother into traffic, into market stalls, into the madman who sings scripture all day as they walk through the bazaar, a test of strength. Watch the other's fear, memorise his defence for another day. A strategic play. A test of bravery, power and skill. Take the hit. Wear the bruise. The joy of a battle scar.

Midnight tightened its noose around their heads. Its soft touch lingered, whispered into their ears and licked their necks, promising to keep their secrets, kissing them until they confessed their desire to bleed a river crimson. The music of a clay heart makes mist of an orange night. The rhythm of the fight. A place to shine, to meet with honoured ancestors, the ancient ones, to kneel before history beside them. To forge an old man's games with a young man's blood. To one day become, like them, an ancient fable.

Hardened in the kiln under the hands of a skilled practitioner, they marched for God, for glory, for play. Until clay marked the land with fateful footsteps, its boots etching lines between heart and homeland, its shades and shadows erased under the hungry fire. Traitors pointed the way through the marshes, the bushes, the windy, whirly roads to nowhere, until the soldiers emerged ready for a fight-play. A play-fight. The countdown to the kill.

On the other side of midnight, academics pleaded in an alien tongue, their anguish extinguished down the barrel of a bondhok. Embers of orange shone at the end of black sticks setting fire to buildings whose fuel was men and stone. Thin brown bodies which had resisted for so long rested in muddy pools, faces down, curled fingers pointing towards the sky. Tears slid back into sockets as men fell. That night, everyone prayed for mercy, some even for the one whose hand was pointed at them, for they were still brothers in faith.

A flaming body walked across the fields, falling unwillingly into prostration. Until the night was a burning graveyard.

Lucky was crouched over a mortar filled with garlic, crushing the fleeing cloves into a paste, when the army opened fire on students in Dhaka, starting the war. Unaware of what was happening in the distant city, she was complaining to her mother-in-law about the cunning market vendor who had sold her half-spoiled garlic cloves.

'He patched them up himself,' she said, peeling another clove only to find it rotten inside like the others.

'Haramzadah!' her mother-in-law cursed. 'How else could dying cloves have such beautiful skin?'

When the news came to their small town, her mother-in-law insisted the shooting had shaken the subcontinent, that it had sounded like the premature cracking of baby coconuts. Lucky concluded that she herself had heard nothing since it had taken place over two hundred kilometres away.

It was an ancient story that could be traced all the way back to Habil and Qabil, thousands of years before the British came, conquered and cut them into pieces. It was a tale of two brothers and their nation of two tribes: West Pakistan, East Pakistan.

Greed was first to grip the western brother. He pledged allegiance to family while holding the hand of his eastern brother with miserly fingers. Accounts were kept secret and trade routed one way until the people of the East, who outnumbered the people of the West, became thin and gaunt.

Pride came second. Urdu, lingua franca of the West, would be the only national language (*and English,* someone whispered from the back). The western brother mocked the tongue of the eastern Bengalis, took their script off their notes and stamps, taunted their culture, customs, dress and palate.

It was all too Hindu-like.

This was Muslim land.

In the East, the students of Dhaka rose up for their language. They bled against police batons that swung through the air to silence them, warning their brother in the West that he would one day be regretful.

Envy came third. After decades of being squeezed between short-changing hands, the East chose a leader. He spoke a message of hope, dignity, rights, leading his party to a majority in the nation's first direct general elections. It was December 1970, and the people had decided: the leader of the East would be the next one to rule over the two tribes.

Wrath came last. The West overturned the people's vote. The land of the small, dark and dirty could not raise a king. In spring, the leader of the East stood at the podium, the square beneath him filled with bespeckled businessmen and bare-chested, sweat-slicked farmers, the homeless, the sick, the hungry, the thin, the angry, shoulder to shoulder, ready. He declared the East, free in people and in tongue, independent Bangladesh.

At midnight, the army arrived from the West, with support from even further west, to arrest the leader. Paramilitary forces of razakars, volunteers from the East who supported the state, formed committees tasked with whispering into towns and villages and mapping a straight path for the army to enter. Academics, physicians, engineers, writers and students were killed first. Major towns fell. Everyone knew a missing woman. The Mukti Bahini, a guerrilla army of mukti joddhas, freedom fighters, spread across the East to regain territory. For eight months, victory and defeat shuddered and screeched in the wind like rumours, until the dull December of 1971 fell upon them.

While leaflets calling for the independence of Bangladesh circulated in secret, and men and women gathered arms, Lucky set the table like she did every day. Meat bowls in the centre, surrounded by vegetable bowls, and bone plates on the outskirts within arm's reach. She served generous spoonfuls of steaming rice to her mother-in-law and son, Rayan, their knees jiggling, their faces alternating between approval and distress as they scrutinised each mound.

Five spoonfuls for her mother-in-law.

Three spoonfuls for her son.

Outside her kitchen window, old men with knitted brows paced. They paced around the veranda, paced in front of the bazaar and paced knee-deep in the river, nets limp in their hands waiting to catch cory and clarias catfish. The men disappeared and reappeared, talked in hushed tones and requested that their wives again make one last cup of chaa. They gathered on the mosque veranda each evening, circled around Iqbal Nana's son's radio and listened to the news, cursing and spitting out betel nut juice, staining the floor like a fleet of birds, when the station changed to a love song at a critical moment. Their hearts hastened towards a land of their own, but their aged legs could not carry the burden of the freedom fighter.

Frustrated cries made their way to Lucky's ears through the window, but she paid them no heed. To manage a spotless home for a pernickety mother-in-law was no small task. Her mother-in-law was a shrewd woman in her fifties with a serpent's tongue that skewered anyone who challenged her with a fatal slice. Ruthless but polite, making it difficult to condemn her, Lucky's mother-in-law was feared by everyone, including Lucky's late father-in-law. Even children trod cautiously around her lest she turn her forked tongue on them.

Visitors came to their home after lunch each day and Lucky stood on the sidelines of their conversations, hovering over their teacups, ready to refill as soon as they were three-quarters empty. Timing was everything. If the snacks became spare, the ladies would be embarrassed at having eaten too much, and no self-respecting woman reached for the last samosa. Lucky waited for the plate of savoury treats to dwindle to the last three before removing it discreetly and replacing it with a towering plate designed in an inviting geometric swirl. She stood and smiled until they left. To sit was to be idle, and an idle wife was a bad wife. And she preferred to save herself a talking-to from her mother-in-law.

Gossip, pitch-perfect with the rise and fall of a lazily hummed lullaby, always made Lucky doze, but she willed herself to remain alert. A trick question, aimed to disgrace the family, might be cast her way at any moment. Her mother-in-law waited for those moments. If she did not answer with the correct vague aphorism, her mother-in-law spent the following week muttering about shameless women. After years of warfare, some lost, some won, some overcome by treaty, some forfeited by enemy demise, Lucky had armed herself with the perfect set of Quranic verses and generic sayings to quell the women's bloodthirst. She smiled the smile she had perfected long ago, responded with the proper response, maintained her mother-in-law's respectability within the community and, most importantly, peace within her home.

Several murmurs and lazy gestures to leave later, the last of the women departed and the Maghrib azan sounded loud from the nearby mosque. The balls of Lucky's feet throbbed as she cleared plates and cups away, eating leftovers she didn't want to repack. The faster she worked, the sooner she could nap, maybe while her mother-in-law readied herself for bed. By then the maid, Shaheda, would return with Rayan from the market. The markets around town were stocked with different produce and goods each day, and if you missed a day, it was possible not to find the same items again for weeks. Usually Lucky nodded off waiting for them to arrive, and if Rayan could not poke, cuddle or kiss her awake, which was the case most evenings, she woke after he had fallen asleep. Like each cycle of sunrise, the guilt she felt rose and fell as another day passed where she had spoken only a few words to her son.

Tasks snatched her time, filled her to the brim and left the threat of war but a passing whisper that touched the edges of her familiar day. Now, eight months into the war, her persistent fingers hovered around her son's lips.

'We're at war!' her mother-in-law hollered as Rayan protested the last handful of rice. 'Eat up, nati. Who knows when our next meal will be?'

Frightened by his Dadi's words, Rayan choked in haste, worried the military would personally pluck the biryani out of his mouth.

They were short on essentials, but Lucky was not worried. War had not touched their small town beyond small bursts of exodus as Hindu neighbours made way for India. They had enough cooking oil, kerosene and rice stocked for the following summer, and while meals sometimes became tight for Lucky and her mother-in-law, they never did for Rayan. They made sure of it.

Nothing big ever happened in their small town. They were far from the big cities, the big protests and the big call to arms. Yet, somehow, the children and animals smelt the violence wafting in from miles away. A deadly hush hovered over their fun and play, and no matter how many times parents and farmers tried to fan the smell away, they still walked around in quiet fear.

'Don't worry, moyna. The soldiers promised they wouldn't come here, and when we win, we'll eat all the biryani we want!' Lucky whispered to her son, rubbing his back as they both giggled.

At night, Lucky and Shaheda exchanged stories while they tucked Rayan into bed. Their neighbour's relative's son told tales of houses burnt, men and cattle killed and women abducted. The military scattered through the country, extinguishing any shimmer of uprising. Independence had become a filthy word.

Death had become the land. It was in every town and every street, even when it was not. It was a black mist that entered the bodies of men and women and made the revolutionaries and the soldiers roar. It strolled leaving large footprints and stood atop the peaks of towns, looking down at their barefooted people with its shadowy, featureless face. It was a devil who would bite a person with a terrifying cold if they got too close. And when it saw their eyes dim with the humiliation of defeat, it pulled back its horned head, spread its wings and disappeared, only to reappear in a different town, casting a shadow over the clouds so its people ran blind in the darkness.

There were sightings of angels too. One told a child to run the other way. Another sat with them while they hid in the bushes. The angels carried with them sweets, water and stories. Children reunited with their families claimed their parents had been with them the whole time, covering them with their wings. Then there were the witches and the demons who goaded those with weapons, whispering instructions. *Look behind the trees, look behind the wardrobe, look under the dead mother—her child is still alive!*

'Children! Can you believe they would go that far?' Lucky shuddered, turning a wooden hand fan at a steady pace towards her sleeping son, his hair flapping like cricket wings on his forehead.

'There's no shame left in the world, Apa.' Shaheda shook her head. 'None.'

In the early hours of the morning, while Rayan slept soundly next to her and Shaheda snored on the floor beside her bed, Lucky lit a small candle and reread the last letter her husband sent to her.

Waleed was a chef in London. In the evenings he adjusted Indian food for a gora clientele, but his mornings were spent organising demonstrations between Trafalgar Square and Birmingham city centre. The international community needed to know what was happening and they would send help, he wrote. Any day now, help would come. His last letter was dated eight months ago.

For months leading up to the war, Lucky's greatest fear was that the postal service would close. Waleed's letters were her lifeline. Whenever one arrived, she would unseal it over an open fire. The flame set at the right temperature, a blue-orange rather than an orange-blue, the envelope raised high enough that the flame would not turn it brown, low enough that the steam would soften the edges of its lips until they curled outward, the glue unwinding on its own before crisp white paper appeared. If she tore it open she feared a piece of him would be lost with the dust that blew out from the ridges. One of his whispers. Mostly, she feared her mother-in-law would read her page, the page addressed to her that Waleed tucked in at the end. She woke early each morning to wait for his letter to arrive so she could open it carefully, take out her page and reseal it for her mother-in-law to open later.

At night, she examined her page and all the pages before it which she had tucked under a drawer. She had memorised the scratches, the dirt smeared on both sides of the paper, the ink smudges and the partial fingerprints, the creases bent left and right in the corners, and the different smells it had acquired as it passed through different hands in different lands to get to her. Those imperfections comforted her until the next page arrived.

They were almost there. Just a little longer and he would have money to build a big home in their town. A house with more rooms for more children. Separate quarters for Shaheda, who slept on the floor beside her. A stretch of land to grow vegetables. A lake of their own.

There was solace in his words. Her husband knew a lot about a lot of things, and naturally, he knew about the war too. He had been to university, unlike most of the men she knew, and he read books and spoke about them in ways she had never heard before. As a young man he had wanted to be a barrister, but fate would have it that he become a chef. Theirs was not a climate for pursuing dreams, even less so with a wife and son. Fulfilment was within the careless grasp of those who lived under clear skies, but here the heart rationed fulfilment's portion to the stomach, which demanded its share now.

Tracing her fingers over the months-old letter, for the first time, she doubted her husband's words. When she spoke excitedly about his efforts abroad, people only smiled, and as the war pushed on their smiles turned into curt nods. She thumbed the words '*the world will not watch this injustice pass by idly, we have seen it before, and we have learnt'*. The line lay deeper in the page than the rest, the curve of each letter cut into the other side, written with faith. In the dark, under the shadows cast by the mosquito net, she smiled at his conviction.

In England, Waleed's friends and cousins protested with him armed with flags and insults, but Lucky knew her husband's gentle nature would only permit him to cry out in the most measured manner. His heart rattled like a boiling teapot but he always remained calm, so calm that birds rested on his back during prayer on the mosque rooftop, mistaking him for a tree. It was his most radiant quality. Looking at the letter, charred under her frequenting fingertips, she wondered if his way to freedom was possible.

Outside, her mother-in-law's soft morning thuds, measured bumps and heavy huffs sounded distantly, until a succession of thwacks and mad mutterings reached Lucky's ears. She hummed along with its cadence, waiting for her mother-in-law to finish with her theatrics so she could enter the kitchen. Her mother-in-law was among the half of humanity who needed a couple of hours in the morning to acquire manners. A plate clinked against three others. A summoning call. Lucky tied her saree around her waist and tucked the pleat into her petticoat, crooning to a daydream where Waleed returned with his bright, handsome smile and they were a family again.

Turmeric?

Check.

Cardamom?

Check.

Coriander?

Check.

Clove?

Check.

Green chilli?

Check.

'We'll run out of garlic paste soon,' Lucky said, opening a letter from her mother, while her sister, Jamila, made an inventory of the cupboards. She had woken to find Jamila at her door, wild and sweating, with nothing but a small bag on her shoulders.

'We need to hurry,' Jamila said breathlessly, before Lucky could open the door fully. 'I found letters from Ammu, wills for each of us.'

Lucky's mother and sister lived two towns away, in the pink house where Lucky had grown up, overlooking a cauliflower farm. Lucky's Abbu had wanted to paint the house red. After months of fighting, they had settled on pink when Ammu warned that they were inviting the devil into their house. The house was surrounded by cauliflower fields that belonged to Abbu while he was alive. When the season was bad and the produce rough, the house smelt acrid and Ammu, who hated the smell, cursed the day she ever married a cauliflower farmer. Now the house was a faded pink-grey, the fields almost empty, and Ammu too sick to care about the smell.

Until now, Lucky had not heard from Ammu or Jamila in months. Letters were not being delivered, and Ammu forbade her from visiting them after the war began. Jamila took great care of their mother, but Lucky worried. Ammu's sickness was consuming her.

Ammu was in her forties. With no grey hair and not a single wrinkle, beautiful and confident, in the way young widows were, she betrayed nothing of her illness to a passing eye or genial ear, until she had become weak. It hurt to move. She could not eat anything that was not watery. With Jamila's help she slid her feet across the floor to remind her legs they still walked. Most nights, thoughts of Ammu kept Lucky awake. They appeared between the clouds of heat and ribbons of aroma that rose from the pots and pans, into her nose and eyes as she stirred lunch and dinner. They floated with the dust from the floor onto her tongue and into her ears as she swept the rooms. Lucky had only just learnt to love Ammu with the gratitude of a daughter-become-mother, and Ammu's illness threatened to cut her discovery short.

'I left when Ammu was asleep.'

'Did you tell her first?'

'I left a note.'

'She's going to be furious.'

'She doesn't want us to worry but it's bad, Boro Apa, you have to see her now or otherwise...' Jamila didn't finish.

The war had not touched Ammu's town but many of her neighbours had crossed the borders, including Ammu's maid, who had helped Jamila feed and bathe her. Hindu families fled as the first fights broke out, promising to return once there was peace and leaving their keys behind for safekeeping. Now, Ammu and Jamila kept watch over several properties for the owners. Each day, before dusk covered the keyholes, they walked around the neighbourhood making sure the doors and windows of each house were locked, fearing the day when they would rattle a door and it would swing open.

Every night, I pray the war ends so I can be rid of this burden. What should I say to my neighbours if thieves come and take their possessions? Ammu wrote. *Would God forgive an old woman's aged efforts? Would man?*

They would leave in the morning. Lucky ignored her mother-in-law's objections as she packed her bag and avoided her son's pleas to join them. Jamila sat in the corner of the room, her eyes rimmed tree-bark brown, her sandals worn until the wooden soles spiked in all directions. Lucky knew her sister would not have come to her if it were not serious. If death were not circling their family. She had to see Ammu. And when she got there, whatever Ammu's condition was, it would be God's will.

2. THE SWEET-SHOP GIRL

Lucky saw Jamila first. She spotted her curled under the counter of the local sweet shop from the kitchen window. Narrating the sweet-shop girl's movements to Ammu while she cooked became her pre-lunch and pre-dinner activity.

Every afternoon, when the owner left for his midday nap, the sweet-shop girl would appear, like a hungry baby fox, picking the floor for roasted peanuts and fallen peas, before folding herself into the shade cast by the counter to nap. Like clockwork, an hour before dusk, she would rise and begin knocking on doors, asking for a meal and space to sleep for the night. Busy mothers who already had many children shooed her away. Wives whose husbands were too eager to take her in shoved her back into the road. Sometimes a kind stranger took her in for a short time, but eventually she returned to her spot under the counter. Lucky waited for the day the sweet-shop girl would knock on their door so she could ask Ammu and Abbu to let her stay with them forever.

Lucky had no cousins nearby and no close friends at school. She was too interested in her worlds of make-believe that other girls could not imagine, and it didn't take long for others to be annoyed by her. When Lucky told Ammu, she said, 'Friends shouldn't be chosen in a hurry. Wait for one who chooses what's good for you even over your friendship with them. One friend like that is better than a hundred who do the opposite.'

Lucky found no such friend who fit Ammu's description. In their growing faces she saw proclivities towards the desperate, the jealous and the cruel, and other things she had no name for but knew she should turn away from. Only one pair of eyes seemed sincere to her, and it scampered along the edge of everyone's vision like a crow mistaken for its shadow.

Blank-faced, pale and covered in dirt, the sweet-shop girl was fascinating. Her waist-length hair gave her the air of a woman rather than a child, especially to those who looked for those kinds of excuses. Her aged brows sat heavy above distrustful eyes that spoke of loss, her shoulders held no expectations, and she had a stare that looked through the colours of the horizon and into the darkness that congregated at its foundation. A concoction that did not belong on a small, scrawny body. Bare feet already hardened, face set in hushed resignation, yet with a childlike anticipation twinkling in her eyes that at any moment something good might happen. To this there was only one solution.

'Let's ask the sweet-shop girl to live with us, Ammu,' Lucky said one evening, impatient that Jamila still hadn't come knocking at their door. 'She'll be my friend and she can help at home.'

'Hush! Keep your voice down, Lucky,' Ammu said, looking around for Abbu. 'These things are not done.'

'Why? I always hear Abbu saying he wants another child in the house. She's my age. It's perfect.'

Ammu was quiet for a moment, long enough that Lucky grew uncomfortable with the loudness of their breathing. The uneasy feeling building in her stomach told her she had done something wrong.

'You shouldn't speak to grown-ups like that, and you shouldn't listen to their conversations,' Ammu scolded with a firmness in her voice that scared Lucky. 'Never bring this up again.'

Lucky never mentioned it again.

But she hoped. When their eyes met in passing, she smiled at the sweet-shop girl, sending her a secret signal to visit them next. Each evening, Lucky hovered by the front door waiting. She peeked under the curtains and sang songs loudly so the sweet-shop girl could hear there was a friend inside. But the sweet-shop girl never came.

There were nights when the sweet-shop girl was not under the counter and Lucky stopped seeing her knocking on doors. She wondered where she had gone and worried that she had moved under another sweet shop. When she appeared again, she returned with a face painted in pink and blotchy purple arms and legs. Like a spring lake with its flowers in full bloom. She returned sadder—Lucky could tell by the way she dragged her feet and tilted her head down so her hair covered her face. After she came back with the flowers, she stayed under the counter for days. The owner pulled at her until her shoulders clicked and tried to prod her out with his foot, but her dead weight and the empty eyes that glanced up at him made him pause and give up. He let her sleep. Dream in daylight. Forget. Curl up like a cat, arms wrapped around her knees, nose lodged in between, feet tucked under her butt. After a few days, when the dust of bare feet that passed her no longer made her jump and the slap of worn-out wheels hitting potholes no longer made her limbs twitch, the sweet-shop girl returned to the markets and knocked on doors again.

Lucky knew Ammu saw her. She caught Ammu glancing at the sweet-shop girl as they went on errands, but she would look away quickly, bite her lip and ask for forgiveness under her breath. Forgiveness for what, Lucky didn't understand.

Over time, Lucky became obsessed. She documented the sweet-shop girl's activities in her schoolbooks, wrote scripts of conversations she planned to have with her once they were introduced, and prepared a speech to convince Ammu and Abbu to let her move in. That was until Ammu was called into school by her teachers, who showed her the tiny drawings of the sweet-shop girl in the corners of all of Lucky's textbooks.

She got a thrashing that night.

'You're hard-headed, just like your father!' Ammu cried, raining the jharu down on Lucky's back. 'Why can't you let it go?'

That night, Lucky gave up on being friends with the sweet-shop girl forever. For some time afterwards, neither Lucky nor Ammu looked for her. If she was around, they didn't see her. And if Lucky did see her accidentally, she didn't dare mention it. But while she stopped keeping record of the sweet-shop girl's escapades, it wasn't long before she began to follow her again with her eyes.

One day, on a rickshaw back from school, Lucky saw Ammu arguing with a man who pulled at the sweet-shop girl's arm. Ammu's eyes were red, her voice like thunder and her chest heaving so much it reminded Lucky of a rising paratha ready to burst. She had never seen Ammu so angry. A small crowd gathered around them, older women heckled the man, two young men shoved him back, until finally he released the sweet-shop girl and fled. In the crowd, a cluster of bones, with her head hung and her tangled hair a curtain between them, the sweet-shop girl stood deliberating. Everyone's attentions followed the disappearing back of the man who had wanted to take her away. No one looked at her but Lucky. By the time Ammu turned back to the sweet-shop girl, she had run too far in the other direction. For the next week, Ammu hovered around the kitchen window with Lucky, both pretending not to look, but the sweet-shop girl had gone.

She returned the day of Abbu's funeral. That day, with Lucky crying at her side, Ammu tapped the sweet-shop girl's sleeping nose and offered her a home. She didn't say yes, no, or even raise her head to indicate she had heard Ammu, but she allowed Ammu to take her hand and lead her into their house. From then, Lucky and Jamila were sisters.

Jamila was quiet. She shied away from everyone, including Ammu, and whispered only yeses and noes, hid behind walls and pillars and ate when everyone else had left the table, sat in strange shapes with her elbows and knees in the wrong directions as if ready to wield them as weapons should anyone get in her way. But Jamila loved Lucky. At that age, she felt what she came to understand later was the recognition of two souls. A divine connection. A celestial gift. She had felt it when Lucky desperately squinted at her from the kitchen window with eyes which held no judgement or irritation, only curiosity and fascination. And need. It was a look Jamila had never seen before. It scared her at first. It felt like the first shiver of crisp lake water on her bare skin. She spent a long time searching for its name. When it didn't come and she found no way to hold on to the feeling in her chest, she decided it was best ignored. She avoided the house with the little girl who needed her. Just when she thought she had squashed the yearning to know more, she surprised herself at how easily she accepted their hand when Lucky and Ammu reached out to her.

Ammu spent a long time preparing Jamila's room, laying out her best pillows and most colourful blankets, ones she had spent months stitching flowers onto, but the sisters always fell asleep together in Lucky's room, Lucky on the bed and Jamila on the floor facing her. It took another season of midnight whispers for Ammu to find two sets of arms and legs hanging off the bed. When winter blew through the windows, Ammu gave in, bought a big bed and pulled out the big blanket, and turned Jamila's bedroom back into a sewing room.

The sisters watched everything together. Baby frogs that hopped onto the pathway to be pointed at, bold, colourful stickers stuck on the inside and outside of rickshaw hoods, stray dogs that growled at old men who followed them, red chilli salt powder sprinkled on green apples sliced into flowers, a rich person's motor car stuck in poor mud roads, agreeing that it could all be laughed at. Words were not necessary. Small gestures made with their fingers, toes, elbows, knees and the midnight eyes of one were enough for the other. And though hardly anyone heard Jamila speak, they both got into trouble at school for talking too much. Her stoic stare, the straightness of her lips, the flatness of her brows spoke to Lucky, and she understood perfectly. As punishment, Ammu had them sit in silence. The girls complied easily, sitting on the floor facing each other for hours, able to make a game of anything.

They disagreed on only one thing. Lucky was younger by two years but still Jamila called her Boro Apa, big sister. It caused many fights.

'It makes me sound old!' Lucky complained to Ammu after they had fought again, this time with nails and teeth. 'And it doesn't make sense.'

'Remember, moyna, Jamila had a hard life before she met us, and this is her way of showing she cares about you. Give her time to drop the formalities,' Ammu said. But she never did, and Lucky learnt to live with it.

Years later, when Lucky grew into Ammu's round chin, small eyes and undefined nose, she realised Jamila was beautiful. Boys at school offered her sweets. Old men made lewd gestures at her on the road. Teenage girls disliked her for no reason. She swerved rickshaws off dirt roads and pacified rowdy village children into shy smiles. Ammu cautioned Jamila about her fair skin that shimmered golden in the sunlight, her wide eyes that enticed like thick, juicy dates and her oval face of uncertain age. Jamila always shrugged, uninterested in people's compliments or Ammu's caution. To happiness, sadness and surprise, she showed the same straight face. It was a comfort to Ammu, who didn't want to tell her yet that a beautiful girl couldn't smile because it was an invitation, and an ugly girl couldn't ask for more because it was ingratitude. That this was the way of the world.

'Happiness isn't real,' Jamila told Lucky one day.

'What?' Lucky laughed at her sister's coarse statement.

They lay under a jackfruit tree in their uniforms. They had just graduated secondary school and could think of nothing better to do but count the jackfruits under their neighbour Mr Ahmed's tree.

'All right, it is, but I don't know why we're all searching for it so hard, it barely lasts an evening.'

'And those are the evenings we live for.'

Jamila bit her lip. 'I'm not sure I've ever felt it.'

'Happiness?'

'Happiness, real happiness. Most of the time... I feel nothing inside. Like an empty mishti box.'

'What mishti was inside before?'

'Laddoo.'

'Then it's sticky inside.'

'Sticky is sad, not happy.'

'Aren't we happy now?'

Jamila said nothing. Her head toppled sceptically to the side to look at Lucky, like a pineapple carved in unskilled hands.

'Are you saying you're not happy in my company?' Lucky said. 'You'll hurt my feelings.'

'This is different.'

'It's not, this is happiness too.'

'How do I know that?'

'Once you decide that's what you'll call it.'

'Ha!'

Unlike Jamila, Lucky never got a second glance. Her aunties noticed. Ammu worried about it. Born milky-light, she later grew into a heavy brown, the shade that was fine on fathers and brothers but became difficult if it spread to their daughters. When it came time to be noticed by men, Ammu slathered her in a holud mask each day. Turmeric, gram flour, milk or yoghurt, and two squeezes of lemon juice for extra power. Face, neck, down her chest, the tips of her fingers to above her elbows and the tips of her toes to above her ankles. Places that could be seen if her dupatta unravelled in the wind. Standing like a terracotta Lakshmi statue draped with marigold garlands, she waited each morning for the sun to crease her skin so yellow clay would break and peel like the first layer of soil under a drought. So her brownness would become whiteness. So someone would marry her.

When she married Waleed, it was a first for them all. He was the first man to approach Ammu for her hand in person and not through his parents' string of communal checks and balances. The first to hold Lucky's hand in his, though his hand was lighter than hers. Waleed was more handsome than she was beautiful. *He'll turn away from you,* they said, so she worried about the different shades of darkness that coloured her body, and whether when his skin touched hers, he would notice the difference too. She avoided the sun, watched the day turn into night from inside her home and waited patiently to become beautiful.

It was Jamila who told her the story about the sun and the moon. Jamila's Nani hadn't stepped into sunlight for seventy-five years because her husband liked pale women. At ninety years old she was free of brown spots, hardened creases, and still had soft hands while others her age had leather touches. But when she looked upon those faces that cried for her in her last moments, in their range of shades, with their creases, spots, scars and marks, and saw that they loved her as she was and that she loved them as they were in return, she knew she had been mistaken. She feared she'd die a sinner if she didn't leave her granddaughter Jamila with a word of goodness.

'The sun is not more beautiful than the moon, the sea is not more beautiful than the rain, and lightning is not more beautiful than the trees that bend with fruit. There is no difference in beauty in the different-coloured flowers, just as there is no difference in beauty in the different-coloured skins,' her grandmother told fair little Jamila, who had a chance to live differently.

When Lucky kissed Ammu and Jamila goodbye on her wedding day, it was the first time she saw Jamila cry. Her sister wiped at her eyes with a fist like a child, and Lucky loved her even more for it.

3. CLEAR PROOF

At noon, Lucky kissed her son's face and hands, unfurling his fists from her saree with the help of her mother-in-law and Shaheda, who pulled at him from behind. Her chest tightened at his wobbly lip and big, wet pleas not to leave. It was the first time she would travel without him. Before her mother-in-law could interject, Lucky pushed Jamila out the door with a rushed salam and damp lashes. With clothes strapped to their backs and a tower of tiffin carriers in each hand, Lucky and Jamila set off to return to Ammu.

The roads were lawless and busy. Children ran between rickshaws and cars, knocking on windows and tapping knees for spare rupees, stomachs protesting another drink from a muddy puddle. Pickpockets strolled through gridlock, bumping into bags hanging from the sides of open vehicles. Stray dogs lay curled up like jilapi behind street vendors and empty clothes shops. A layer of dust and broken stone, crumbled from homes and businesses, blew over Lucky's skin, clothes and mouth as she gaped at the ruined town.

'The army passed through here,' the driver, Shahzad, said, filling the silence at the back of the tuk-tuk. 'We're taking a longer route to avoid the schools. They were razakar camps for a short time and we don't know who might still be there.'

Razakars occupied mosques and schools as bases to detain Bengali nationalists. People entered the buildings and never came out. When the Mukti Bahini took back the territory, they found bodies piled to the ceilings, abandoned before they could be hidden from history within mass graves.

'The devil sows discord between brothers!' the local madman shouted as they passed him.

'He gets saner by the day,' Shahzad joked.

Charred temples stained the landscape like broken ink pots. Debris from mosques lay across the ground in small piles. The skeleton of a door was all that was left standing of an orphanage.

'And they call themselves brothers in faith. The people here were simple people with no interest in politics. The mukti joddhas have reclaimed the town but they can't rest to rebuild it. People are coming back and by Allah, the Merciful, children will play here again.'

Just then they passed a group of children sleeping by the riverbank, some of the older children asleep with toddlers in their arms.

'Let's move along quickly,' Jamila said, cutting the conversation short.

They stopped at a small market halfway to Ammu's house. Lucky bought biscuits, bananas and mangoes. A small golden light caught her attention while she waited for her change.

'You're wearing the earrings he bought you,' Lucky teased, cocking her head towards her sister. Hanging from Jamila's ears were gold-painted earrings in the shape of a birdcage. Little balls dangled around the edges of the bottomless cage. Lucky could hear them jingle when she stood close. 'Do you admit you're excited to marry him? Dare I say it, is my stone-hearted Jamila in love?'

'Stop!' Jamila said, pushing Lucky into the dirt path with the side of her body, the bags in their hands swinging dangerously near pond water, her face tinged pink. 'The date is set. There's nothing more to talk about.'

Lucky laughed at the terrifying scowl on Jamila's face. Her sister never admitted when she liked something and it was unlikely she would confess her feelings for Rahat, even on her wedding day. Her heart was a fortress, guarded by suspicion and disbelief, having discarded sentimental illusions long ago. She had never liked a man, let alone loved one. What was there to like? They were silly and uncertain and expected too much. Or so she said.

The two sisters walked around the pond bickering, hidden behind a band of palm trees and bush, when the thunder of military trucks pierced the air.

Jeeps stopped in the middle of the road. Soldiers stepped off shouting and cursing, booting barefoot drivers from rickshaws, patting customers down for plunder. Market vendors fled, leaving hard-earned harvest behind them.

Dragged from his tuk-tuk, Shahzad struggled against a barrage of blows. Their bags and tiffins were flung to the ground.

Jamila grabbed the arm of her sister, who stood trembling in disbelief, and pulled her into the bushes behind them.

An argument arose. Bangla clashed with Urdu. A rickshaw fell sideways. Shahzad stumbled over his lungi to the ground. Black boots stomped on his face like bay leaves caught under a hailstorm. Blood splatter darkened the mud road.

Beside Lucky, Jamila drew short, hard breaths. Taking Lucky's bag from her, she grabbed her sister's cold hand and squeezed hard.

'We're going back,' Jamila said, pulling them further into the bushes, until the scene behind them was lost behind dense trees and the arguing made faint by the brush. 'We're halfway from your husband's town. We can make it.'

'No.' Lucky dug her heels into the ground, stalling them.

'Boro Apa!'

'They're passing through. We'll wait for them to leave and go by foot. We're closer to Ammu,' Lucky pleaded, her voice breaking as her eyes flitted between each shivering branch. 'She needs us.'

'It's too dangerous to wait.'

'Then you go back.'

Silence. Jamila pushed down the sting in her eye. Beyond the bush, the sound of gunfire shook birds out of their nests. Inside the bush, they only heard each other.

'We're no good to Ammu dead.'

'We hide until they're gone, there's nothing here, they won't stay.'

'They'll stay wherever they take!'

'Please, Jamila. We have to see Ammu.'

Jamila's face was stone. She wore this expression whenever she stepped aside on family matters as the daughter who came second and who had less right over Ammu than the first. Lucky spent years delicately assembling their lives to prevent its appearance, but now she cast her creed aside and pulled Jamila's hand to her chest desperately. 'Please, Jamila.'

Toes tumbled over wayward roots and loose rocks. Sarees tore against twigs. Branches stabbed at their bodies. The ruckus became a dim hum in the distance and gave stage to their heaving chests. Lucky fell to her knees, her burning calves giving way.

'Let's stop here,' Jamila gasped, sliding down a royal palm tree. Sweat seeped through her blouse attracting wayward leaves. Her juddering arms and legs shook holes into the ground. Above them, small specks of light peeking through the leaves spoke of the setting sun.

They sat in the foliage. Beetles and crawlies creeped on their bellies, trespassed over their toes. Every so often, a jeep roared past and a twang of Urdu disrupted the night. Like twin mushrooms, huddled amongst the undergrowth, Lucky and Jamila watched the sky change from an inky black to indigo to navy to blue, and then to a bright white. A spectral show reserved for masked palm civets and small muntjacs.

Moonlight cast scattered shadows across the treetops. Bamboo trees hung like nooses from the sky. Under a canopy of gloom, heavy breathing was approaching.

Lucky and Jamila sat stone-still, clutching hands, faces hidden behind broad sal leaves. With her other hand, Jamila held the sharp metal edge of a tiffin container above their heads, ready to strike, murmuring prayers under her breath.

'Hurry, Mihir!' said a small voice.

'I can't!'

Stifled sobs and whispers startled nearby squirrels back into their burrows. Lucky rose slowly against Jamila's remonstrating grip.

'Children,' she called into the darkness. 'Walk towards my voice.'

Dawn's dam spilled over, and the sisters met Minna and Mihir, siblings aged nine and six. Their village had been set on fire. Abbi instructed them to run, promising to follow soon with Ammi. That was four days ago. The children ate the bananas Lucky gave them quietly. Neither of them cried. Lucky looked to Jamila, who shook her head.

The next morning, the women split a biscuit between them. The food they had bought would last their group of four another day or two.

'Lucky-ma, are we going to die?' Mihir asked.

The boy's courage to ask questions that adults shied away from made her tremble. Such brazen questions from Rayan were hushed to protect him from the machinations of God and man, but faced with Mihir's mortality, Lucky realised she had only hurt her son with her silence in a world that would not spare him. Mihir sat in her arms looking up at her. She struggled to give him an answer.

'No, my darling,' she said, smoothing Mihir's hair out of his face. 'We'll find your Ammi and Abbi when it's safe to move. Nothing will happen to you.'

'Ammi is in the house,' he whispered. The lump in Lucky's throat blocked her words.

'We don't know that,' Jamila interrupted, poking at Mihir's stomach. 'I hope you can cook, mister. When we get to your house, you'll make us delicious sweets, won't you? We shared ours with you, it's only fair.'

Mihir nodded. Minna sat apart from them. She was old enough to understand what had happened and wise enough to let her brother hope. Jamila pulled her close and waited. When Minna's tears seeped into her blouse, she rocked her. Minna cried politely with no sound and no shiver, like a girl used to being forgotten.

'I'm going to tell God about this,' Minna whispered into Jamila's breast.

'As you should,' Jamila said.

A long way away, gunfire pushed the birds out, ceasing sunlight's song. Lucky counted eleven stars that shone so bright they eclipsed the moon, which stood shy behind a cloud. The stillness of the bush unnerved her. Its silence smelt like a cold, musty grave. During the day, she asked the children to tell her stories to distract her nose, but when it was her turn to keep watch of the night, the smell seeped into her ears and eyes and through her fingertips, pulling her into the ground with it.

'I'll fast today,' Lucky said.

'Will our fast be accepted if we can't break it with food?'

'I don't know.' A booming noise ahead shook the ground, disrupting the journey of the coral kukri snakes around them. Birds shrieked back in outrage. 'We'll be fine, but the children won't last long.'

They watched the children sleep, shooing cockroaches and fanning mosquitoes away. Mihir scratched at his bites, drawing blood. Lucky placed his mud-covered feet on her lap, gently massaging them to bring the flesh colour back. He was a few years older than her son, with eyes too big for his head and baby fat still clinging to his bones. In the dark, she was afraid each leaf and twig would draw his blood and the animals and insects that orchestrated the night-song would devour him if she didn't keep her hands on him. Next to her brother, Minna shivered in her nightdress. Her arms and legs bare, unblemished by womanhood and its expectations. An oasis to innocent and filthy eyes alike.

The war would not touch their town, Lucky had promised her son. Now, her face against the soil of the forest floor was clear proof that it could reach them all. Her thoughts drifted to Ammu. Would the soldiers have mercy on a sick woman all alone? Then her mother-in-law. Would they spare an old woman and her grandson? The stories she had heard told her otherwise. She pressed her hand across Mihir's forehead, then placed her cheek against his. Fever scorched his skin, the moist air and soil becoming a boiling pot.

'I'll bathe him in the morning, that'll fix his temperature,' she whispered to Jamila. On one of their excursions looking for fruit, they had found a small pond nearby.

'We'll go together,' Jamila said.

Wrapping the head of her saree around his shivering body, Lucky burrowed close to him, resting her nose in his hair as their heads lay on a mosaic of leaves. Minna huddled against Jamila, cocooned under a tali tree. Small palash, tuberose and madhu kamini flowers grew around them in litters. Night-blooming jasmines woke while they slept, daylight's timid bud unravelling its luscious fragrance in the hours of darkness. In the stifling silence, they became new points of focus for night-time creatures in their green home. A garden of delight.

'There's only one truck left on the main road. The gunfire is fading. We'll take the children to Ammu's house once it leaves,' Lucky said, knowing they would be betraying the children, who believed they were returning to their village. Jamila was silent.

Jackals howled all night. But it was the roaring of army trucks that rattled their hearts with sleeplessness.

The bulbuls ceased their dawn twittering and the markets stood calm ahead of the trucks that terrorised the roads. Lucky slept entwined with Mihir, like a spotted crake sheltering its new-born, when she woke to a baton to the face.

Blood spilled onto her tongue with fury. Stunned by her ringing ears, she dug her fingers into the ground to stop her swirling vision. The air burned with metal mixed with tangy male sweat.

The soldiers had found them.

Large vultures swooped down and plucked Mihir from her side. 'Lucky-ma!'

She lunged after him. Grassland green clashed with khaki in front of her as she struggled to stand.

'Please, don't. Please!' Jamila cried, her pleas ignored.

A soldier hauled Minna out of the backwoods and passed her into another pair of harsh hands.

An alien tongue spat at them. 'Put them in with the others.'

Hidden behind the bushes, alone on a mud-beaten path, stood two jeeps. Beside them, a soldier urinated into a muddy spring. He turned his head towards them and winked.

Exposed to the hazy humid heat, piled on top of each other in the jeeps were half a dozen blindfolded, half-dead women. They sat in silence. Shivering. They smelt of ripe banana leaves and sun-dried mud roads recently doused in monsoon rains. *God help us,* Lucky prayed.

A baby masked palm civet peered from behind broad leaves and listened to the thump, thump, thump of metal on flesh. It sprayed its scent towards the soldiers as Lucky and Jamila cowered on the ground. It squawked as the soldiers bound the sisters' eyes and threw them into a jeep, knocking them into the skeletal women sitting numb with fear.

The jeep rocked side to side, dipping low, thrusting upwards, until limb knocked limb, making clanging sounds. With every few potholes, the soldiers cursed and complained of the low-lying land of low, lying people.

Under the darkness of the tight blindfold, all the aches and pains Lucky had ignored over the years now touched her. Once, her smile had become lopsided from all her overworking. 'Ammi, your laugh is wonky!' her son had pointed out, its miserable weight sliding her eye down on one side, but she didn't stop to look or attend to it. Now, as the truck slipped in and out of sinkholes, the clarity of each wound and the sorrow of the side of her face that pulled downward more than the other gathered in her eyes, and she cried.

After some time, the air chilled and the smell of salt filled their noses. The smooth rush of waves drowned out the noise of crunching wheels. Planes shrieked above, entering and exiting the airstrip occupied by the Air Force. Unbeknown, navy gunboats pointed at them as they passed, punishing the sea for echoing the noise of procession and slogan.

The jeep came to a stop.

On a day when the musky heat blazed forth, almost bursting with rage, and seagulls flew alongside military planes, the room drew its breath as soldiers pushed Lucky, Jamila and Minna inside.

The women in the room were all different. Some were young, a few years older than Minna, teens separated from their families as they fled. Others were older, perhaps in their thirties. But the limpness of their bodies was the same. They sat in curved shapes, like the skins of green beans which curled inward once the beans had been pulled out.

Snippets of song interrupted the silence. A prayer. The Quran. The Vedas. A lullaby sung to the children.

A woman sat in the corner without a blouse, the thin, sheer material of her saree exposing the sharpness of her ribs and the cuts along her back. Another hummed, rocking against a woman who knelt face down in perpetual prayer. They sat in petticoats, their bloated bellies hanging from frayed belts. Their greasy hair, unravelled and knotted, touched the ground, gathering dust and ants.

Lucky, Jamila and Minna huddled in the corner of the room. Arms tight around each other, the thumping heart of one shaking the hearts of her sisters. Small fists gripped the edges of Lucky's blouse so the material dug into her skin. The women stared. Empty-eyed. Numb with knowing.

Out of the lone barred window, Lucky saw the sky had fallen low on the small village-made-camp where monsters wearing human masks congregated. The soldiers occupied every house on every side of the camp. The room lay in the middle, surrounded. Designed perfectly to chain wayward men to an unholy mission. She heard soldiers laugh and joke in the distance.

A tall soldier strolled in, rifle strapped across his back, eyes appraising the inventory. The bones of their ankles raised his brow, their bare legs made him salivate and their open torsos made him smile. He took in Minna's small fingers and toes, her skinny body engulfed by the two women holding her beneath their breasts. A yolk between two sides of a cracked shell. He hadn't eaten an egg since the war began. The soldier strode over, kicked a shell to the side and snatched the yolk from its cocoon, pulling it towards the door.

'Khobis!' Lucky yelled, clinging to Minna, terror swelling in her gut and stinging her cheeks.

The tall soldier turned his rifle and hit back. When Lucky fell, no one said a word. When he crushed Jamila's hands with his boots, some women looked away, others closed their eyes. When Minna shouted for her Ammi, they covered their faces.

Another soldier sat on a chair inside the room by the door, watching them with one crossed eye on Minna and another on Lucky, finger resting on the trigger of the rifle butt balanced on his knee, its mouth kissing the ground. Ready.

Lucky charged forward, grabbing hold of the tall soldier's leg. He gripped Minna by the hair, dangling her to the side, and crouched beside Lucky's ears.

'You'll be well taken care of here,' he whispered, in broken Bangla. 'If you're good, we'll treat you like a queen. If you try to escape, we'll kill you.'

As he dragged Minna from the room, she looked older, her

edges sharper. The whites of her eyes had become wide with understanding and her small fingers quivered at her fortune.

'Don't speak to them,' a woman said to Lucky as she cried. 'You'll die sooner if you do.'

Lucky turned to Jamila, gripping her hands. 'The mukti joddhas are everywhere. It won't be long before we're freed, we'll take Minna and leave, Waleed—'

The look on Jamila's face stopped her. There lay a wildness in her eyes she had never seen before.

'Waleed isn't here,' Jamila snapped. 'We must save ourselves!'

The room howled with distant screams. Its shadows passed over their faces as jeeps entered and left the camp. A missile screeched in the distance, drowning out the last breath of a little girl crushed beneath a man, never to be seen again. It landed on the edge of a small village, scattering tin homes and haystacks, leaving a great black moonscape in the ground. The mark of the night when Lucky first prayed for death upon a man.

4. THE WOMEN

The waste bucket was potent at night. It drove away birds and foxes, leaving only the static of festive flies. Cockroaches and rats competed with mosquitoes to pierce flesh and feast on the women who lay motionless, sleeping, knitted together, limbs touching, neither dying nor living.

Most stayed silent during the day. Once night fell, some wept loudly, some softly. Some sang a wordless song that came from the gut, a mournful a cappella.

A lone window was squished between several patched-up panels, nothing visible from the outside but the thick black threads of hair of the women inside, shimmering liquid under moonlight. Some nights, even the moon deserted them. Nights so dark Lucky could not see her hand in front of her face. Only hear the thump, thump, thump of the ants marching on.

The mud floor was a patchwork of browns. Pistachio shells from a life long ago peeked between the network of dried, connecting rivers that ran between them. A chalk grey-brown river where the soil cracked. A moist orange-brown river where their warm bodies lay. A deep fertile brown river where their tears landed, creating a pit stop of plenty, an oasis for travelling insects and flower seeds to reawaken. From this land rose green stalks that walked with black boots.

The soldiers never took off their uniforms. Khaki hung from the sharp edges of their shoulders, rested on their pointed ears and gathered loose around their hips. A jagged khaki trail of mountainous ravine for the women's attention to drift into while their bodies left the world. They remained silent, watching, clawing, tasting, while the women listened to the violent clanging of gold and silver medals beating on their chests, smiling down at them. A smile that lingered in the women's stomachs, like a gathering storm, long after the soldiers left.

Now, you are pure, they whispered once they were done.

When the sky lightened to a deep-sea blue, the soldiers left the room long enough for the women to reach for their hearts under their torn blouses. In the room, young girls yet to grow into their breasts learnt to scream without moving their lips. Lucky and Jamila watched as they clutched at their chests in their sleep, fingers clawing to reach inside and hold their hearts with their hands. To soothe. To make sure their heart was still beating, and if it wasn't, to squeeze it with their fists. Pump their veins with their fingertips. To scatter the fear that it would betray them, enticed by whispers to surrender its duties to the flesh and make it all go away.

At night, under the soft glow of the lantern, Lucky counted twenty-two heartbeats rising and falling. The tin roof shook with each murmur of the wind and bellowed with each patter of rain, until their bones echoed with its nocturnal melody. A tangled sea of tired limbs stretched across the floor, each drop of sweat spreading like ink onto another. In the room, if you saw a woman, you saw them all, and if you saw them all, you saw a woman. A gathering of souls in a single body. The room swayed with the rhythm of their weak, limp bodies and after a while in the darkness she no longer remembered where she began or where she ended. Her hands, her feet, her flesh belonged to all. Each night, she feared she would soon wake up to see herself with someone else's eyes.

'Stop thinking terrible things.'

Lucky turned to Jamila. 'There's nothing else to think about.'

'You're forgetting I'm here with you,' Jamila said, winding their hands together. They sat for a moment feeling the warmth of the other's grasp, enjoying the welcome embrace between palms that had never lied to each other. Its softness felt like summer, of fields heavy with wheat and vegetables, of trees dropping gifts into the hands of two sisters drowning out the yells of chasing farmers with their girlish laughter. Sunrise filled the room and Jamila's fingers became thoughtful around Lucky's. Small strokes circling the joints. A loving, considerate heat. The slow crawl of light over their bodies, up the walls and into the roof confirmed to Jamila what she had been debating. 'I won't let anything happen to you,' she vowed.

The soldiers came every day. In the reflection of their black eyes, Lucky saw herself shrunken. She discerned a slight figure, with downcast eyes that tilted sad; an undefined nose, good for measuring sweetness and spice, now shrivelled and crusted over with a layer of dried blood; thin lips, a musky berry, crumbled and parched grey; a dark complexion made darker by their darkness; and long, wavy hair, the only beauty about her, afraid that one day soon it might be knotted in clumps beneath a soldier's fist, as if he had the power to stretch and shrink the ocean with his hands.

If only you were your mother's colour. Family and friends had lamented her dark complexion her whole life, and even here, a woman's worst crime was to be ugly. But today, the reminder that she was no great beauty comforted her. There was nothing to be mistaken. No invitation. No sultry smiles. No longing looks. When the time came, no one could say she had invited the ocean to drown her.

'Close your eyes,' Jamila said. 'The longer they stay open, the more you'll remember when you leave.'

'What I see with my eyes closed is worse than what I see with them open,' Lucky replied. Terror possessed her body once again. 'What will happen to Rayan if I don't return?'

'You will return, heaven couldn't stop you from getting back to him.'

'What am I against the heavens?'

'A praying mother.'

In the morning, when soldiers arrived refreshed, some women showed determination. They stood up as soon as a soldier entered, a mango in his hand, chewing loudly, sucking on the seed, letting the juice drip down his chin and onto the small, colourful square accolades on his lapel. The women smiled a smile they rested all night to raise, took his outstretched hand, and walked out with purpose. Those women didn't return for days. When they did, they returned carrying a plate of ruti and daal for all to share. Food that went down Lucky's throat like thorns.

Lucky neither stretched out her hand nor pulled it back. She remained a migrating bird, in search of seeds, soaring between shelter and predator, without a place to land. Jamila took food for them both, forcing Lucky to eat from her hand when she had missed so many meals she could no longer sit upright. When Lucky pushed Jamila's hand away, Jamila reminded her, 'You're no good to your son starved.'

'How does it go down your throat?' Lucky asked.

'Easily, this food is ours, not theirs.'

Whenever a new woman came, the old ones asked her about the outside. Which side was gaining? Did she know of so-and-so of such-and-such district? Was help travelling their way? Silence, clear for all to understand, was the reply.

Once again, night fell. Clouds drifted through Lucky's heart as she watched a shadow fist pull a shadow girl through a shadow door. Strange questions entered her mind at rest. If she touched the candlelight in the room's corner with her eyes, would it melt like ghee under the sun or shine like glazed sugar on jilapi? If she rested her forehead on the mouth of a soldier's gun, would he shoot her or take it as an invitation to have her for the night? The questions haunted her until sunrise.

The women were of different ages, the youngest of them still on the edges of girlhood. Muslim, Hindu, Buddhist, upper, middle and lower classes and castes. Most of them, like Mohini, Rabia, Chanda and Suhana, the camp cook, came from villages. A handful came from towns, like Rokeya, a university student, and Sumayyah and Noori, secondary school friends.

Zoleyka, the oldest of them, somewhere in her thirties, never spoke. Each day, her fingers creaking with the smallest movement, she braided her hair in different patterns. Plait braid, single braid, lace braid, ladder braid, fishtail braid. When the soldiers came, they grabbed at the end and pulled her head like fishermen pulling a net full of bounty back from the sea.

Each morning tears pooled in her sockets, swished side to side, settled in even puddles and fell silently from both corners. Two streams from each eye. As if she had four eyes, feeling twice as much pain as the rest of them.

The only time Lucky had seen Ammu cry, she also cried in four streams.

The day was stripping away into the night and baby frogs pounced onto their veranda, peeking inside for shelter. Ammu shooed them away, but not before Lucky had placed the smallest into her frilly pocket, just as Abbu returned from the cauliflower fields with muddy sandals, a sweat-soaked shirt, and a lungi in need of patching up.

Ammu and Abbu's routine was as follows. First, Ammu followed Abbu into their room and laid out clothes for him on their bed while he washed from a bucket that she had dipped her fingers into exactly four times to make sure it was warm-hot like he liked. They discussed how many men had come to work that day, how many cauliflowers Abbu and his employees had picked, how big the leaves were, how many snakes and rats had got to them first, how many had gone bad, how much it had rained the night before, how much rain would be best, if they had more or less to sell than last year, how much they would sell for in the struggling market. Ammu listened until Abbu was clean and happy in a fresh shirt and lungi. Then she dried his hair before they joined the dinner table, where an impatient

Lucky pinched rice from the bowl into her mouth one grain at a time.

One Tuesday, and Lucky knew it was Tuesday, because Abbu always came home with a roll of money from the week's sales on Tuesdays, Ammu and Abbu remained in their room for a long time. So long that she released her baby frog at the door herself instead of waiting for Ammu to scold her, then set the remaining dishes on the table, walking snail-slow to and from the kitchen so as not to spill anything.

Under the buzzing lantern light, for the current had gone off across town at lunch time, Lucky heard thuds through the thin walls between the kitchen and Ammu and Abbu's bedroom. When tapping the sticky rice had lost its appeal and licking the paisley patterns around the bowl was complete, she slid her feet along the tile lines without lifting them and looked into her parents' bedroom, her eyes level with the keyhole. Abbu stood in front of the keyhole, his back covering half the room. The door hadn't closed fully and only rested against its frame. Lucky slid her fingers up and down the gap, feeling the coolness of the room on her fingertips. Somehow, she knew not to pull it open. Or close it shut.

Abbu suddenly pushed his fist into the wardrobe until it rattled, growling words to Ammu that Lucky couldn't make out. Ammu fluttered around him like a butterfly and pulled on his arms. Lucky heard Ammu say her name. It made Abbu's back stiffen. Then, he rushed forward and dug his fingers into Ammu's arms. The house was silent for a moment and Lucky felt the pressure of the sky in the room. One. Two. Three.

Thunder came from Abbu's chest before he shook Ammu so hard her face disappeared under the keyhole. A wet thud. Like the sound Lucky's butt made when she slipped and fell on the bathroom floor under the grip of Ammu's scrubbing hands. Lucky's chest began to pound until she saw the beating of her heart in the squiggles in her eyes. The air curdled thick and clumpy so it was hard for Lucky to breathe. The back of Abbu's lungi brushed Ammu's face as she sat on the floor, the shawl of her saree strewn across the ground halfway to the keyhole and Lucky, whose small fingers lay frozen on the side of the door.

Two streams fell slowly from the corners of each of Ammu's eyes. Not racing, not arguing, but waiting to meet each other's step, until all four streams dropped in perfect lines down Ammu's face and into her open palms. They tiptoed quietly to the middle of her hands until Lucky saw them turn into a puddle in the window's reflection. The puddle grew into a pond, and Lucky thought of all the lotus flowers and fish that could live in Ammu's palms if she never moved her hands from that position again. When the pond, now a vast lake, grew legs and travelled down the side of Ammu's hands like a waterfall, Lucky felt a clock ticking in her chest, so loud it began to chime in her head.

The rice was becoming cold. Ammu and Abbu needed to sit at the table quickly or they would need to heat everything again. Abbu liked to eat on time. Lucky walked to the table backwards, her feet no longer following the tile lines. She touched the tip of the rice mound with her little finger. Warm. Not hot the way Abbu liked it. The clock ticked louder. She kept her eyes on the table as Ammu's slow shuffle reached the bedroom door and made its way to the dining table. When Ammu reached over Lucky's head to pick up the rice bowl, Lucky hoisted herself on the edge of the table with her palms, swinging her hovering legs to rattle the plates until Ammu told her to stop, just like always. When Ammu disappeared into the kitchen and Abbu came in and sat down at the head of the table, he took a slow sip of water with a sigh of *bismillah,* just like always.

'Abbu, did you find the Frog Prince between the cauliflowers today?' Lucky asked, just like always.

'Not today! I'll look harder tomorrow,' he said with a wink, just like always.

Ammu returned with the rice, once again bursting with hot little clouds. She placed a mountain on Abbu's plate, a mound on Lucky's plate, exactly three spoonfuls, and lastly a hill on her own plate. Just like always, Ammu placed a spoonful of chicken, then meat, then fish on Abbu's plate throughout the meal, and like always, she laughed at Abbu's stories about the sneaky sellers at the fish bazaar. And though she stayed up for a while wondering how hard she would have to fall in the bathroom to hear that sound again, Lucky slept well that night, just like always.

When Ammu's sister, Lucky's Chotto Khala, came to visit months later, Lucky overheard them whispering in the kitchen.

'I can't give him more children, no son to ease life's burdens. So his cousins tell him to give all our money away. *What reason is there to leave so much to one daughter? She'll only enrich her husband's family.*'

'Pah!' Chotto Khala scoffed. 'They're jealous the stupid son works hard and has more than them, and they're angry that he's generous too. Didn't he buy them a shop last year?'

'And a tuk-tuk the year before that.'

'And they're still asking for more?'

'They ran the shop to the ground and damaged the tuk-tuk in an accident. They can't afford to fix it.'

'The Khans are already stealing from us, and they refuse to farm?'

'They're too proud to work.'

'Proud enough to let their children starve.'

Ammu shot Chotto Khala a disapproving look. She didn't like it when Chotto Khala spoke so cynically. When the onion had browned to the right shade, Ammu continued. 'Lucky's Abba became a partner in his uncle's fishing business.'

'Again? He's bailing them out of their failures!'

'He starts, he fails, he starts, he fails, he gives and gives, and they take and take. They're the only family he has, so he lets them drain him just to keep them close.'

'Isn't it enough to have a loving wife and daughter?' Chotto Khala fumed.

'What's a woman's opinion of a man compared to another man's opinion of him?'

The sound of boiling daal popped in the air. A small yellow firework. Like sunrise after a rainy night.

'Have you spoken to him?'

'I can't hold him back from his own destruction.'

Chotto Khala stirred the pot, clenching her fist around the wooden spoon. After a while, she said, 'We're women. We tolerate everything, like Mother Nature does. People shave off the mountains and disturb the balance of the land, cut down too many trees, pluck too many plants, take too many fish out of the river, and every day Mother Nature renews herself with less and less until she is destroyed. Then, the people wonder why she no longer bears fruit for them.'

The daal continued to pop.

'It's a woman's curse to foresee the world burning and be able to do nothing about it,' Ammu said.

Ammu was proved right when, not long after, Abbu died of a heart attack at the ripe age of thirty-four.

A knock came from behind the door, shaking Lucky from her memories.

'It's time to go,' the Slightly Cross-Eyed Soldier said.

Zoleyka nodded, wiping four streams from her eyes as she stood up. A soldier stood waiting for her with a slow, lazy smile, too drunk to recognise how she seethed with a hatred that could boil him.

'Come,' the Slow-Smiling Soldier slurred, tugging her braid.

As Zoleyka disappeared behind the door, an ocean of guilt pushed down on Lucky. She lay lost upon its waves, chastising the ugliness in her heart that shuddered in relief that it was not her. Ashamed, and worried it would turn to something worse, she countered its foul odour with prayers for the woman with the braided hair and streaming eyes. For them all.

5. RUBI'S LULLABY

The sound of artillery fire merged with the sound of the sea, a sleepy symphony that resembled the lullaby Lucky hummed to her son. As the trees whispered of a cool night and the ducks dove deep into the marshes to huddle close and pick at their feathers, Lucky met Rabia.

Rabia liked to speak. When soldiers came in she spat her words at them, stopping only when she was hit with the butt of a rifle or dragged out the room by her hair. Later, she would return bruised and bloodied, snarling, 'I can't understand these devils' language.'

The soldiers didn't understand her either. So she chose her words precisely. Purposefully. Rattled her brain to find words they both shared. 'Hell exists for the likes of you!' They recognised the word 'jahannam' and hit her twice as hard for it, as if her words were prophecy and the force of their punches had the power to extinguish its flames.

Rabia knew war was coming, and that she would bleed with it, when the state forbade the broadcasting of Rabindra sangeet, her favourite Tagore songs, on the radio. 'Joy Bangla!' she shouted until her words were lost between thick red gurgles as soldiers squeezed her throat. But the more they shouted at her in Urdu, the harder she lunged at them, baring her teeth.

'I'll never learn that damned language!' she vowed, her face a singed blue. Black, purple, red, green, she was always the shade of a burnt shadow. Still, beneath it, you could see her beauty. It was the kind of beauty that made you forget yourself.

Wild, curly hair, floating like fallen feathers from a summer sky and glinting like meat hooks hanging in the dark corners of the markets. A dark body that moved like the rushing river, its curves and corners pulling the string that tied the eyes to the heart. Downturned lashes that whispered trouble. A touch of darkness on her fingertips. The kind of beauty that men loved, and their mothers hated.

The Slightly Cross-Eyed Soldier let her poke and prod him, ignoring her attempts to rouse him from his chair. Lucky watched, not having the courage to join in. She had seen that spirit of freedom in other women. It was stubborn. Fierce. Jamila had it, that thing. Her mother-in-law had it too—Lucky had heard the whispers of old women who knew her when she was young and had seen her terrorise her husband. Then there were stories of Ammu from before Lucky was born, when she was another woman altogether.

Ammu had been the rebellious type when she was a girl. Despite her parents' threats, she had sneaked out of the house to join a Bangla language movement rally in 1948. The shouts of certainty and cheers of hope embraced her, but it wasn't long before a man's off-beat chanting made her irate. She went to move away just as the police advanced on the students. In the midst of the fighting, the off-beat man saved her from being trampled and took her all the way home before her parents realised she was missing. Every night for the next week, he trudged through marshes and backroads to check on her injuries. From the window of her room, above a sprawl of jasmine vines, she proudly presented the tiny cuts on her arm where she had fallen, making sure to complain about the pain so he would visit again. Night whispers of hope and sorrow gathered what had started as camaraderie and sealed it as love. Against the wishes of both families, after months of arguments and tears, Ammu and Abbu wed in a small ceremony in Abbu's friend's living room. It took the birth of Lucky, a year later, for their parents to speak to them again.

'The lure of the grandchild is powerful,' Abbu said, after Ammu's parents had left after a visit. He never failed to ask, 'Do you remember when I asked for your hand and your mother chased me out of the gates of your house with a jharu?'

With a pointing finger, Ammu accused him of slandering her mother, and they both fought into the night about whose version of their engagement story was true until Ammu stomped off to bed with a small smile playing on her lips. As the last of her saree disappeared around the corner, Abbu's eyes widened with mischief and he whispered lies to a giggling Lucky—who only half understood—knowing they would make their way back to Ammu the next morning. *She was swinging it over her head! I couldn't tell if she was trying to take me out or herself!*

Rabia reminded Lucky of Ammu. She scratched at the soldiers, whether they dragged her roughly like a beast or guided her gently like a lover, fighting them with her fists and her feet.

One evening, after spitting at one soldier and being hit across the face by another, until her eyes became so puffy they disappeared into her face and the tired soldiers left to perform the Maghrib prayer, Rabia told Lucky the story of her baby.

A soldier had thrown Rabia's baby on the ground so hard something fell out of her head. Another stomped on her so no one could pour her back together. The last Rabia saw, her baby was flowing onto the road, a ruby red washed away with the rain. Every night as the koel sang, Rabia sang with it.

Go away, O black clouds,
My moyna will have her bath now,
Go away, O disease and harms,
I have charmed my house against you.
Hills in the east, sea in the south,
And hear me, O stars and moon,
Release the anchor, O magnificent ship,
My dear will set sail on waters calm.

'A part of a mother's soul passes on to her child when it rests in her womb. That's where love comes from, a sharing of souls. It's why we cry for each other, laugh with each other, die for each other.'

Rabia faced Lucky on the floor, their eyes and mouths parallel so when she whispered, Lucky could hear her through the movements of her lips. Sunset cast sporadic shadows over them; one moment Rabia's face was cast a passionate pink and the next a melancholy blue. Under the changing skies, they held each other's stories.

'I hadn't realised how much love I had in me until I had my son,' Lucky agreed.

'Do we know what patience is until we have a sick child? What fear is until we've lost him in a crowd? My mother always told me that as the terrors of the world descend on a mother as her child grows, the beauty of her character ascends to make room to protect them both.'

Guilt seized Lucky's chest, curling her inward. 'I'm a bad mother.'

'You're not,' Jamila objected. Lucky hadn't noticed her listening. Her face was sunken, her mouth tight, but underneath, Lucky could still feel her sister's warmth, reserved just for her. 'You haven't had time to become a great mother, that's all.'

'There's no difference.'

'There's plenty.'

A tired frown pushed Lucky's eyes closed. Jamila was an unforgiving interrogator, a merciless judge and a remorseless executioner. And Lucky tried never to look at anything too closely. To look too hard was to think too hard, and to think too hard was to make it impossible to live with herself and impossibly easy to live without others. And to live without others, that was to blaspheme against the laws of the heavens and the earth. Yet something lay heavy, hard and cold against her rushing veins. The skies burned hot all year round, and her wrists were encircled by small, clinging fingers so its weight was almost forgotten. But in moments of silence, it held down her arms when she tried to reach higher and pulled her low when she tried to push herself off the ground. Its chains that jangled in front of her all day, leading her to the promise of an unknown salvation, made themselves known.

'I could've tried harder.'

'Your time hasn't been yours to give.'

'All my son will know is that his Ammi was too busy to tell him she loved him. That she never played with him or taught him anything. He'll remember the loneliness. And there'll never be a good reason for it, he should have come first.'

Jamila fell quiet at the pain in Lucky's voice. The sisters saw less of each other after Lucky's son was born, and for the first time Jamila realised that there might be something she didn't know about her sister. A pain she never realised she harboured. A pain she wasn't privy to.

'I'm sorry,' she whispered to Lucky, who flinched as she reached over to wipe away her tears.

'You underestimate the love a child has towards his mother,' Rabia said. 'The agony of birth is a divine partition. Love passes through a small tear from a single soul, so painful only love could make you forget it. The joy of the first sight of the baby is made greater than the pain so a mother can smile down on a bundle of bloody flesh.' Rabia's voice was filled with understanding. 'It's wicked people who draw lines between us with blunt pencils, claiming love. Love of the land, love of the people, love of God, but they find at the end of the night, alone with themselves, they can't cry for us.'

'They'll learn one way or another,' Lucky sniffed. 'In this life or the next.'

Jamila frowned. 'Some people never learn a thing. They'll barter with God claiming he made them that way.'

'Like the bastard banana seller from the market,' Rabia muttered, thinking of the village she had left behind. 'He wouldn't take a rupee off, no matter how much a child cried or a beggar begged.'

'Their minds are murky,' Lucky pondered. 'Like the water when you first wash rice, so cloudy you can't know what's underneath or how many times it needs washing. But they can learn to be better.'

'They won't learn because they think they already know,' Jamila said. 'And when they grow tired of themselves, they burn the past so no one can hold it against them with anything but their memories.' Impatience sprouted from her chest in hard, fast words. 'Don't mistake traitors for fools, it'll only call your grave forward.'

'No one needs to *learn* not to push a child into a lake and hold their head under it,' Rabia agreed. 'Only the child needs to learn not to trust every man or woman who smiles at them.'

Jamila closed her eyes, deliberating, before she said, 'Every child must one day set fire to the belief that every aged face is a friend, and that is the day their childhood ends.'

At night, Rabia dreamt of a burning building. As she ran, she looked back and saw a burning body walk towards her. The first night, the body was her mother-in-law, but as the nights went on, it was her mother, her sister, till on the last night, before it extinguished its light forever, it was her baby made woman, her body grieving the future she would never have.

'What was her name?' Lucky asked Rabia one night when they couldn't sleep.

'She didn't have a name. They came before we gave her one.'

'What did you want to name her?'

'There's no use thinking of that now that the rain has washed her away.'

Lucky rested her cheek on Rabia's bare shoulder. The mourning waves in her heart seeped under her eyelids, ringing in her ears, and settled heavy and wet in the bridge of her nose.

'There's power in a name. Often it takes giving something a name for us to realise its beauty.'

An owl hooted its last as the sun rose.

Footsteps crossed the veranda towards them.

The smell of rain-soaked leaves roused small creatures from slumber.

'Rubi,' Rabia said.

On a night when the moon drew far away and the wind blew nests apart, in came the Fat Man.

His shirt strained against his bulging stomach. His trousers, struggling to contain the meaty thighs above, were too long below, bunching around his black boots, half hidden beneath the material.

The Fat Man's upper lip was heavy with perspiration, though the night was cool. Waleed always told Lucky to stay away from men who would sweat for no reason. These men were slimy men.

The Fat Man smiled.

Too much in the cheek and not enough in the eyes.

The smile of a slimy man.

The Fat Man scanned the room until his small, slanted eyes fell on her.

Jamila, whose skin still shone golden in the light, whose hair still fell like satin around her shoulders, watched closely. When the Fat Man slid his feet forward, she swayed into his eyeline until her face eclipsed Lucky's.

Entranced, walking straight to Jamila, the Fat Man tapped his baton on the floor, drawing her face to his. He tapped his baton on her bare foot. He tapped his baton on the edges of her saree. Sliding underneath, he tapped his baton on her calf.

Flicking his wrist to the side, baton swishing, he brought his baton down on Jamila's breasts.

He looked her in the eye.

Baton still tapping.

'You, come with me.'

The Fat Man turned on his heel.

Jamila stood, fingers shaking, and followed.

She returned to the room the following night. She sat quietly beside Lucky, facing the wall, her body stone still. Goosebumps lined her skin. Yellow bruises sat like little islands on her bare arms and legs. Small cuts lined her lips.

Neither of the two sisters spoke.

That night, with her eyes closed, Lucky listened to Jamila tap her forehead against the wall until her lids glowed white with sunrise.

The sun and moon rotated, each only staying for its appointed time. The birds followed suit, as did the clouds and the leaves. New animals replaced the old and departed, and new, pleading prayers replaced the tired ones, but Lucky's prayer remained the same. If God would only let one of them live, let it be Jamila instead of her. God already knew Jamila was a greater good to the world than her. It was always Jamila's hand that stroked her hair while she dreamt, quietening her desperate murmurs as she chased after her son, who turned his smiling face toward her, his mouth shaped by her name, and stretched out his small hand in search of hers. And when she woke up, in a gasping sweat, it was Jamila who comforted her by saying, 'It's okay, it's okay, I'm here, Boro Apa. Remember, dreams are God's reminder that reality is just an illusion we must work hard to distrust so we can reach that place where its mask falls away.'

Come back. Lucky felt her mouth move in her sleep. She jolted upright, worried her heart had spoken aloud.

Jamila was gone again. A couple of women had been taken to join Suhana, the camp cook, to prepare a feast for another section of soldiers who were stopping by.

Sharp like spades, Lucky's fingers, toes, elbows and knees dug into the soil as she lay waiting for her sister. Each day, the sun glided down the sky with anticipation and the moon arrived silver and strong, but Jamila did not arrive with it. Fear gripped Lucky's mind as one day turned into two turned into three. Occasionally, a woman's scream could be heard in the distance. A whip. A sob. Then, silence. The fourth day turned fear into bile that shook Lucky's body up and down and left and right, until Rabia wrapped her tight, and in her consoling grip, her head dangling from Rabia's arms, Lucky had no choice but to look for herself in the spaces where the petals that blew in from the window changed from white to pink.

When she returned, two streams fell from each of Jamila's eyes.

6. PERPETUAL GARDENS

A tortured hum trapped inside Rabia's chest woke her.

The soldiers kicked her awake, mistaking the sound for evil incantations. The country was overridden with witches and whores. The soldiers had seen too much. Heard laughter in abandoned villages. Felt a whisper in their ear in the forest. Smelt perfume where bodies were piled up. Saw shadows pass by in darkness. A thing they couldn't shoot or burn. Tasted sugar when they bit into the flesh of bloodied girls. This was nothing new to the women. The night stories they had whispered in girlhood were coming to life for the invaders, and now, as womanhood pressed down on them, the stories began again.

There once was a witch who lived in a village nearby. Children loved her and the elderly advised her. Men despised her because she was ravishing; women despised her because she ruined marriages with a passing glance. Men proposed, but when she showed interest, they grew mad with worry she would leave them for a wealthier man. A trail of broken engagements stained her name. Women, ripe with envy, spun tales that lingered after her every step. If the oceans were turned to ink, it could not record how many times she was made a whore. Her beauty so bright they made her a sinner to dim it. In the bazaars, lecherous eyes hung on her curves. When she grew tired of their lustful looks and depraved calls, she wore full purdah in the deepest black and learnt to walk without a sound. Still, they followed the waves that flowed around her feet, where the wind whispered compliments to her.

Her father feared that the men who remained caged in the day were plotting to snatch her away at night. He took her out of school. Locked her in her room. Left her with books, a needle and thread. Years later, when he died and money fell short, her mother sobbed with grief in the day and sent her daughter to fulfil her duties at night. To live. The death and rebirth of many moons spun truths and untruths until the woman became a fable, a witch behind purdah by day and a siren by night.

Men swore she jumped from tree to tree, singing her siren's song. She appeared, in a blink of an eye, in front of their tuk-tuks and rickshaws, forcing them to stop, crying that she needed help. She sat silently at the back of the vehicle until they had almost forgotten she was there, and when they looked up and noticed no reflection of her in the mirror, they swore she grabbed them by the throat and kissed them. When they woke the next morning on a pile of old, dirty blankets in a wooden house with holes in the roof, alone, with their buttons undone and their wallets lighter, they swore she cast a spell on them, stole their money and fled, leaving them with no recollection of the night before. To their crying wives they placed their hand on the Quran and pleaded the influence of magic spells, tied knots, evil eyes—the trappings of a demoness—so the incident should be forgotten immediately, as agreed upon with the village elders.

Talismans made of numbers, letters and shapes to counter the magic were written for the ailed man by a kobiraj and sealed with wax in a silver pendant to tie around his neck, arm and waist. A bottle of water and a smaller bottle of oil, with the same hexagonal drawings floating in them, were given to him as aids.

'Drink a small cup of this water every night and rub a few drops of oil into the scalp and belly button. Should the demoness possess him again, to escape the house at night or run after another woman, recite Surah Baqarah,' the healers said to the wives, counting the notes presented to them and quickly tucking them away in the folds of their jubbas. 'If that doesn't work, come back and I'll give him something stronger.'

Now that demoness, who never saw the brightness of flower petals in the day, only the grey cast of gloom that curled them inward by night, sat across from Lucky in the room.

'I'm a good woman from a good family,' Mohini said.

Mohini had eyes that whispered. A solid gaze with the assurance of a sapling peeking out of the soil, laying bare its young heart to the burning sun. Her plump lips were watered while the rest were parched from drought, the face of a woman who was visiting a friend, not of one held in the room for more than half a year. Her eyes glowed when the wind cast the candlelight out, and Lucky pondered that while you couldn't see clouds at night, maybe Mohini could.

'When I close my eyes, I see the rainy season in my village when the ground washes away beneath my feet. It brings a smile to my lips.' Mohini smiled at Lucky, feeling her curious eyes on her. 'Isn't that funny? Even when we find that our homes and shops have slid a foot down from where they were before, we can't help but laugh in awe of nature's power.'

Unlike the rest of them, Mohini still smiled, and it was a genuine smile. It looked strange, like a mockery, but it fit her gentle face and piqued a morbid interest in Lucky. She wanted to know how she did it, even if it was just to confirm that she was insane. Mostly, she wanted Mohini to teach her how to smile too.

'Look at how this tiny flower greets us with so much cheer! It worked hard to get to us.' Mohini pointed to a small pink bud that had grown in a hairline crack in the concrete, brushing its petals gently like a mother would her new-born's face.

'It's strange that it should travel all the way here to make itself a home,' Lucky mused.

'Flowers have a rare beauty. Their beauty is final. Complete. A rose is beautiful in a poor man's shack just as it is in a rich man's mansion. It brings life where it grows and makes melancholy where it dies.'

'Maybe we should wait to cry until this one begins to wither.' *Flowers die far too quickly to be so enamoured of them,* Lucky thought. It didn't seem wise to attach emotions to something so short-lived.

Mohini paused dreamily. 'I think one day flowers will grow over these minefields and the ground we sleep on. And people will take pictures of this place that shudders now with our cries.'

Mohini answered whatever she wanted to answer and not what Lucky was asking. But her response was better than what was asked of her, as if she could see beyond the pleasantries and into Lucky's fears.

'My son points to flowers wherever we go,' Lucky said. 'I can't name half of them when he asks me.'

'Do you notice them?'

Lucky couldn't remember the last time she had seen flowers bloom or remarked on their colour. The small window in her kitchen looked out towards the backwaters of the communal lake; dry summer soil and dark winter waters held the corners of her eyes hostage all year. Sometimes, small flowers emerged, bright and proud, from the mud. But their shape, colour, name, smell, their feeling on her fingertips, evaded her. She had forgotten to look at them.

'No, I don't.'

'That's a shame.'

'A wife forgets to notice a lot of things, a mother even more.'

'That's an even greater shame, when she's the one who teaches the future how to see.'

She didn't have a response and Mohini moved on, not expecting one. Mohini gazed at the little pink flower with a curiosity Lucky had only seen in children her son's age. An appreciation of the beauty in small things. It was sincere and innocent, just like Mohini herself. Her presence was inviting, her spirit warm and joyful. Others could see it too, and it drew them in.

The commander of the camp, a moustachioed army major from Multan, had found Mohini waiting in an empty house for her customer, who had been killed on his way to her. She didn't scream or fight when they found her, and her eyes didn't widen with shock or fear. She simply picked up the rest of her clothes and walked past them to the truck. The Major liked that, so he made her one of his favourites.

Major Moustache was a big man, built like an untouched mountain. He could wrap his hand all the way around a woman's throat and touch the other side. The only part of him that wasn't made of stone was his full, black moustache that stabbed at everything it touched. He liked that Mohini didn't grimace when his moustache brushed her face. He enjoyed her soft, girlish smile, which never betrayed how she felt, its gentle, slow curves remaining on her face no matter what he did. Each night, to test its resilience, he devoted himself to breaking it.

'Where's my honey?' Major Moustache sang whenever he wanted her. He took her away in an extravagant fashion, twirling her around, watching to see if her smile slipped before it came back round to him and being disappointed that it remained firm. The women watched her mouth too and found Mohini returned to the room the next morning with a small smile and a plate of food to share. She fed those who couldn't sit upright, stroked the hair of the girls until they fell asleep, hugged tight those who shivered when the night blew cool. Cared for those who would never have cared for her on the outside. It was clear in her kind words and generous smile that it didn't matter to her what she was, it only mattered to others.

And others loved to remind her. Major Moustache reminded Mohini that she belonged in the room, that she should be grateful to serve a man of his stature, compared to the low-borns of before. He loved everything about her, but when her smile grew too soft, too warm, he tried to break it in front of the other women, curious to see if it would slip, slide, falter for a second when her eyes met with theirs. In the middle of the room, he undressed her and pulled her hair back, hoping for a grimace of pain, or better, humiliation. Instead, she peered at the women shyly without a sound. The others were given less mercy. Major Moustache slapped those who looked away in protest, who sobbed, who pushed at his arms and legs to free her from him, until their noses and mouths dripped red and they feared they would lose their eyesight if they did not look. They watched him squeeze her face, crush her throat, tear her legs and trample on her smile until only an unconscious memory kept it in place.

'The world has seen too much of me against my will. I don't mind if it never gets to see me again,' Mohini said one night. Lucky lay by her side. The other women had been taken out of the room, leaving Lucky and Mohini with the Slightly Cross-Eyed Soldier and a few sleeping girls.

'I fear no man,' Mohini went on. 'I lost my fear of him long ago. I want to be rid of him, and I want to be free from this world, from this place where I'm hated for being wanted, where man keeps me alive with his money freely but despises me for taking it. I want to go where no eyes have seen, no ears have heard, and no hearts have imagined my flesh, a place entirely my own.'

In the distance, a belly rumbled.

A low, long hum.

A dry gulp cut through its complaint.

'You smile when they call you names,' Lucky said. 'Feel fully, even after they touch you without feeling.'

'The least I can do is be unhappy, you mean? Oh, it angers people like nothing else when I'm not, as if I've stolen from them what should have been theirs. The witch dares walk with a smile, while those who hold legitimate jobs, the type they introduce themselves with before their own names, who have respectable families and make honest money walk without one!'

'We can never really know who's happy or unhappy.'

'We can. It's in the eyes. Everything but the eyes can lie, the eyes can only look away.'

'I've seen lying eyes.'

'You've seen shameless eyes that told the truth and a mouth that did the opposite.'

Mohini had many grown answers trapped in her young body, ready and willing to strike should the right question arise. Though Lucky could never envy her life, she envied her wisdom, and the certainty with which she held the world.

'God doesn't leave women so defenceless,' Mohini continued. 'We always know. The feeling that settles in the pit of the heart and the pit of the stomach at the same time. Like a dried leaf tumbled by the wind, it touches the base of the heart and disappears quickly so you're free to make your choice, to accept or reject that it's not just creatures of the night, any mouth can be laced with venom. Unfortunately, I usually crush that leaf beneath my foot before it can rise into dance.'

'I sweep mine into a corner, out of sight.'

'And here we both are.'

For a moment they said nothing. The Slightly Cross-Eyed Soldier was leaning back on his chair with both eyes on the roof. Lucky's gaze fell to his unlaced boots, and she balled her fist at memories of bowing to touch an elder's feet, to seek their blessing—for what, she never knew. To die without having done that would have been better.

'You know, it's true what the elders say,' Mohini said. 'The light of the sun isn't valuable to those who've lost the light of their eyes. Look how beautiful the sun is, how lovely this flower is, but man's favourite thing to look at is a woman!'

Lucky laughed, enjoying Mohini's damning insights and lack of propriety. If she were to die as young as Mohini, she would die complaining too.

'God must've given us different eyeballs, men and women, they only seem to see the tree and never the direction of its branches,' she joined in.

'Or any of the leaves that wither and fall off.'

'Or any of the birds that fly up there and lose their footing.'

'Or any of the fruits that rot away unnoticed.'

Mohini's fingers trailed around each petal until she reached its bud. Lucky wondered if the first people ever to see a flower were as enchanted by it as Mohini was now. Had they traced it with their fingers, drank in its velvety touch and seductive sheen, marvelled at how it held a single droplet from the sky, and found comfort when it became too heavy and tilted its body, returning the water to the ground to help another of its kind rise? Did the first leaders of the land see the great, green hills of Bengal, its perpetual gardens and luscious lotus flowers, and become mesmerised? Or did those first leaders vote on the beauty of the lotus and whisper down their verdict, ear to ear, until it reached them as truth and lie? She asked herself if that was why they fought over it, so their people might fight over it again and again. If the rise and fall of nations was not an ancient beauty like the moonrise, but an ancient whisper that settled, like a moving shadow, over the poisoned hearts of each people.

'How did you do it?' Lucky asked, knowing Mohini would understand her question.

Mohini looked at her for a long time in search of something. When it seemed she was satisfied with what she found, she drummed her fingers on the floor and turned her head toward the roof, exhaling quietly until her chest looked like it would collapse and pierce her heart, the smile on her lips still in place.

'First, you look at him and think about what you have to do. You think this is immoral, and your soul shouts, *I must leave*. Then you remember your baby, or your mother and her fingers that are becoming crooked, and you're scared, scared for them and scared of him. Both fears fight inside your heart, almost tearing it to pieces, but fear for your family wins out each time. Pride isn't as precious to you as your life. Men are kind to you if you make them forget their guilt, and a man forgets his guilt within the curves of a woman's body. Then, you close your eyes, and work.'

Lucky gasped around the lump in her throat. She had sown stitches across her heart, securing it in place for whatever answer would come its way, before asking Mohini her question. But now her eyes pulled at those seams, and her chin trembled, unable to bear the weight of Mohini's words.

'Cry,' Mohini said, averting her eyes so darkness could shroud Lucky. 'Cry until your heart turns to warm dough. Don't wait until the day you forget how, when your heart has hardened so much that only fire by someone else's hand can soften it again.'

The night looked away as a hot stream slid down Lucky's face and into her ears.

Above, a gecko scurried into the corner of the room as moonlight set on them.

'Even now? Does your heart, your family, win each time?' Lucky whispered.

'The heart shows you the truth, if you have courage enough to listen to it.'

'What does it say?'

'That these men have open, bloody wounds. They want to pierce and poison us with the diseases of their hearts, to keep from feeling it themselves, and so their appetite for pleasure intensifies the crueller they become. They live for the moment of false bliss. It's why they look into your eyes and not your face, to see the reflection of themselves in pleasure, to see their faces unburdened with the evils of the day, once again.'

'They search for themselves in us.'

'But they're mistaken. We can never make them forget their guilt and they hate us all the more for it.'

Reaching her hand out the window, Mohini tore a leaf from the vine that crept closer towards them each day and placed it between a family of ants. After a moment of hesitation, once they were certain her generosity was sincere, the ants rested one by one around the edges of the leaf and carried it away.

'I'll live through this, as I've lived through much before. They call me witch. Whore. People don't look down on their shoes as much as they look down on me. But I don't look to people for kindness, for understanding, I would only come up short. I look to the world for beauty, and I find it in abundance. I feel it. Do you want to know why beauty is divine?'

'Why?'

'Beauty is water. It falls on any surface, even the darkest, most jagged rock, where the gentlest touch draws blood, and makes it shine and glimmer under the sun as if it were a smooth pathway. Beauty existed before us and will remain after us. If the world destroys itself, its beauty will remain visible from the sky. It's our greatest hope, our guiding light, the origin of our patience.'

'I've never known patience to be beautiful,' Lucky frowned. 'It's bloody and painful.'

'It's part of the cycle we were created to witness. We're patient because we know beauty will appear in our lives again. We yearn for union with the divine, the eternal beauty, search for it in illusions and are disappointed when they fall short. So we distract ourselves with love and desire, substituting perfection for its mortal imitation.'

Lucky felt tired. She wanted a simple answer. Something she could apply easily to her life without requiring the last part of herself that kept her standing.

'I've been patient my whole life and I've nothing to show for it. How much longer will it last?'

'A lifetime. If it's not this time, it's the next time, and if it's not this thing it's the next, one thing dies, another is reborn. In this life, the only life we remember, we must witness the cycle of beauty come and go.'

'And then what?'

'We learn to look forward to it.'

'Is it really so simple to talk of flowers and come to know people,' Lucky pondered.

'When the lotus flower opens its eyes in the day and joins us in sleep at night, or like me the night jasmine does the opposite, man tells me I'm better off lost and buried somewhere if I don't live for his pleasure, and through it all the beauty of my resilient heart still beats louder over the darkness of his.'

The rain hit the leaves outside as the weight of Mohini's words washed over Lucky. The earth pulsed beneath her. The ground, like the sky, had a heartbeat. It was bright, and it was alive.

'It all breathes,' Lucky murmured.

'It does. When you've been kicked to the ground as much as I have, you learn the enemy's trick is to remind you of your past, to keep you in your dull memories, darkened and made fanciful, the dead world of the mind, tempting you to forget that the trees, the rocks, the summer breeze breathe. Your mistake is to believe him. But remind that miserable mutt of his future and watch him flee.'

'I haven't thought of the future for a long time. It never seems to arrive.'

'Think about it now.'

'Well, my husband will build us a bigger home once he returns from abroad, and it's time we give our son a brother or sister to play with. I can tell he's tired of us grown-ups.'

'And what of beyond here? Beyond this world?'

Lucky thought for a moment. The slow thud of drizzly rain hit the tin roof until the air hummed with life. A rustle above their heads. A squeak. A chirp. A cry. She heard it all, and it settled heavy on her heart like a humid day.

'I want a mango orchard. Coconut trees. Pomegranate trees, Jamila likes pomegranates. A garden as far as my eyes can see, filled with flowers and the green birds that my son loves. A river for my husband to swim in, with colourful fish. The finest silks for my mother to wear. That's paradise to me.'

'It's beautiful.'

'It's a fantasy, I've done nothing to deserve it.'

Mohini began to laugh. 'And I have? We don't get things because we deserve them, we get things because we ask, so ask.'

'How do you know what to ask for?'

'We only find out when we live through what we didn't ask for.'

We only appreciate the brightness of day by feeling the fullness of night. Ammu had told Lucky that. Lucky hadn't understood the words until Rayan was born. The enhancement of her love, care, joy came from him, and she felt its great absence in his absence. Always, she failed to see life's beauty until it was a faded figment of her memory, more imagination and yearning than vivid truth. Less colourful than her dreams and nightmares, less heartfelt than her daydreams and fantasies, a catacomb of regret within an album of disjointed images.

'I've seen the truly ugly,' Lucky said. 'From now I wish only to see the truly beautiful.'

'One day, the scales will be in our favour,' Mohini vowed, entwining her fingers with Lucky's. 'And these gardens will be ours to run in.'

Releasing her hand, Mohini stood and walked towards the Slightly Cross-Eyed Soldier, who guarded the door from the inside, and smiled as he jumped under the playful tap of her fingers on his shoulder.

'Open the door,' Mohini said. 'We're hungry.'

7. HONOURED GUESTS

'Do you know my brother loves you?' Sumayyah said to Noori.

The Slightly Cross-Eyed Soldier's lips twitched, and for a moment his eyes came together in a temporary pact to plan an escape.

Sumayyah and Noori were classmates and best friends. Captured on their way home from school, they were tied to trees for three nights and two days before being taken to the camp.

'He's going to propose,' Sumayyah said, with twinkling eyes. 'We'll be sisters.'

One by one, the women turned to Noori, who covered her face with her hands. At fifteen, Noori had all the signs of a silly girl. She laughed more than she smiled and cried more than she argued. She joked easily and spoke hastily with little thought. The women grew concerned at the news.

'Don't marry a stupid man,' Rabia warned Noori before she could reply. Darkness came over her eyes and deep lines cut into her forehead. 'Stupidity is harmful. Dangerous. A stupid man will harm you, himself, his children, his mother, his favourite uncle, his dying Nanaji, the imam, the mango seller, the djinn that lives in his toilet... everyone around him. And you'll have to comfort this stupid man for his stupidity, because he's too stupid to understand how stupid he is!'

The women pressed their sarees hard against their mouths, their shoulders shaking with laughter. Even those whose minds had fled long ago lifted the corner of their lips.

'He'll live forever too, that stupid man!'

'Alhamdulillah,' Rokeya praised, laughing. 'The people with the worst personalities have the most indestructible health.'

Whispered words of wisdom sailed across the room, free from the proprieties of the civilised world.

'Never marry a man who needs to make a mistake to learn.'

'I rejected any man with more than two siblings. I'm not learning all those names!'

'Look at your mother-in-law's hair. If she has a full head of hair, she's the one giving everyone stress. The one with thinning hair? She's the one taking stress from her stupid son.'

The room buzzed with warmth and candour. The women rushed their words with what little spark they had left, making sure not to speak over each other. They waited for those who burst into a fit of giggles to calm before interjecting, pushed each other away when the counsel grew outrageous and pulled each other into an embrace when the words flinched with vulnerability.

'Take a good hard look at him. You'll be intimate with this man for the rest of your life. Don't marry him if he looks like a shondesh, you'll never forgive yourself.'

'It doesn't matter how wealthy he is, if his personality is drier than shutki, you'll go searching for death earlier than you should, leave the gas on at night every once in a while, to tempt fate.'

'There's nothing a daughter can do to make her mother lose all her hair like a son can!' Rabia shrieked, jumping to her feet, poking her finger at the phantom son.

Lucky stifled her laughter with her saree, her empty stomach rattling with a painful joy. The Slightly Cross-Eyed Soldier lowered his chin and covered his mouth with a fist that stood resting on his knee.

'He's very handsome,' Noori gushed. They could see the shape of her heart from the way she spoke.

'They're all handsome at first, before you wash their mud-slicked lungi for the second time that day.'

'He's handsome because he fills your stomach with sweet talk. Let us take a good look at him.'

'Remember, Noori, marriage is the hard half of your deen, your husband is your paradise or your hellfire. You can marry the most handsome man in the world but if he has a great character flaw, that'll be the only thing you see about him for the rest of your life. A beautiful character, a beautiful manner, a beautiful mind, those remain beautiful beyond the grave, so marry someone you want to meet again in the afterlife.'

'My brother is a good man,' Sumayyah stressed. 'And he loves Noori.'

'Dhhur, dhhur! *Love.* Does your brother have crazy eyes?' Rabia slapped Sumayyah's knee. 'People with crazy eyes only look to see what you can do for them.'

Beside Lucky, Jamila watched a mushroom sprout with hurried steps. It pushed uneasily against the air, fighting itself, groaning at the effort. It whispered sad stories to her. And when she became overwhelmed by its grievances, her hand reached for her ear and twirled the dangling bird cage around and around until her lobe bubbled with blood.

Lucky grew afraid at Jamila's erratic behaviour. Ever since her return, her sister's gaze swayed each day from wild to dim to wild again, floating further and further from her, but whenever she began to ask, Jamila turned her back so she could no longer see traces of either.

'What will Rahat think of your ruined earlobes?' Lucky said quietly, rubbing the redness from beneath Jamila's fingernails until it vanished into her own. 'He said he'd replace these earrings with real gold ones when you get married. Don't you want to return to him as beautiful as you were when you first wore them?'

'I will never marry,' Rokeya announced, drawing Lucky's attention before Jamila could reply. The conviction in her voice made them all turn.

'Why the hell not?'

'Because I've never met a man who didn't want me to empty myself of me and place him in there instead. Who didn't only see in me what he wanted to see and wanted me to be, not what I am. I've never met a man who could hold my heart in his hands without trying to crush it.'

'Ya Allah, you've met some terrible men...'

'Who hasn't?' Chanda jeered.

'Let me guess what village you're from.'

'Oh, stop that!' Mohini laughed, pushing Rabia away from Rokeya. 'It's fine to take your time thinking about it. Once she's married, she'll be married for the rest of her life. Now is the only time she's free to live for herself, let her enjoy it.'

The women hummed in agreement.

'She'll die a married woman and enter paradise as a married woman!' another woman teased.

Around the room, whispers blended with snorts, snickers and splutters. Jamila leaned her head on Lucky's shoulder and smiled into the folds of her flowing hair. The love of women reviving forgotten joys.

'My first husband, may God forgive him, was a wonderful man. A man of few words but tender character,' one woman said, reaching into a memory that made her eyes water. 'His strength didn't come from his hands but from his gentleness towards me. He died only four years into our marriage. He was so special I could only have him for a short while. He was my first taste of paradise.'

A hush descended on the room. The women's hearts leaned heavy across their ribs and beat with yearning. Kind eyes, kind ears, kind mouths and the men to whom they belonged stood before them in the room. Vivid and in motion, shades of brown and burning reds, with fingers as hard and soft as they were on a day that had already passed them by, touched their eyelids until they dreamt under daylight, wide awake, in a crowded room of menless women. Across the floor, the Slightly Cross-Eyed Soldier shifted in his chair with neither understanding nor allegiance, his chest heavy with something he did not recognise.

Mohini broke the silence. 'Marry a man who can look past the little things. Men look at women's past, women look at men's future, and we pick at the little things in the days that lie between them,' she said. 'And the difference between happiness and hell is in little things.'

Noori's face flushed with concentration, trying to absorb the women's advice. Lucky listened wistfully, while Jamila watched on in doubt. The sun fell slowly in the sky, and the river rushed warm. It fell silent behind their chatter and withdrew from the edge of the bank, so still that birds could dip their mouths into its surface and touch the skin of the fish inside. The river endured the birds' piercing cries and the assault of their hurried, hovering wings with grace, all to listen to the laughter of women on a cold and dark day.

'Let's not live like our mothers,' Jamila said, the seriousness in her low tone silencing the remnants of the women's laughter. 'They lived in a different time. They were told to have patience until they destroyed themselves and now they say the same to us. They were wise, but their wisdom was only a shield to protect themselves, telling them to give everything to the very hands that crushed them. Better to shape a marriage with our own hands, not the hands of all the women before us.'

'Our mothers survived, but they didn't live,' Mohini murmured.

'There was no time to live,' Lucky replied, rising to Ammu's defence. 'All there was time for was patience and endurance. Sabr, in all of its pain, with none of its beauty.'

'And at what cost?' Jamila demanded. The whites of her eyes were inflamed with anger. 'They held heaven's weight in patience in one hand but couldn't hold on to love for their children with the other.'

'It's the same now as it was then,' Chanda said. 'Our husbands and sons marched yesterday, fight today and will lead tomorrow, while we're told to wait patiently for the world to fall around us, and be ready to rebuild it once it's beyond repair!'

Rabia shook her head. 'This world wasn't made for a woman's heart, only her hands. And should she break a nail, or worse, a finger, they'll cut off both her hands and ask her to separate gold from soil with the stumps.'

'And tell her to have patience with the one who cut off her hands!' Jamila scoffed.

'Real patience starts at home,' Mohini concluded. 'Only then can it reach the streets and the chants we shout and pray for. And everyone has a part in it.'

Mohini's words reminded Lucky of a time before love. Before her husband, there was another man. Lucky should have loved him. He was everything she sought, tall, sensible, smart and more reasonable than most. But while he would laugh at Lucky's jokes and listen to her stories, he could never entertain her dreams, even in jest. No matter how exhilaratingly honest she dared to be with him, he brushed aside her hopes and ideas, wanting her to be as small as he felt.

Lucky knew that having time in the day to sew, alone and without interruption, would be an impossibility as his wife. With him she would have to pack away all her needles, threads and materials into a box that she would place at the bottom of her cupboard and see again only briefly in the summers when she aired out their clothes and dusted the floors so the sand would not harden at the bottom.

And so, despite the loveliness of his laughter, she ignored his letters for weeks on end, until they grew distant and finally apart.

Ammu could not understand. To Ammu, a kind man with a good job could be taught what he was deficient in, taught to love her how she wanted to be loved, taught to care about her and about what she cared about, never mind that Ammu herself had never been able to teach her own husband anything. Abbu had died early so Ammu had forgotten, but Lucky did not forget how Ammu refused to marry again. Widowhood suited Ammu. She grew younger in it; the girlish smile that had disappeared after those early marital days came back sunnier than before and never dimmed again, blazing towards those who pointed in scandal that she did not cry longer for her late husband. And while hopeful suitors lined the doorway to steal a moment of conversation with her, it was to Ammu as if all men had been wiped from the face of the earth when the last of the soil was levelled over her husband's grave.

Ammu saw Waleed first. She pointed him out to Lucky one day when she didn't notice him noticing her. He was beautiful in the way men were. Tall and curly-haired, with a wickedly witty sparkle in his eye that glistened like lake water in the dead of night. He spoke gently and asked more questions than he answered. He was interested in the shade of Lucky's lips as well as the shape of her thoughts, especially the ones she dared not tell others, and cradled every one of her words delicately in his palms as if it were his most precious treasure. After their marriage, they would stay awake into the early hours of the morning, ravelling and unravelling each new idea together to nurture between their joined hands.

Beautiful, that's what Lucky became when she met him. He rewrote her damning judgements of herself as placid curiosities, her declarations of sadness as strength, her anger as comedic delight. She was not just a woman but his wife, the part of him that required the best of him, and he was unafraid to show it.

Waleed's lazy smile rested in front of Lucky. She could hear his kisses on their son's cheeks, feel his tight embrace at the airport as he left to build a better life for them, see his careful handwriting on cheap, thin paper she knew omitted the pain of being other in another land so she could dream of a future. In return, she hid the pain of raising their son alone, of missing Waleed so much she cried herself to sleep, so he too could dream of a future.

Beyond the barred window, half a world away, the ringing of a rich and deep laugh pulled Lucky's heart to pieces. An unusual desire to speak of what she felt bubbled from her chest.

'It's beautiful if you choose well,' she began, resting her chin on Jamila's shoulder. 'There's no greater joy in this world than a good husband. No one will support you more, love you harder, forgive you faster. You become the closest people on earth, so close the pain of parting for travel feels like the pain of death. There's more affection between you than between friends, more mercy than between mother and child. Affection shows itself during good times, and when times are bad and affection naturally dims, mercy rises in its place. When children come and love's early fever cools, and life makes you forget one another, those children who have your husband's eyes will remind you again why you fell in love.'

As Lucky spoke, Jamila's thoughts drifted to her fiancé. They met at the bazaar. While she slept under the sweet-shop counter and wandered in and out of the market to grab a grape, pinch a hog plum, shimmy a bean shell out of a basket to peel later, until she was full for the day, like a bird returning to its nest after setting sail early in the morning, Rahat helped his father at his fish stall. He watched her weave between sarees and lungis, between chatter, chants, slogans and furious haggling, until she finished the day with a scattered meal. When the prawns fell short in their own baskets, he did not tell his father about her quick fingers; when a single lime slipped off its tower beside him, he did not turn his head until she had woven her way back into the crowd with her bounty.

Late one evening, father and son passed Jamila while she crouched over a puddle, her cupped hands seeping with muddy water. Rahat turned his head before she drank, his heart, still too small to hold the answers of the world, unable to explain why his stomach twisted tightly and told him to avert his eyes. The next day, as she hopped towards them like a cunning squirrel, approaching their stall from the side, he was ready. He pulled out a carton of mango juice from the strap of his trousers and shoved it into her pinched fingers with rehearsed precision. Eyes wide with fear, she grabbed the carton and ran. The next time he saw her, she held a woman's hand and shielded her face between the folds of the woman's saree. Another girl prattled beside her, jumping around her from all sides until she returned an uncertain smile. That day, the sellers greeted Jamila as she pointed shyly to the grapes, hog plums and beans with a joyous smile.

Eleven years later, Ammu sent Jamila to the fish stall to collect ingredients for Waleed's family, who were coming to set a date for the wedding. Rahat waited nervously for her to arrive. Since his father's passing, he had run the stall successfully and made enough to think of a future. The sellers at the bazaar saw he was sweet on Jamila. They teased him when she came, wiggled their eyebrows as he took extra care to wrap her order. He hoped she would pick up on their signals too, so he could take the coward's way out of making his intentions known.

But Jamila hated that Rahat knew her from before. To forget the fact, she avoided his eyes and never touched a mango again. Still, she couldn't help but be drawn to his sweet smiles and liked that he placed extra prawns in her bag because once, years ago, she had told him they were her favourite.

Today, when he saw her approaching, he planned to tell her how he felt. Yet by the time courage touched his lips, her orders sat packed on the table, and she looked at him expectantly for the total. Panic gushed from his chest into his mouth.

'Let's get married?'

The mango seller looked on in dismay. Nearby, children stopped fighting to listen. Haggling aunties turned their way.

'Who?'

'Us.' When Jamila didn't reply, he flung a box into her hands. 'Here, this is for you.'

The old hog plum seller muttered, 'Inna lillahi wa inna ilayhi rajiun.' To God we belong and to God we return.

Jamila noticed Rahat's erratic breath and the sweat gathered in his hairline. Slowly, the pinks in her cheek deepened to a turnip red as his intentions became clear. The aunties shook their heads, covering their mouths with the ends of their sarees, and pushed their children to move forward.

'Thank you...' Jamila spluttered. Grabbing her bags she sped through the crowds, forgetting the extra prawns.

Rahat watched her shawl disappear and exhaled long and hard until he felt light-headed.

'I should drown myself,' he groaned to the sky. It shone bright despite the storm that lashed his heart. The world giving neither heed nor cover to his humiliation.

'Do it before the end of the day. We can bury you in time for Zuhr tomorrow,' the old hog plum seller said, arranging his hog plums. 'You're in luck, it's Friday.'

Rahat sat in a daze, stroking the smooth skin of the boal fish for a long time, before he said, 'She took the earrings.'

At home, Jamila and Lucky howled with laughter into the night recreating the event from different angles, switching characters with each re-enactment to get a better reading on what had happened. Tears spilled from their eyes each time they opened the box housing the dangling golden earrings shaped like birdcages.

Now, in the room, Jamila's cheek rested on the flesh of her sister's open thigh. A moment of clarity touched her lips.

'I won't marry him.'

'Don't say that.'

'It's different now.'

'Do you hate him now?'

'No.'

'Then nothing has changed. You'll see it's just the same when you meet again.'

Rahat had left some weeks ago to join the Mukti Bahini in a southern town, promising to marry her on his return.

Upside down, Jamila's wry smile was a full-crescent frown. 'It wasn't a good idea to begin with.'

'If you hate him when we get home, we can consider breaking his heart then. For now, continue with the engagement.'

Jamila was silent. Lucky rocked her in her arms. They sat like that for a long while, each lost in the velvet smoothness of the other's sincerity. Was there anyone else to whom they could expose their ugliness and have it held without judgement? They were two beech trees that had grown separately and, at some point, grafted together and remained conjoined in the face of a sneering world.

'Do you feel bad for him?'

'Yes. No.'

'Then what are you thinking about?'

'I made him wait for years, Boro Apa, it's unheard of. You know I've never wanted to get married. Sometimes I think I still don't. Maybe all the natural desires have been sucked out of my heart and I should just wander the earth, filling my emptiness with its wonders, alone.'

'Nobody is meant to be alone.'

'What good is it to be married to me? When I can't love like other women. When I hardly know what it is?'

'You do know what love is. You love me, don't you? And I love you just as much. You know, in many ways your love is greater than mine. You're more considerate, you have sharper eyes, a deeper heart. It's just wrapped up a little tighter in your chest.'

'It's not enough.'

'It is.'

Jamila sighed. 'It won't go well.'

'What makes you so afraid?'

She paused, deliberating as to how honest she should be. Across from her on its back, a decaying gecko lay forgotten between the legs of numerous women. Death sat with them in the room; there was no use hiding from it. For the first time and probably the last, she would ask for help.

'If I marry him, will I still be me or will I become someone else?'

Lucky was surprised at her sister's question. She had never known Jamila had these kinds of reservations.

'That's for you to decide, you can become his limb, or you can become a better you with him. You get to choose.'

Jamila fiddled with her fingers.

'If he were to cover my freedom with even a grain of dirt, I'd leave him and never look back.'

'He wouldn't do that.'

'I know that.'

'Then what's the problem?'

Jamila groaned in frustration. 'I can't understand it, how others feel it so easily, the love that poets write about, and he deserves nothing less.'

This was the most Jamila had ever spoken about her feelings and Lucky sent a silent prayer for the skies to remain still so nothing would cause her to stop.

'Not every love needs to composed into a sonnet, Jamila, and the only heart you need to understand is your own. Tell him everything you want from him, and he can spend the rest of his life trying to give it to you. He'll be slow, it'll be hard, but that's what makes it special.'

'Is it worth it?'

'Yes.'

Jamila pushed her face into her sister's thigh, the contour of her nose and lips pressing into Lucky's flesh. Her hair slid down covering the side of her face exposed to Lucky. A curtain to cut the conversation.

'What do you want from him?' Lucky asked gently, moving Jamila's hair away.

Jamila looked away in embarrassment. She felt like a child, worried about what others understood instinctually. As a young girl, she had realised she was different. Deficient. She read faces while others felt each other's words. Sat quietly when others jumped for joy. While others loved easily, she wondered what love was. Her life was spent avoiding people, to push aside the signs that showed her she was different, and now that people had come to her, she was lost. Deficient, again. Age had given her some comfort, some courage, and though she did not know what direction she should walk in, she knew where she stood.

'It's not just what I want from him... it's what I want from us, for each other. For us to give each other the freedom to pursue our different paths to paradise. To hold the soul that lies deep within the other and give freely to the heart that yearns to meet our Lord...' She broke off, cupping her hands before her face. 'Ya Rabb, I'm lost without your love to make me understand love. I don't know what I'm looking for, or what I'm even asking for, but I ask for the greatest version of whatever you give to me, because you are the greatest.'

Outside, the river sang in time with her private plea. Lucky became teary, mesmerised by the depth of her sister's heart, which was more generous than any she had ever known.

'You're more loving than you believe, Jamila, you're just cautious with it. You protect people from the parts of yourself that you're afraid of, and that's more loving than anything I know. It's just you walk in a world where people's love touches only the surface of the heart, while yours stems from the soul.'

Jamila's eyes drooped, exhausted. 'If I'm so loving, shouldn't I get some of it back? I'm tired, Boro Apa, I want to rest too.'

'You can teach him.'

'Ha! Is it that simple? A woman who thinks too much isn't a wife, remember? Especially if she can think better than a man. Who would want to be taught by me?'

Lucky smiled. 'Rahat would be more than happy to be taught by you.'

Jamila closed her eyes. A yellow hue covered the room. Warmth settled on the women's faces and the cast of winter leaves rested on their closed eyes. Jamila's fingers traced the small flowers on her blouse before reaching for her earrings. The women's whispers had simmered down with the sunset, and they settled into a restful silence, basking in the aftermath of the joys of their strange sisterhood.

'Promise me you won't end things just yet.'

'I promise.'

'D'you think there's still time for me to get married?' Mohini asked, her wistful voice gliding around them like summer rays.

'Only if you leave with the soldiers.'

Mohini slapped Rabia's leg, her offence echoing across the room.

'You're all invited to my wedding,' Noori piped in, her young love lingering on the soft edges of her words.

As footsteps approached, the women quietened, moving away from each other, each lost in their thoughts, wondering what their pasts would now mean to the men they loved. None considered the question of whether they had anyone to return to. Not even those whose ears rang with gunshots in their waking dreams.

8. A PROMISED DAY

'Hey, Sahib,' Rabia sang, her legs splayed open. 'Won't you touch us? Or do you believe in God?'

A shawl was wrapped loosely around Rabia's thighs so the night air could cool the bite marks that darkened her skin. Lucky watched the Slightly Cross-Eyed Soldier trace every mound, every tear, every droplet of dried blood and close his eyes when he had finished, brows furrowed with a weight he could not conceal.

'Where were you before the sweet shop?'

Jamila turned, surprised at the sudden question. She was met with Lucky's hesitant expression, as if she might cry if Jamila didn't answer her.

When Jamila had been gone, her image had remained just behind Lucky's eyes even in wakefulness. It leapt in front of her thoughts and rattled her chest so hard she forgot the stench of the soldiers' sweat and the waste bucket in the corner of the room. As night terrors began to consume her, instead of sleeping, Lucky opened her chest to look inside and found her heart lay where two oceans met, between salt and freshwater. She was always there, in the middle. Never brave, never cowardly. Never angry, never at peace. But in a much worse place altogether, in wait. Spirit apart from body. A breathing inhabitant of the barzakh.

Now, Jamila was back with calloused hands and bloodshot eyes, and in a desperate attempt to close the distance that had settled over their silence, the questions Lucky had put off asking for years rose to the surface of her tongue.

'I wondered when you would ask.'

'I was afraid you wouldn't tell me.'

'And if I don't?'

'Then I wouldn't know how to feel.'

Outside, the heavens hummed with fervour, but the women could not hear the cries that accompanied it. Jamila looked towards the scorched sky for answers. When her eyes were made heavy with its bright light, they fell upon the jasmine flowers crouching under the window's edge, steadily creeping towards them.

Jamila's memory was still fresh with the first jasmines she held in her hands as a girl. White flowers filling her open palms like moonstones. A jewelled prayer.

The year after Lucky and Jamila became sisters, when summer's heat crawled down from the skies, Chotto Khala got engaged. All the women in the family volunteered their needles and thread to create a piece of the special day, while the girls were tasked with trawling through the bushes to collect white jasmines for the garlands.

Jamila, the taller of the two sisters, saw the jasmines first. The vines crawled up a tree, their heavy clusters just out of reach. Plump, pearly buds, still unopened by nature's call. Lucky sat on Jamila's shoulders throwing down a single bud at a time, filling the sky with a fragrant hailstorm. Bags, pockets and hands full, they returned home.

Ammu gave clear instructions. Hold the string away from the body. Place two flowers facing away from each other at the base of the string. Loop the string around the flowers. Twice or thrice, for extra strength. Tighten the knot. Make another loop and pass another flower through it. Pull to get a knot. Keep adding pairs. Again, and again. Every so often, Jamila found a cluster attached to its stem. She placed her hand under the flower, angling it under sunlight until the ray of light caused the stem and petals to stretch up her arm and onto her face, and she wondered if this was where the spirit met the bone, and if it crept back up into the body when they woke.

As Jamila stared at the jasmines, deciding what she should say, Lucky trembled by her side. She turned from her sister, deciding never to touch the question again, until she felt a firm hand on her waist, accepting her request. Jamila scooted her towards the wall so they could be alone.

'A secret lasts longer in a boy,' Jamila began. 'Did you know that?'

Lucky shook her head. Jamila regarded her puzzled gaze, so removed from the grip of depravity that it never considered how it could be so easily harboured within another. She didn't want to spoil it. But her sister's confusion only thinly veiled her desperate plea to know her, and Jamila found in her eyes, after all these years, finally, their capacity to hold her.

'Abba returned home one day without my brother. I had just started my menses, so my father stopped taking me to the backstreets behind the markets where men would hand him a bottle and he would hand me to men.'

'Jamila...'

'He was the first to see the blood,' Jamila continued, ignoring Lucky. 'The day had come where I had turned old enough to cause problems. And we couldn't have people talking. So, he took my younger brother. I only had one brother, two years younger than me. His teeth were still growing in his mouth, so he hated to laugh aloud. Amma was a mute, so it was easy for Abba to lock her in the house when he left with us. And no one came to visit because our family was cursed. If she tried to keep us in the house, he beat her, if she tried to break out, he beat her too.'

Lucky sucked in her breath.

'The police hired a magician to find my brother, but they never did find him. It's easy to disappear in this country, there's too much forest and too much sea. And no one cares about a poor boy from a poor home, he's just one less beggar on the street.

'A few days after my brother disappeared, Abba was dead in his bed. Amma shook her head when I tried to call for the neighbours. Only when the house started to smell did Amma point at the door for me to leave. I cried, *No, Amma! I want to stay with you. Please, I'll be good.* But she pushed me out the door and locked herself inside. I knocked and knocked and waited and cried, but she never let me back in. Not even at night. Not even when I went hungry. Soon I realised I couldn't hear any movement inside, and that nobody would be coming out.'

A cricket jumped between the bars and into the room. It chirped erratically on the ground between the women, surprised by how many of them were sitting in the small space. Moved by the creature's panic, Sumayyah and Noori shuffled upright and competed to see who could catch it first and release it back out of the window.

'What was your Amma like?'

'She didn't have shoes, so her footsteps were as silent as her tongue. She never took anything from anyone and was never given a thing but gave of herself to everyone. I loved it when she played with my hair. Her touch was soft, it made me shiver. She nodded at everything I said. And when my brother and I fought, she held our tongues between her thumb and forefinger and pulled them upwards, higher, higher, higher, until we were on our toes and couldn't go higher, and then the three of us would fall into laughter. She liked to see us laugh with our teeth showing. When we were sad, she'd pull the corners of our lips into a smile and hold it there until we laughed for real. She ate the least. I never saw her eat a single piece of fish or meat in my life, she would just mix her rice with water. She loved to hug us and would pull our fingers and toes to tell us she hoped we'd grow taller. At night, she'd unwrap her saree and wrap my brother's legs and mine together in knots that only she could open in the morning. That was what my Amma was like. I never even knew her name.'

'Then you came to the sweet shop.'

'I stayed in other places, but people didn't want me near their homes and stores. They'd chase me away with sticks. I'd have left the sweet shop too if you and Ammu didn't find me.'

'Thank God for that,' Lucky whispered, her throat croaking as grief gathered in it. She wiped at her eyes quickly, not wanting to disrupt Jamila.

'Alhamdulillah,' Jamila affirmed. 'You know, for a long time, I didn't want to know God. He'd shown me too much too young, so I no longer wanted to see him. I imagined he was a big book in the sky, and no one had taught me to read, so I figured I wouldn't ever know him. He was invisible to me, so I was invisible to him too. Abba told us God was angry with Amma, so he made her mute. We were poor because God was angry with our family and that's why my brother and I had to work. God was always angry with me, but I still couldn't hate him. At night, I'd ask him if I could do something to make him happy. Maybe then Amma would speak, and Abba wouldn't take us to work with him. Only when I left the house did I learn that my father had lied, about everything.'

Lucky's chest rose off the ground in waves of anguish. Finally, she understood why Jamila's love was buried so deeply within her and why she was so reluctant to exhume it. Life had been unkind to her and its people cruel. Her cold demeanour shielded the kind of love that had to be excavated by gentle and patient hands over a lifetime, for anything rougher might crack the treasure beneath. Hers was a love not golden but made of gemstone, to wear around the neck, close to the heart. A carefully guarded jewel that would enrich a land for centuries to come, worthy only of a king who could be entrusted with the keys.

Lucky's tears fell until their weight consumed her.

'I'm so sorry I couldn't help you all these years.'

'Don't do that, Boro Apa, I didn't tell you because I didn't want you to think differently of me. I don't really think about that time anymore, although I wonder sometimes, did he wrap my brother's body when he buried him or throw him into the sea nude? On good nights, I dream he ran away that day, away from Abba and his friends, and now he's a handsome man living freely somewhere.'

There was a knock on the door. The Slightly Cross-Eyed Soldier rose from his chair. The women shuffled close. Silence.

'I'm glad you came to us,' Lucky whispered.

'Me too.'

The door flung open and in came the Slow-Smiling Soldier with unsmiling guests. His eyes held a glimmer, a secret sliver of a smile. A true smile is fast, lifting the face like the curled edges of a bedsheet shaken upwards in the air. A true laugh is faster; it betrays the mouth and fills the air with fever. But the Slow-Smiling Soldier smiled slowly. The corners of his lips rose slowly like the corners of a daphne stalk and wilted into his chin even slower. Cruelty sat in the borders of his mouth in wait, sharpening his tongue until it was strong and smooth. His big, straight teeth flashed white when he cursed them and seeped red when he clamped down on their flesh. Thin, dark lips spread across his face until the creases reached his eyes, in his slow way, like a pebble through a puddle. When he was done, he licked where he had bitten, a promise of next time.

'Sit up, ladies, let's take a look at you,' the Slow-Smiling Soldier said, his slow smile settling in the pit of Lucky's stomach. With his elbow resting on the Slightly Cross-Eyed Soldier's shoulder, he leaned down until his face was level with his ear.

'Aren't you lucky? Sat with the women all day while we fight for the country,' he sneered. 'Did your father send special instructions for you to guard every naked woman in the land or were you chosen because you can't gawk at the Major's favourites?'

The guests laughed. The Slow-Smiling Soldier smiled slowly. The Slightly Cross-Eyed Soldier looked on without a word, but Lucky saw his fingers clench tighter around his rifle.

'Come now, darling,' the Slow-Smiling Soldier said to Jamila with an outstretched hand. 'You're too beautiful to be sitting here gossiping with a eunuch.'

The Slow-Smiling Soldier turned and winked at Rabia before he left. Lucky watched Jamila's back disappear. The new soldiers came forward eagerly and took their pick. A dozen bare feet followed the crunch of a dozen new boots. The Slightly Cross-Eyed Soldier closed the door after them.

'These men aren't worth the weight of a single mosquito wing,' Rabia scoffed, as she scratched at the bite marks that bloomed like roses between her legs.

The soldiers marched outside, chanting, 'Pakistan Zindabad!' Khaki helmets reflected sunlight, casting sporadic spotlights into the room. All at once the chanting stopped as the Shaytan returned with gifts for the Major.

The Shaytan was the tallest man Lucky had ever seen. When he walked past the window, only his shoulders and torso were visible. He stood within the shadows of the camp, forgotten by everyone, until night arrived, when the orange light of the cigarette that always hung from his lips burned between the bushes, the only indication he was there at all. He walked with no sound and spoke in low whispers. Not even Suhana, who had been there the longest, knew who he really was. Major Moustache was different around him. Alert. Wary. Lucky couldn't tell if he was giving orders to the Shaytan or taking them from him.

The Shaytan never touched them but he liked to watch. At night he slithered out of the shadows, bringing with him a sudden cold, and stood in front of the window to listen. He stood for hours. With no striking features, the image of his face was hard to recall, except for his eyes. Eyes so dark Lucky was certain he had no pupils. In certain hours of the night, they seemed to slant into the eyes of a cat or a snake; in daylight they disappeared altogether. Though he was rarely violent himself, he helped others brand themselves sinners. Glee bounced off his dark eyes as others sliced, shot and set people alight. Once, Lucky was unlucky enough to meet his gaze. He peered into the depths of her despair, moving his jaw from side to side unnaturally as if his tongue skittered with excitement. Neither vicious nor vocal, but altogether something worse, the Shaytan made the women shrink into themselves with his eerie presence. Like they were facing the devil himself.

'These cockroaches were hiding along the border of the southern village,' the Shaytan said.

Major Moustache removed the cigar from his mouth and spat on the ground. He looked at the dirty young men crouched on their knees before him and snarled. 'Truly, all the people of this land are disbelievers and traitors!'

His rifle swung in the air.

Smack.

'Bol, Pakistan Zindabad!'

Smack.

'Bol, penchod!'

Smack.

Major Moustache raised his rifle and cracked it over the head of a captured mukti joddha. The young man fell with a sharp grunt, his forehead splitting into two red banks. Reunited with a lost vigour, the women crawled over each other to look through the single window in search of a father, a husband, a brother.

'Joy Bangla!' an older man yelled before his tongue gushed with blood at the end of the Shaytan's boot. As he lifted his foot, the Shaytan's tongue wriggled across his lips in wicked glee.

Six men knelt in front of the Major. Blindfolded. Hands tied behind their backs. Bloodied feet angled in painful directions. Green lungis damp with water and mud. The boys shivered with their heads pointed to the ground; the men raised their faces at the Major with their mouths set straight in defiance. Gaunt bodies, hot, cold, and rattling with the remembrance of death.

'Here to kill us? Rescue your women? Both, if it's a good day?' Major Moustache's lips curled into a snarl. 'It's a shame you're so weak, it's why we came to help you. Did the Indians give you these weapons? God doesn't help the kuffar, or anyone who makes a deal with them.'

Fury coiled at the ends of the women's tongues. It was wondrous how much of another language they could grasp when it was spoken with contempt. Rokeya translated a few words under her breath, and whether or not they heard her, the women's hearts hardened with understanding.

Suhana trembled behind the Major with a tray of ruti and daal in her hands. Next to her the Fat Man tore around the edges of the ruti, Suhana's shaking hands quickening the process, and slipped a hot piece into his mouth.

Two more boys were led to the Major by their shaggy hair. Students. Their gangly bodies frozen in youth, stunted from running from gunfire and shooting at men. Rokeya's breath trembled as she watched the boys grind their teeth, like she did each night, to keep from begging the enemy for mercy. She pushed away from the window, searching wildly on the ground, and picked up a small pebble with an even smaller insect burrowing inside it. To take a chance.

'Bismillah.' She blew on the pebble, squeezed it in both palms, then launched it out the window toward the students.

Later that night, Lucky wondered how Major Moustache and his soldiers missed the sailing pebble hitting the side of the boy's bare foot. How they missed the boy raising his head slightly toward them and, through a sliver of a slip in the blindfold, locking eyes with the women and giving them a small nod of acknowledgement. In that moment, she asked herself, was the soldiers' sight covered as a mercy from God, or was it just a trick by the devil to prolong a painful hope that still beat in her heart?

The Slightly Cross-Eyed Soldier pushed past them to reach Rokeya. He pulled the women from the window one by one until they sat behind him, away from the Major's line of sight.

'You must stay back!' the Slightly Cross-Eyed Soldier warned.

'You should go back,' Rokeya shot back in Urdu, her eyes alight. 'Your time here is coming to an end.'

Rokeya crawled back into her corner. Her fingers drifted across the dips and ridges of the mud, like a gentle wind. Lines scarred the soft ground in the room's corner—one line for each morning that rose and each night that fell while Rokeya lived. A record of her time in the room. So, when the Mukti Bahini entered the camp that day, Rokeya knew help had come seven weeks into her captivity.

The Slightly Cross-Eyed Soldier stood before the window, the mouth of his rifle petting the ground, waiting for the women to settle back into their spaces, into the dips in the floor and the curves of the walls that remembered their bodies. Except now, their hearts remained outside with their brothers as renewed hope pumped in their veins.

Footsteps crossed the veranda. The Slightly Cross-Eyed Soldier moved across the room and into his chair as the Slow-Smiling Soldier appeared at the door. He surveyed the women one by one in search of a light, a shimmer, a drop of defiance. Lucky closed her eyes. Mohini smiled at the pink flower pushing through the cement. Jamila fixed her gaze on the mushroom that grew between her feet. It bloomed beyond itself, cracking under its skin, peeling itself open. The Slow-Smiling Soldier walked past them, satisfied at having found what he was searching for, and locked the doors of the window, covering them in darkness, leaving only small rays of light to seep through the uneven panels.

That night, as they entered the room one by one, the Slow-Smiling Soldier smiled more slowly than usual, Major Moustache offered no 'darlings' or 'honeys' to his favourites, the Fat Man forgot to bounce his baton on their breasts before taking his pick, and the Shaytan stood closer to the window, his torso and shoulders pressed against the bars, his lit cigarette giving an orange eye to the khaki night.

The waves were loud and near, tossing Lucky like a dandelion on a windy day, until she emerged, cleansed of all the dirt and smells of the room. Walking to the bank with easy strides, she stepped out of the river, completely dry. Before her hovered purple and blue skies. Rolling meadows and perpetual gardens. Ammu had told her stories about this place when she was a child. A place with no sun or moon, where none died and none were sad. Hanging from branches lost among the clouds were fruits of every kind, fat and full of colour. The smell of jasmines and roses wafted through the air. Between melodies of bird-song, the sound of familiar laughter echoed through the mountains, soothing like the song of martyrs flying free. Lucky ran. Sand parted beneath her feet, opening a path for her, until she saw the back of Waleed's wild curls and Rayan's smile splash the ocean surface.

'Look, Ammu's here!' Waleed called.

Rayan ran to her, his excitement tumbling towards her until his tiny arms wound around her neck and his legs wrapped around her waist. Gripping his head to hers, she breathed. Fresh grass mixed with what remained of his baby smell. At last, peace. Just then the tides pushed her back until Waleed was a speck in the sea. The sand disappeared as water rushed in, filling her nose and lungs, pulling her arms apart until the last of her fingers fell away from Rayan and she was swallowed by darkness.

Go away, O black clouds,
My moyna will have her bath now...

Lucky moved her fingers erratically across the ground, shuddering with relief as they were met with Jamila's hair. Outside, the Fat Man snored and stray cats screeched at each other. Rubi's lullaby filled the air.

'Rabia, I'm afraid I'm going crazy,' Lucky whispered, so quietly the calm winds almost carried the sound away.

Rabia's singing tapered off into the warm darkness. Silence sat between them. The faint whites of Rabia's eyes searched Lucky, looking for something within, and Lucky felt her friend's fingertips press into the rooms of her heart until she grew restless against her assessment.

'Yet your eyes remain clear,' Rabia said finally. 'And when they lose their focus, you bring it back with sheer stubbornness.'

'Only by remembering my son.'

Rabia shook her head. 'We're all mothers and daughters here, but some of us will wander into darkness and never return. Others, like me, with nothing to live for, just hold on to sanity for vengeance's sake, to see a day when justice demands that what was taken from us be returned.' Her chest rose again with Rubi's lullaby. 'What do you live for?'

Lucky searched the patchwork roof. She looked for herself in each crack where starlight sparkled against the corrugated tin. Tiny, twinkling specks of rainbow sat in the rust. A day would come when the soldiers would slump dead to the ground in different directions. Fall on their foreheads, sides, and the unlucky ones on their backs, to be pointed at in the afterlife. In this life, certificates would mark their deaths as those of martyrs, the ground above them dignified and their memory honoured, while she lay in the open plains of hell. Yet, under starlight, the sweet scent of jasmines called to her through a pathway to an open beach, where a handsome smile and tiny outstretched arms waited for her.

'I live for a promised day.'

9. MARKED ARROWS

The sun pricked Lucky's skin, making it bubble with water. A magpie-robin perched on the windowpane. It looked around, jerking its head quickly, before its neck turned backwards and Lucky saw, reflected in its pupils, tiny jets zipping in between drifting clouds, marring the blue sky with a sickly black. The Slow-Smiling Soldier had opened the window in the night as an unnatural lightning torched the skies, to show the women the hideous conquest.

Lucky's thoughts drifted to Ammu. Ammu's face had faded in her mind's eye. Did the beauty spot lie on her top or bottom lip, was the crease around her mouth more prominent on the left side of her face or the right? She couldn't remember. Had Ammu realised what had happened to them? Was the worry making her sicker? And, if she never saw Rayan again, would he remember her? Clearly or faintly? Would his memories be of their laughter, her hugs, the songs she sang to lull him to sleep, or the back of her head as he waited at the kitchen door while she murmured distractedly that she would be just a little longer? The burning, jagged rhythm of regret kept Lucky's palms, held in prayer, pressed against her face.

'We have to leave, now,' Rokeya said.

She stood in the middle of the room, looking down at the women. The Slightly Cross-Eyed Soldier sat behind her, resting his chin on the butt of his rifle, which stood beneath him like a walking stick, eyes on his boots, thoughts far away, but listening. Those who had been in the room the longest confirmed he showed no indication of understanding Bangla, but as a precaution the women switched words that were similar in Urdu with local dialect. The older women no longer cared if he understood or not, having as little regard for him as they did for his comrades. He was another leg on the chair, and everyone, including him, seemed to accept it.

'The war is turning in our favour. The Mukti Bahini came all the way here, on foot! It's only a matter of time before others come this way. We must help them escape,' Rokeya urged, looking at each of them for support. 'The students who came in last are from my brother's class. I know them. If we help them get away, they'll tell my brothers to come for us.'

The room was silent. Women turned their backs to her. Empty-eyed girls looked on. Jamila rolled her earrings in doubt. Faced with the women's silence, Rokeya grabbed Lucky's hands in appeal.

'It's our only chance to live, to see our families again, to set ourselves free from this torture. It's a risk, yes, but better to die trying to escape than die under the fingers of filthy men!'

A murmur lifted the room. Those whose voices no longer served them reached towards Rokeya and Lucky and squeezed the pair's hands. Whether in agreement or dissuasion, it was difficult to tell. Rabia slapped their backs in agreement. Uncertain, Mohini bit her lip.

'Why? To reveal ourselves and cast doubt on our honour?' said a voice behind them.

Chanda's head was permanently tilted in that sour way telling of a bad lot in life. She huffed at their talk of fight or freedom, scorned their attempts to placate their captors or brawl with them, stuck her nose up at those who prayed and those who cursed, and turned away from those who cried readily and those who feigned dry-eyed strength. Each day she lay under the beams that fell through the roof, shimmying across the floor until the light fell directly onto her eyes like spectacles carved by the sun, calling to the heavens to let her enter or to strike her blind before the door opened again.

'People draw false lines across the world and call it power. What remains true is that we are women and they are men, and after a while, the men outside will spit on us just like the men in here. Should we run towards disgrace? Cheer for our humiliation? Is that the freedom we should escape to?' Chanda paused to let the weight of her warnings settle over them. 'We are women—even in death, while we are soulless and cold, our bodies are so valuable that we must be wrapped with more cloth and buried with tighter knots. We are taken, tortured and returned, only to be rejected later by our own. That is the truth.'

'Our families are waiting for us,' Lucky said softly. 'They're praying for us to come home.'

'They'll use the same prayers they plead to God now to heckle us with later. Don't you understand? Our freedom comes at the cost of the peace of those who love us! Humiliation lies beneath our every step, and the step of everyone who walks after us. It's better to rot here with these devils.'

'To die as martyrs,' Zoleyka nodded.

'Exactly. Make peace with your rotten destiny, don't test the love of those who love you by asking them to endure something they won't be able to bear. Our families will forget us one day if we never return, but if we step foot again on our own doorsteps, they'll *wish* to forget us.'

'You're too harsh on people, Chanda,' Mohini said. 'We don't know how our families will receive us.'

Chanda shook her head. 'It's better to be a happy memory than a living pain.'

Lucky's support for Rokeya's appeal had vanished from her lips. Instead, her breath came out in short, hard bursts at the remembrance of her husband's parting promise, her son's parting tears, and the possibility of their ruin. Beside her, Jamila's fingers paused around her earlobes.

'If the price of our freedom is the peace of those we love? Let them pay it,' Jamila challenged, breaking the silence that had descended on the room, her calm, sure cadence commanding the night. 'Why shouldn't we free ourselves? They're not some great undefeatable enemy. These soldiers aren't monsters, they're not mad or evil, they're no mystery. War only brought forward what darkness was already in them, and with defeat it'll slip back in. And our families? If they're disgusted by us on our return, it was always in them to be so. That's what we must accept, not that we're dishonoured but that those we love were always heartless.'

Chanda blushed with indignation. 'D'you think we'll leave here unchanged? Go back to making tea and stitching pillows cheerfully? We're slaves in body here, but we'll be slaves to our minds once we're free. Are you fine to return like that to your children?'

'I'll not live or die for someone else's love. I live for my right to live.'

'So, you'd dishonour your family just to live a torturous life.'

'Nobody holds your honour in their fists,' Jamila said to Chanda, her eyes lit with a ferocious spark Lucky had never seen before. 'God granted no one that power. Don't you see that every man becomes a politician when it suits him? They speak of honour only to tie your wrists to their ankles. And a woman who crawls on her hands is never thanked for being on her knees. So let them forget us if they must, there are rewards in our pain. For a start, we can use it to free the mukti joddhas, so they can free us in return.'

'This is a mistake,' Chanda said, shaking her head. 'We'll curse our families once we walk out of here. And we'll break our own hearts doing it.'

'We can think about that once we're free,' Mohini concluded, ending the dispute.

Rokeya sat cross-legged leaning her head on her hand. Her fingers trembled over the lines she had drawn in the ground. 'A people doesn't change until they first change what's within themselves, and we've a lot to change as a people,' she said. 'But neither fear nor comfort is worth the price of our freedom. Please, think about this.'

Rain murmured down on the roof in gentle waves. No one spoke. The dark sky lulled their eyes closed but the women did not sleep. Each was lost in memories. Lucky's thoughts returned to her son's milky smell, to her husband's warmth, to Ammu, to her mother-in-law, to the little joys in their days together, to the catmint that poked onto her veranda and waited to be watered each day. What she should do, what was right, these answers evaded her, but she knew one thing with certainty. Her family would not forget her.

On Fridays, the soldiers lined up to pray, removing their caps and covering their medals with their hands, to murmur for forgiveness and a victory that history would celebrate. Lucky wondered if angels ever scoffed at what they wrote down. If they shook their heads at those who rested their foreheads on the ground, obedient at the level of their limbs and wetting their throats with remembrance five times a day, hoping to wipe away the terror they had caused between prostrations. Or if the angels tightened their grip on their pens as they watched the devil dance by their kneeling heads in triumph.

Each week, before the Friday prayer, the soldiers welcomed Lychee Bhai, who brought boxes of fruit, vegetables and spices to the camp. Lychee Bhai had a face that reminded you of the devil, though he spoke gently and greeted the women with a salam whenever he came. He was a local merchant, the lychees from his farm famous as far as the eight surrounding districts, their seeds smaller and their pulp juicier than those grown in other orchards. People whispered that he travelled to China for seeds. When the war began, half of Lychee Bhai's employees made way to India and the other half joined the Mukti Bahini. But Lychee Bhai was not deterred. He continued to sell his lychees to those few customers determined to remain home, until even those neighbours dwindled, and he worried about the tonnes of lychees unsold and uneaten in his gardens. So, when khaki uniforms stood before him in the ripest season, he sold his lychees to them instead, pleased business was up again. Lychee Bhai's lychees were so juicy, the army spared him and his farm from incineration and employed him as their personal merchant. He shook hands with them eagerly. It was better than letting the lychees go to waste.

Every Friday, Lychee Bhai and the soldiers laughed and joked and spoke about the rain and the sun, forgetting the bombs and the fires. Lychee Bhai gave them alcohol and they gave him foreign cigarettes. After the harvest passed, he threw in extras, not as seedless or as juicy as his lychees, but enough to keep them pleased. And each week, when Lychee Bhai turned his back on the soldiers as they wrestled over their bounty, he whispered words from the outside to the women behind the barred window. The women counted the days till Friday when Lychee Bhai would return with snippets of news. But it had been two weeks now since they had last seen him.

As the sun set on another Friday without Lychee Bhai's lychees or news from the outside world, the women grew restless, and Rokeya, noticing their dwindling morale, decided to tell them her story.

'Boro Bhai helped organise the '68 uprising against the regime,' she began. 'When we were children, our father told us to always challenge what's unfair because you have nothing to live for if not your values. So, when relations between the East and West got worse, I heard Baba tell Ammu, *I have my sons, I have my daughter, and I have you. I have my two hands. I have the support of God on my side. Everything will end well.*'

But at night, Rokeya's father did not sleep restfully. Small sounds woke him. He would pace around the house, checking the locks on the windows and doors, and stand on the balcony looking out towards the night. Rokeya would find him there in the early hours of the morning with cups of tea around him, as if he had not slept at all.

'Did he see an ominous sign when he looked out? I don't know, he never told us.'

The chill night gave her words a silver smoke. In the candlelight, Lucky saw the outline of her lips touch the moonless night sky.

'By the middle of March, there were already incidents of violence being reported in our town. Baba was a doctor, and people came to his hospital after they were beaten by razakars living next to them who supported the army. How easy it is to betray one another,' Rokeya sniffed. 'Still, we believed we were united in our town, our neighbours were our friends, our businesses were honest, our love for each other and for our land was enough. We were confident we could fight if the enemy arrived on our doorstep. The night they came we had to close our eyes to keep them, fearing the fires would burn them away. They tore away our confidence and united conviction, forced us to forget our families, our friends, our neighbours and our homes, to run without looking back and later hope that our loved ones had run with us.'

Lucky's eyelids lowered with each word. Tears bent her lashes threatening to pierce her eyes. Shame turned them inwards, the grief of her own naivety come back for vengeance. She had been silly to believe the war would never reach her.

'They announced that the army had attacked over loudspeakers and that we should prepare. Baba's practice became a hideout for injured mukti joddhas. There were so many injured that they came to the doors of our home at all times of the day and night. Baba didn't have enough hands to help them or the heart to send them back, so Ammu and I became his nurses. He knew my two brothers had joined the Mukti Bahini but he kept quiet. As a father, he couldn't tell them to join and risk death, but as a man of principle, a patriot, he wouldn't stop them from holding on to their freedom by force. So, he said nothing. Nothing when Chotto Bhai didn't return for days. Nothing as he treated Boro Bhai's injuries. Nothing when Ammu and I hid arms under our beds in the day and buried them under our chilli plants at night. Nothing when I went to the markets to send messages to other factions. He knew it all, but he said nothing, so he could remain both a father and a patriot.'

Rokeya cleared her throat. The women moved towards her voice, facing her in the darkness. The Slightly Cross-Eyed Soldier turned one eye to her. Night creatures stopped their chatter to listen.

'What Baba didn't know, towards those last days, was that Chotto Bhai was injured and trapped behind enemy lines. Boro Bhai returned without him to regroup. They needed supplies for the rescue mission. When I heard, I told my parents I was going out to send a message, but I followed Boro Bhai into combat. We didn't tell our parents, *they must continue to treat the injured and shelter the sick,* we thought. Boro Bhai had taught me how to use a gun months before the war began. He was the pessimistic type.'

'You fought?' Jamila scanned Rokeya's body for signs of battle. A slight girl with even slighter arms, Rokeya looked too gentle to point death at anyone. 'They let a woman fight?'

'Boro Bhai didn't think a woman was any less a fighter than a man, as long as she had a weapon in her hand. I didn't understand him for a long time, his readiness to fight, but when we went to watch *Jibon Theke Neya* in the cinema together, before it was banned, I cried when "Amar Shonar Bangla" played. That day, I decided I would do something if the time came, something, anything, woman or not. So, when Chotto Bhai was taken, I put on trousers and a shirt, cut my hair short, wrapped my head and chest with a gamchha and covered my face with dirt. I was as skinny as the rest of them and didn't speak. They couldn't tell I was a woman.'

'Did you kill anyone?'

'I shot when the shooting began.'

Lucky furrowed her brows at Jamila's questions. It was a bad habit of hers. Often her curiosity came across as cruel, but for Jamila, only truth was important, and it held its position above all.

'I don't know if I've killed and a part of me doesn't care if I have. They came here with their guns first. Should we catch their bullets with open palms while we plead with them to stop?' Rokeya questioned.

'You must feel different now.'

'It feels like a part of my soul has left me forever.'

'You were in the right,' Lucky interjected, comforting Rokeya.

'The rights of life and death are beyond what I think I know,' Rokeya said. A faraway look crossed her face, but she gathered herself quickly before it could settle on her. 'At some point, as the bullets flew, I lost Boro Bhai and was pulled away by another man. We ran through the bushes, but I knew it was no use. I felt the angel of death run with us.'

'They caught you.'

'The Slow-Smiling Soldier caught us. He shot them all and smiled at me in that slow way he smiles, like he's all-knowing. He saw something in me that the other men hadn't. He knew I was a woman. *Lower your trousers, prove you're Muslim and not a Hindu*, he said. All the men laughed. Later I learnt he called me a warrior princess. It was amusing to him they were being shot at by a woman. He brought me here to torture me slowly, instead of killing me like he kills men, to take from me the certainty of death.'

Jamila exhaled. 'Death is too great a mercy for women in the hands of merciless men.'

Boots splashed on still puddles outside. The Fat Man's snores became irregular, shifting the chair beneath him sideways until he woke. The Slightly Cross-Eyed Soldier tilted his head toward the candle in the corner of the room, suddenly tired. The crickets took their silence as a cue to recommence their song. A woman's shadow hesitated outside the door.

'Your brothers will look for you,' Lucky said.

'If they're alive. I want to return to Baba and tell him he was right. You fight oppression to the death or fight yourself each day to accept it. You know what I hate the most about this war? These people, politicians, they all think a poor man can't have a sophisticated thought, but everyone knows when they're being cheated and when they're being laughed at. They call the farmer stupid but print papers and posters to condition him and use the radios to belittle him until he thinks as they tell him to, and when he still doesn't, because his heart hungers for truth, they call him an enemy and throw him in prison or kill him. They lie to our faces and call us conspirators for questioning them.'

'They're hypocrites who deny our humanity,' Lucky murmured out the window, glimpsing her own heart on the other side of the river.

'And try to make us forget it. They kill our teachers like we'll lose the desire to learn, they kill our preachers like we'll forget God in the face of oppression, they kill our friends of different faiths like we'll never worship side by side again, slide their filthy hands down our bodies like we'll never long for love again, release their desire in us to ruin our futures like we'll never rebuild again, demand our silence like we'll never speak truth again. What they don't know is that we see small pins of light in the darkest nights, like marked arrows set sail for the moon.'

As the night merged into day and the day into night, Zoleyka braided her hair. Plait braid, single braid, lace braid, ladder braid, fishtail braid. A wavy wand.

Now she sat quietly beside Lucky and Jamila and picked up a feather that had fallen from the sky into the room. With four streams falling from her eyes, she began tearing at its wispy veins, ripping into the strands one by one, grabbing the flesh of her fingertips at the same time until the soft grey feather kissed red. Jamila sat up, watching her cautiously. She placed a hand on Lucky's knee in warning, but Lucky ignored it.

'Apa, do you see the birds above us spreading and closing their wings?' Lucky asked, feeling Jamila's disapproval as she gently wiped Zoleyka's fingers with the corner of her petticoat. Lucky could sense she needed someone to talk to, and unlike

Jamila, she wasn't sceptical of everyone. 'The Lord of Mercy holds them up there.'

Zoleyka reached over and stroked her raw fingers across the top of Lucky's hand. 'I don't believe in God.' Her voice was low and scratchy. Unused.

Lucky sat up straight in surprise. She had never met anyone who didn't believe in God. 'Why did you stop believing?'

'A year ago, the cyclone washed away my Amma's family. I was visiting them at the time, and they found me far away in a field between bloated sheep and overturned trees. They planned to bury me with the sheep when they realised I was still breathing. That day, I lost my Nani, the sight in my right eye and my Amma's love. My Abba sold land to pay for my treatment and Amma resented me for it.'

'None of that was your fault,' Jamila said. She had seen women like this before, whose pain had settled in a place forever changed. They became a fixture in their own macabre memories, still unable to rejoin the world long after it had forgiven them.

'We grew poorer because I didn't die, and it was during these days that the soldiers came. The birds were the first to flee. If we'd noticed them, maybe we could have run too... but we never listen to the birds. Only your God understands their language,' she said with a wry smile. 'They killed my father and brothers. *Cooperate and we won't kill you,* one said, but the other didn't listen and flung the coal net over them to set them alight.'

'I can't understand it,' Lucky shuddered.

Zoleyka thought about this for a moment. 'It's best if you don't try to understand them.'

While Lucky was astounded by Zoleyka's thoughts, so different from her own, Jamila sensed a volatility that was being fuelled by her sister's enquiry. She signalled to Lucky to end the conversation. But it was too late.

'My hair was always beautiful, long and thick, everyone said so,' Zoleyka continued. 'That night, the soldiers said the same thing, in their tongue, but I understood. So did Amma. Her resentment left her when she saw how they looked at me. When they dragged me by my hair into the truck where the other girls sat, she pleaded with them to spare me, to take her instead, to kill us together, until I heard two shots and there was no one left to pray for me. Your merciful God could have let us die together.'

Fearful of the savage pain she saw in Zoleyka's gaze, Lucky prayed that night to be dealt a lesser pain, pain that blew like fresh petals fallen on a river's surface, rocking with the tide. A ship of solace for small-winged insects to land on, their weight pushing it only slightly further into the water. A pain that sat without settling, that trembled and flipped away whatever fell on it, turning under the water again and again, to rise, renewed, shining under a new sun. A pain that could overcome and reopen its heart to the world.

Zoleyka closed her streaming eyes and hummed against the beat of Lucky's silent prayer. Her fingers stroked her plaited hair until it shone.

In the small hours of the night, she lay still in the blind spot where the Slightly Cross-Eyed Soldier's crossed eyes conspired against each other. Her back towards him. Her braid, long and thick, curled close around her neck.

The next day, when Lucky woke up, Zoleyka was gone.

That afternoon, the Slightly Cross-Eyed Soldier cut their hair off.

One by one.

Until it reached just below their ears.

10. MAJOR OR MINOR

The plan moved in the rhythm of a spider's web, built and abandoned, built and abandoned, until it was perfected. They needed one night. Perhaps only a few hours. They would wait to hear from Lychee Bhai first before picking a day. Everyone was in agreement.

They whispered the scheme to each other one by one, careful not to alert the soldiers who came in and out. Even those whose minds were locked away in their broken hearts opened their mouths long enough to pass on the message. What was left to settle of the plan was the last central strand, to which each other strand pointed: Suhana.

Suhana was Major Moustache's favourite of all his favourites. She had travelled with him since the beginning, chained to his feet as he collected others like her. She slept in his room, listened to his stories, kept her eyes to the ground the way he liked, low, and never cried. She spoke Urdu fluently. After seeing one of Waheed Murad's films on her friend's TV, she had memorised all his lines and then all the other lines as well, then watched each of his films, perfecting their accents and expressions until she was indistinguishable from a Punjabi except in blood and colour. To Major Moustache, a small part of home lay in Suhana's body.

Major Moustache returned with gifts for Suhana after each expedition. When his laughter swam through the gates, Suhana, who came to the room only to deliver food, came in wearing a fresh kameez, a gold necklace or new bangles. A doll fit for the Major's tastes. Lucky wondered about the women who died for their wedding bangles to end up on Suhana's wrists, those women who did not satisfy the Major's taste. When Major Moustache's lusts drifted elsewhere, Lucky saw Suhana scratch at her wrists until the red claw marks made it look like the gold had seared her skin, so deep she could hear it sizzle.

Suhana would not meet their eyes when she came into the room. She fled their imploring fingers and hushed their heaving sobs with such a fearful look that they had no choice but to return to their own heartaches. Around the camp she walked with her back hunched, only straightening herself when the Major called for his darling.

In the morning, as Suhana placed ruti and daal in front of them, Rokeya whispered into her ear. She shook her head before Rokeya could finish. 'Stop this now,' she said, her voice level with the clattering of the bowls placed on the floor. 'It won't work.'

'If we free the mukti joddhas, they'll contact my brothers to come for us,' Rokeya pleaded.

'I've travelled with them from place to place. Trying to escape has never ended well for us.'

'We can't give up trying.'

The Slightly Cross-Eyed Soldier's crossed eyes lingered on Rokeya's mouth. Suhana's heart hammered in her ears. He was listening.

'They'll kill us,' Suhana said, turning towards the door, her eyes flickering to the Slightly Cross-Eyed Soldier. 'They watch closely when I walk past the cell.'

Rokeya gripped Suhana's fingers and lowered her voice to a hush. 'We're already dead! Zoleyka Apa is gone, may she be in peace, and the rest of us sit here with death each day...' Her eyes filled with water even as her tone grew steady. 'Please, Apa. Let's have the courage to free ourselves, before we lose another.'

Outside, Major Moustache called out for his darling.

'Let her go,' Lucky said quietly, pulling Rokeya's fingers from Suhana's hands.

In the courtyard, a portly soldier with a patchy beard, spread like the early morning leaves of a lotus waiting for its flower to bloom, brushed a small black comb over his chin, as they estimated he did a thousand times a day. The comb left angry tracks between the patches, so his face was striped like a hog badger's.

'Don't look at him too hard, you'll give him nazr,' Rabia nudged Rokeya, the sun casting shadows of wispy winter leaves across her face. 'Imagine what would happen if those small patches fell off his face like the crust of a crispy paratha. He'd kill us all for sure.'

Mohini laughed, her voice reaching into the ground beneath them, until it reached back up to shake them all. The pink flower swayed with her girlish jingle in its concrete home. If they had looked closely, they would have seen the Slightly Cross-Eyed Soldier's mouth lift slightly too.

'In the time it would take for him to drop his comb and reach for his rifle, we could take him,' Rokeya replied without breaking her focus.

'Look at those arms! Combing his chin all day has given him muscle. It'll take a lot to kill him,' said Noori.

Jamila shook her head, agreeing with Rokeya. 'He gets distracted by his own reflection in the waste bucket. We'd have strangled him with our petticoats before he remembered he came in to kill us.'

Would his meaty limbs fold inward or to the side when they tackled him, Lucky wondered. She smiled at the thought of their colourful petticoats creating a rainbow chain around his neck.

Jamila flicked her sister's forehead. 'Stand behind me when we attack, you can barely touch the fat on meat without squealing.'

Lucky slapped her arm in protest, and the sisters began to squabble.

'If Lychee Bhai returns with news that we've lost the war, let's promise to kill Lieutenant Patches over there with his own comb as our last act of revenge,' Rabia snorted.

The women sat in silence for the rest of the day, sunlight bouncing off their slouched angles while they waited for Suhana to return with an answer. As night dimmed their sight, the depths of hell settled in the gazes of some, the heights of paradise in others', and all its wretched patience in between.

A family of ants marched up the wall and through a tiny hole outside at a steady, rhythmic pace.

Lucky pushed one ant out of line with the pad of her finger. It squirmed and skirted around her nail until she placed a thumb on its body, stilling it with light pressure. Placing it in the pouch of her saree between her folded legs, she watched it try to escape for the rest of the evening, raising the sides of the fabric every so often so it would slide back down before it could get too close to the edge.

Lucky asked God if he could turn her into an ant so she could leave through the tiny hole in the wall too and go back to serving spoonfuls of rice to her family.

Five spoonfuls for her mother-in-law.

Three spoonfuls for her son.

That night, when the new moon shone bright, Lucky gathered the ant in a little shell in her saree and pressed. She opened the ball to find a dark blob and tiny stick legs splayed across the fabric valley. She waited for her heart to respond. Nothing.

'Keep us sane,' Lucky prayed.

As the lizards departed and the room swelled with emotion like an unpicked lychee past its prime, bursting at its seams, and the women covered their ears to block out the tortured screams of the Mukti Bahini from across the camp, Jamila stroked her sister's face. Rough but warm fingertips pulled Lucky back from the smooth, cold sands of her mind.

'I've told you before, stop thinking terrible things,' Jamila said.

'Is that possible?'

'It's possible to be hopeful.'

'What if soldiers are in our town?'

'Your son's safer over there than we are in here. Worry about getting back to him.'

Heat stung Lucky's nose. It was the smell of regret, like burning leaves stoking a fire from a distant house. 'We're imprisoned here because of my stupidity and now Rayan may grow up without a mother...'

Jamila covered her mouth with her palm and the sisters studied each other. Sorrowful sockets whispered assurances to one another, the cavernous lines of one pair acknowledging the other's twin depth, its edging towards emptiness at a terrifyingly assertive pace. Lucky understood that Jamila did not want an apology for the decision made in the forest. She would not talk about it. Guilt gathered under Lucky's lids, and she tightened her brows, determined not to let any spill. A soldier peered in at them from the window.

'I should remember these men to point them out one day,' Lucky said, clearing her throat when Jamila released her hand. 'But it's as though I can't see their faces anymore.'

'They don't look much different to any man you pass in the market.'

'That's a terrible thing to say.'

'It's true.'

Jamila pressed Lucky's eyelids closed, moving the moisture inside from side to side. They hadn't eaten in days or slept for more than a couple of hours every night before being woken by a distant blast. Sleep beckoned Lucky, but she fought to stay awake, desperate to hear her sister's familiar, austere opinions. Her only comfort. Questions that had plagued her since their capture began to leak from her lips.

'How do they feel lust at a time like this?'

'They worship their desires over the laws of man, land and God. Look into their eyes, they're lost. Their actions hold no reason, their strikes have no purpose.' *And when man loses meaning, he seeks pleasure of the worst kind,* Jamila thought.

'I would rather have died than come here.'

'Should I call one of them over?'

Lucky pinched Jamila. 'Be serious! Aren't we the enemy? Why don't they just kill us?'

Jamila looked at her incredulously. 'Well, there isn't much sweetness in all their killing...'

'So they crawl onto our bodies...' Lucky finished Jamila's sentence.

'You'd be hard-pressed to find a war where we haven't become its treasures,' Jamila mused. 'At worst we're a pleasurable release to demons, at best we're tanks or horses, a comfortable seat to take them to their destination. Not really all that different from peacetime.' She wiggled her brow.

Lucky hated when her sister spoke like this. Jamila had a terrible habit of noticing small things and remembering everything, which meant that, most of the time, she could be nothing but pessimistic.

'Rahat doesn't see you as a rickshaw.'

Jamila paused for a moment, as if only having realised that he was a man too. 'We'll see.'

As the night and day wrestled by, an answer appeared to Lucky. Simple and sickening, so cruel she couldn't have realised it sooner. The reason she was here in the room with her sister, not crushed under the weight of a thousand bodies in a mass grave, was that war commanded that a fighter's honour lay not within himself but in what he could take from between women's legs. And to win that honour, the soldiers were ready to sacrifice their humanity.

Ammu had warned the sisters of men like this, those who only sought the approval of other men, when she sat them down and set out the criteria for picking a husband. Though Abbu had died young, leaving her an even younger widow, Ammu had seen enough of the world to know how to protect her daughters from it. She had seen men who were human at home and tyrants outside and men who were human outside and tyrants at home. Both were wicked. Bad men tortured women in ways they could not survive themselves. They used women as fuel to survive in this world and kept them alive only in flesh so they might serve them. They were lost souls, and a soul that abandoned itself would only corrupt others. But before she told her daughters what she had seen, Ammu wanted to know what they already knew of life.

'People lie,' Jamila had said matter-of-factly. 'So we need to be careful. Someone once told me that too many hard-hearted people walk around with soft smiles.'

'Who did you hear that from?' Lucky asked.

'Bibijaan.'

'From the market? She's a bit...' Lucky made circles with her finger near her temple.

'She's not.'

'Well, that can't be true.'

'It is.'

Lucky frowned, not understanding what hard-hearted meant, so she appealed to Ammu. 'Ammu, you told us not to be suspicious of people.'

'Not to be suspicious of the intentions of people we already know,' Ammu corrected.

'We need to be careful of everybody else,' Jamila said.

Lucky was taken aback by the severity of Jamila's answer. It made her shudder to think how Jamila could have come to this knowledge.

When she saw Ammu and Jamila waiting for her response, she grew warm with embarrassment at having nothing to say, so she asked, 'Why do they become like this? Hard-hearted?'

'Some people forget God easily, so God lets them forget themselves,' Ammu said. 'They roam the world looking for themselves with clenched fists, and their hearts become hard. And while a hard-hearted man can learn how to fly in the sky, how to sail in the sea, he never learns how to walk the earth with goodness.'

Major Moustache had the air of a man granted all the blessings of the world—a good wife, a spacious house, a comfortable car and pleasant neighbours—although he was never home long enough to know if he suffered from the miseries of the world—a terrible wife, a small house, an uncomfortable vehicle and bad neighbours. His father was stern and believed a man should make himself distinct from all others, especially women, and there was no better way to do it than with facial hair. A strong moustache. Nose hair. Ear hair. Mole hair. All the hairs that signified manhood. The ways of the world came through his father's harsh words and even harsher hands. It helped Major Moustache rise within the ranks of the army and turned him into the kind of man who licked his finger before turning a page in a book just to leave a mark on everything he touched.

Kindness Major Moustache kept only for his children, and sometimes his wife. To others, he was an ambitious miser with a temper that might well strike a friend like an enemy. Friends eyed the corner of his stache, which twitched downward when he was displeased and hardened when he wanted a fight, and before either could become firm, they would flee his presence with parting well wishes. And so Major Moustache never heard a word to counter his, after his father died, and like all men who have always been told they are clever, he became stubborn and severe.

On a cloudy evening, as the soldiers stumbled into the room, Major Moustache opened his arms to embrace the night and began to slur a story of his military might. In broken Bangla he had picked up along the way, he declared, 'Women are the luckier sex. You see the gentlest parts of a man, the most merciful parts of war, the best of us! We could shoot you dead if we wanted... but we don't because you're women. We're good to you.'

He smiled down at them, appraising each woman's level of undress, in the way drunk men smiled, slow and stupid.

'The soul of a woman is just like that of a cat or a tortoise. No matter how much you torture it, it still lives.'

'It doesn't die,' the Slow-Smiling Soldier concurred, raising a bottle to his lips.

'It doesn't die!' the Major cheered. 'It may cry at first, but it stops crying with time. It may scream, but its tongue unravels. It may glare, but its gaze dims. Ice may freeze its lips, but its body remains warm. Ha! It remains beautiful under filth and dirt, and soft... its flesh and blood never harden. If you squeeze it, it bounces back, if you slap it, it turns a pretty pink, if you choke it, it only gasps. The Lord made you sturdy... useful. But we should always be careful not to teach cats how to climb trees, oh no.'

The sharp glint in his stare hardened as he spoke, and his body tensed, ready to strike. The women shrunk as his voice grew louder. Jamila leaned into Lucky until their backs hit the wall.

'Did you know chickens still run around after they die? Humans are like this too, they shit themselves. Ha ha! Still causing us problems, even after death.'

The soldiers laughed, spilling over each other. Major Moustache smiled, pleased with the thunderous reception of his jokes. At the wave of his hand, Suhana handed him another bottle. Major Moustache grabbed her by the waist and kissed her loudly on the cheek. He pushed his face into her neck and inhaled her with the zest of a charlatan ready to perform an exorcism.

Suddenly, he twirled her around, an opening dance before his men. He tapped his foot to the beat of a phantom rhythm and swayed to its music. A deep hum full of triumph bellowed from his chest. And as suddenly as he started, he stopped. Suhana fell into his chest as he took a breath. Alcohol had turned him into a poet.

'A perfect creation!' he proclaimed. 'A woman's soul flows into every swamp, puddle and hole and performs with perfection! A true comfort and an evil for man, coolness to his eyes, sweetness to his tongue, softness to his lips, joy to his ears, comfort to his touch, what beauty! The only beauty left in war… now understand this, what's a crime in the outside world is admissible in war, and we're good to you, you know. We fight for you, keep you alive and safe.'

Disgust coiled in Lucky's stomach as he surveyed them. She had seen that look before. It was the unblinking eye of a man that circled a woman's body but travelled beyond her eyes and lips into fantasy. A place where he was king and she, whatever he wanted her to be. The ugly heart of a man witnessed through a woman's weary eyes.

Just then the skies rumbled. Lightning snatched away their sight, adding dramatic effect to the bard's show. The spark unsettled the Major's men, a stern reminder of their smallness. They paused around their bottles' lips. Straightened their smiles. Looked to one another for assurance. These were the pains of the Minors, but for a Major like Major Moustache, a man too satisfied with himself to have doubts about the future, his hardness did not thaw when the heavens demanded humility from him. It hardened further.

Suhana staggered forward, pulling the Major close to the women. He stumbled over his footing, swaying like the branches of a swamp willow under a heavy rain, and stubbed the cap of his boot against the Slightly Cross-Eyed Soldier's chair. She peered at him to see if he was irked.

'Those self-righteous eyes, that look… understand this, woman!' He glared at Suhana, who prayed her face did not betray her fear. 'Gratitude, that's the delightful dance between man and woman. You ungrateful whore, I should've killed you long ago… Oh, my sweet, sweet darling!'

He became incoherent, mixing stories and people, and Suhana's legs shook from trying to keep him upright. Pain gathered in the Major's eyes with the impossible recollection of himself killing his Suhana-rani in fantasy, casting a shadow across his face for a life almost lost.

'Devils!' Rabia jumped up, unable to remain silent any longer. 'Hellfire is waiting for you!'

The Slow-Smiling Soldier leapt forward and slapped her across her face. Rabia fell to the floor, cradling the lump on her head. A drop of blood trickled from her nose into her open mouth, staining her clenched teeth a rosy red. She held in her gasp of pain. Mohini threw herself over her cowering body as the Slow-Smiling Soldier moved to kick her.

'I've done nothing to you,' Major Moustache said in a quiet voice, regaining clarity as he looked upon the brutal scene that had disrupted his delirium. 'You betrayed the land your fathers liberated from the Hindus. Pakistan! The dream of our ancestors. In one generation, you betrayed your people and your religion. This is what a Bengali is like. We've used no unjust authority over you. We came to correct the natural order, purify you, establish the laws of the land, restore the religion. We spoke to you gently, gave you choices, and look how you responded. You have only yourselves to blame for all the havoc you've caused.'

The lines in the Major's face became deeper and meaner the longer he spoke. He had aged months each day and his soldiers looked like they had wandered out of their graves, their bodies on loan to be returned to the darkness. Their limbs moved unnaturally like parts hurriedly sewn together with different stitches. A seven-piece puzzle of eyes, ears, tongue, stomach, genitals, hands and feet, clashing and clanging, ready to testify against each other. Lucky seethed at their grotesque conceit. She would wait for a day when these men would stand witness to themselves. When their eyes replayed the filth they had seen, their ears resounded with the cruelty they had heard, their tongues filled with the blood they had spilled, their stomachs boiled with the food they had stolen, their loins burned with the pain they had inflicted, their fingertips scorched with the fires they had set, their feet stung with the lives they had stomped out...

But for now, the Major stood tall and mighty on the land and made a home out of their skin, the only way a soldier knew how. To him a woman's screams were chimes on a windy day, her fists against his chest a lover's warm touch, her sobs at night a gentle lullaby.

Outside, three razakars from the neighbouring village looked in on them. They drank in the women's torn sarees and bruised skin but took care to avoid their faces, fearing they would see something in them to make them falter. It didn't take much for them to forget their countrywomen. The deed to a friend's farm. A handful of gold. A wad of cash. A pack of cigarettes. A promise. Whenever they crossed each other the soldiers' medals made them salivate and sweetened the cries of the women behind them. They spoke in double negatives, with one foot in and one foot out of culpability at all times. Happy to collect the riches of a military victory, and equally happy to return them without question after a guerrilla victory.

Rabia flung an empty plate at the barred window, rattling the razakars' hearts enough to make them turn away.

'Why are they here?' Lucky asked.

Rabia shrugged. 'To confess their crimes.'

'They're not confessing, they're bragging,' Mohini corrected. 'Just like a married man who visits the brothel during the day.'

'They're on two paths to the same destination,' Jamila's mouth curled with disgust. 'Those filthy bastards would follow the devil into a lizard's hole.'

As they moved around the camp, the men cast long shadows into the room. Tall and dark, with thick arms and legs that looked like scorched firewood. Sporadically shrouding the women's heads, midriffs and feet in turn with a volatile rhythm. Ready to roar alight again at the slightest scrape.

'What a lowly place to end up for some trinkets,' Lucky murmured.

Later that evening, Major Moustache came in with a smile so big his top lip disappeared between the wires of his moustache, and his slimy tongue slurped heavy on each word.

'I bring gifts, darlings.'

He flung a pile of clothes before them, tattered lungis and blouses from ransacked markets and homes. The women remained where they were, seeing the garments' owners in each crease and tear.

'Take what you want,' the Slow-Smiling Soldier smirked behind the Major.

The women pulled at whatever was closest to them. They trembled at the small sizes of the blouses and dresses made for young girls. Shirts the size of young boys. Those whose hearts still held the spark of defiance pulled men's vests and lungis towards them, to remind the soldiers that they too were enemies, who could not be lusted after without the reminder of the defeat that awaited them.

Dressed in a blouse and a lungi, Lucky slept with her fingers intertwined with Jamila's to stop her sister from pulling at her ears. The tick had become more frequent, and her piercing had begun to tear downwards. *Just wait a little longer and we'll be free,* Lucky promised Jamila that morning. Jamila only looked at her.

Now as she hovered between sleep and wakefulness, Lucky heard a sound so faint she could have dreamt it.

'I'll try, with Rahat.'

Beyond the windows, white jasmines sat on royal green leaves like soft reminders of a distant love that ran through her life. Like the laughter of women with baskets made of wood and bamboo leaves, who plucked jasmine buds from their roots and eagerly traced their fingers over budding petals, giddy to garnish life's beautiful moments with garlands. Now, her heart burned with a heat she wished she did not feel. A yearning, hellish heat to see those same white jasmines lining the barred windows, stained red with the repentance of men who had sold their hearts in exchange for hers.

Like the heart of a Major or a Minor.

11. BEAUTIFUL PATIENCE

Lucky couldn't remember the last time she had woken before dawn, nor could she recall the smell of the trees and the wet grass before light touched them, or when she had last witnessed the day colouring itself in with its details. A bee flew between dawn's damp leaves and into the room through the window, found its way around their tangled bodies and her knotted hair, and landed on the bud of the small pink flower that grew through the concrete. Lucky's tired thoughts moved slowly over one another before settling on one truth.

Today is beautiful.

'Today is beautiful,' Ammu said, as a little Lucky sobbed for the cows Abbu had prepared for slaughter after the Eid prayer. 'This cow will feed a lot of people, Nanis, Nanas, Ammus, Abbus and even tinier moynas than you. Lots of people will be happy!'

'The cows are scared of Abbu!'

Ammu watched the weary cow's shifty eyes and decided it was best to lie.

'Last night, the cows told Abbu they were happy to help on Eid day.'

'I didn't hear anything.'

'You were asleep.'

'I wasn't, I was crying with the cows.'

There was a time when children didn't ask their parents questions or make fantastical statements without fearing an imprint on their cheeks or buttocks by shoe, switch, pan, broom or the always available rough, calloused hand of an exhausted mother, ready to swat them back into silent obedience. But the small scars on Ammu's back and arms from a swat too hard told her it was no longer the way. She would try something different and throw in a lesson or two for her daughter to remember later in life.

'The cows know they're being made big and special for Eid.'

'Why?'

'God asks us to give him our best cow for his best day.'

'These cows aren't fat enough to be the best!' Lucky sobbed.

It was true, the cows hadn't grazed enough this year, and they looked almost as skinny as the street children. Their ribs scraped their soft-furred skin in envy of the goats and chickens who strutted around plump and delicious; their restless tails wagged in the air like parched wheat. Even their moos were pitiful. But a sacrifice had to be made, as promised, and a skinny cow for a skinny village child would have to do.

'Look how helpful and calm he is under Abbu's hands.'

'It's going to hurt.'

'Only for the tiniest moment. Then the cows will make the villagers' tummies full and God happy. This is a beautiful occasion, moyna.'

Lucky sniffed, doubtful. 'Beef curry isn't beautiful.'

Ammu took a breath. She would try again without the cows, for this was what it meant to be a mother.

'Beauty is hard to see on a sad day but it's still there if we look around, and once we see it, it reminds us that the sadness we feel today will turn into the beauty of tomorrow.'

'Where does it hide?'

'Behind our sad thoughts, we need to shoo those away first to find it.'

'And if I can't find it?'

'Then ask yourself, is there anything beautiful in today? Was there anything beautiful in yesterday? Your mind will magically call to your eyes all the pretty things around you.'

'We'll see the same things?' Lucky grew excited at the prospect of sharing the same eyes as Ammu—it would make playing games more fun. She could direct Ammu to hide and seek her out with her thoughts alone. She had heard that angels had that power but didn't know she did too.

'We don't need to see the same things. You just need to see something for yourself.'

Lucky saw lots of things. A cat on the road, butterflies near bushes, lost frogs splashing in a muddy spring on her way back home. But how often did she see those things? Most days, naked children cried on the streets and slept huddled together, poor men lurked in the shadows looking for work, and women Ammu's age shouted in their homes at children Lucky's age.

'Sometimes I think of more bad things.'

'Well, what will be my next thought? That's what you think when bad thoughts come to you. Then you choose a thought that moves in the direction of goodness.'

Ammu's words rang true now with the buzzing of the bee. Happiness belonged to the bees, who worked diligently and purposefully, having faith in each flower they sought. They moved with leisure, rested regally on the silky petals and drank from the centre slowly, showing gratitude to the bud. A mutually joyful exchange.

Lucky's mind wandered to days when frustration had dripped from her eyes at her new-born's refusal to feed from her breast, at her impotent body which could not satisfy her baby. With that, of course, came the look of judgement from her mother-in-law. A hairline tut in the distance, a reshuffling of the baby at her breast, an impatient *don't worry, Rayan's Amma,* or worse, a sweet, grandmotherly chastisement of the baby that was actually meant for Lucky herself.

She became Rayan's Amma to the world and remained Lucky only to Ammu, Jamila and Waleed. Whenever they were away from her for too long, she began to forget her own name, its lazy beginning and arresting ending, that odd English word that had made its way from another land onto the tongue of her Nani, who had named her as dawn rose between the clouds in the small town where she was born. It took days, and often impatient reminders, for her to respond to it again after she left the small world of her home and entered the world where others lived.

In those days when she had no name, her baby felt the tension in her arms as she rocked him and sensed her sadness. Only out of pity, she was certain—after numerous nights of her tears bleeding onto his face in the dark, causing him to blink in surprise—did he finally accept her. His mouth pulled painfully and she cried with happiness even as her skin chafed sore. She learnt to synchronise with his needs, understand his cries, coos and huffs, and was thankful when his restless squeals told her when he wanted her. Her gratitude made her happy and gave her, like the bees, a good life.

The bee passed out the window to hover over the white jasmines outside. It took its share of nectar before moving on to the next flower that beckoned it when the breeze mixed with its fragrance. Each bud gave happiness enough for the bee to fill itself, spare the rest, and weave honey that later touched Lucky's tongue. Nature, unlike man, regulated its greed with gratitude, so life could go on.

Yes, there is beauty in today, she thought. *And every day.*

Signs of happiness rested all around Lucky. Beyond the barred window, she saw she lived in a world held together by tiny, beautiful things, where sunflower seeds hid in cracks for hungry ants to find, birds stopped to prance before clumsy calves, and petals spiralled down in choreographed dance from summer trees onto small lakes, so tiny heartbeats could travel from one end to another. A world fused together by a promise. Nature's covenant that she did not honour. Rayan saw those signs, his eyes still vibrant where hers had grown dull. Whenever he patted her excitedly and pointed towards them, she had brushed his small hands away. Now regret anchored her body to the ground until her heart beat in step with the heavy beat of the land, jealous it had dismissed the small pieces of heaven that lay on earth.

A cool, smoky sadness seeped into Lucky's lungs and coloured the air she exhaled. She had never caressed the lotus flowers in rivers she had sailed, where sky became sea and sea, sky. Now she wondered if the branches outside the window drooped low over her head to be near to her, if the wind complimented her as it passed and the river whistled with melody so she might enjoy its music. If the rain that fell into the room spread on her skin to feel her warmth, if the bees hovered by her seeking friendship. If they all spoke to her in a language she did not understand.

A lone jasmine had crawled into the room through the window. Its vine stretched like a pointer finger towards the women, having grown impatient with their wistful stares that never complimented them from any closer. Lucky smiled at its bold advance.

Jasmines waited in bundles behind busy roadsides, hidden lakesides, private gardens and gatherings of joy. Their buds grew in clusters towards searching hands. It was said when careful fingers picked jasmine flowers, presented their softest parts to a needle, threaded them into wreath garlands that tied around a woman's hair, hung from her wrists, swung across her neck, swayed from the rooftops and dangled from the bedposts of the marital room, their potent scent cast a spell on her husband to make him fall deeper in love, and only then did the jasmines wither in peace. As a child, Lucky skimmed her fingers across their petals, dreaming of her wedding day when she would wear jasmine garlands too.

Bibijaan was the only woman who had a stall in the market. Her nimble hands were legendary and women from nearby towns travelled over broken roads and through dangerous neighbourhoods to buy her jasmine garlands. Bibijaan's garlands piled high into the air till you almost missed her small, thin frame behind the mountain of white. Each day after school, Lucky and Jamila hovered around her stall and stroked the flowers, whispering and wishing, and Bibijaan smiled her toothless smile, tied a thin jasmine bracelet around their wrists and shooed them home.

Ammu said jasmines were heavenly flowers, placed on earth by God's most favoured angels, to remind them of him during the most precious moments of a woman's life. Lucky remembered filling her hands with them as a girl, how those first jasmines rolled around each other to fit into the curves of her palms like flowing water. She remembered how the same smell had enveloped her as Waleed placed a garland around her head in front of their families. How his nose had twitched at the flowers tied on her wrists when they hovered around his neck, and how the flowers shrivelled and closed their petals at night so as not to see or hear them.

In the camp, the jasmines slumped from loneliness, having realised long ago that no one would pluck them. Though they blinked open and spread their scent far, the soldiers' hearts were too hard to notice their beauty, and the women's too hollow to cherish it. For Lucky, the small stars stretched and squeezed her faded memories and shrouded her eyes with a watery warmth until sleep overcame her.

They say the strength of a woman is to make the best of a difficult situation and the strength of a man is to remain calm when angered. Each morning, the sun tested the strength of the Slightly Cross-Eyed Soldier, who never could tell if he had passed or failed. While his feet had covered the distance of the war, his heart had not covered the distance of his convictions. Beauty did not seem to entice him into becoming a beast, though the women lay bare before him night and day, and so the Majors and Minors sought to bully him into beastliness.

'Say, how do you sit here in silence all day, eunuch? Can you even enjoy the sights?'

Major Moustache's wandering eyes landed on Lucky, and he winked at her as if she were in on the joke. 'How many years have you served, and this is all you're good for? Heh, the sons of diplomats...'

'Must've sent the faulty son to die,' the Slow-Smiling Soldier said.

The Slightly Cross-Eyed Soldier remained silent. One eye remained on his rifle and the other looked beyond the windows as if he lived between two worlds, one in which he wore a uniform and another where he was a traveller looking towards his new destination. After the Major had picked his woman, he rose from his chair, locked the door from the inside and returned to his seat.

Though the Slightly Cross-Eyed Soldier never touched them, Lucky hated him the most. He was shy and awkward, as adorable as a small child and just as brutal. A soldier by misfortune, he accepted the women's glares and abuse with welcome palms and looked over their bruised bodies with cross-eyed pity, dragging his feet when taking his orders as if in apology. Not motivated by pleasure or by cruelty, he obeyed his superiors without resistance, with the readiness of a boy who tore off the wings of a dragonfly out of a curiosity that brought him shame. Lucky despised his efforts to dance on the edges of history while everyone else stood firm at the centre by conviction or by duress.

One night, during the darkest part of the night, a crying crow had beckoned him out of the room. Thinking they all slept, he left the door ajar and walked into the courtyard. Lucky had watched as, with gentle fingers, he unwound the crow's wing from the metal spring lining the low wall. A small act of redemption. His rifle leaned on the wall by the open door. If Lucky was quiet, she could turn it on him. But any act of heroism had stopped short at the image of the Slightly Cross-Eyed Soldier's face at the end of a barrel. Should he fight her, she would scratch at him, but looking at the pitiful slump in his shoulder bowing before the crow, she decided she would not give him the satisfaction of death: his was a hell that had to be lived.

Beside him now, Rokeya dug words into the moist part of the ground. She drove lines into the soil until her fingernails were covered in clotted grain and her hand and the earth were one colour. As soon as a sentence was complete, she shook her fingers until the clumps fell off, lodging missiles at fleeing ants, and wiped the phrase away to write another.

'Why do you do that?' Lucky asked. She flinched at the chafed skin around Rokeya's tireless nails. The erasing of words frightened her for reasons she could not articulate.

'For a simple reason. To the enemy we're weak women who know nothing. So I learn their language one word at a time to use against them at a good moment. If we never leave here, I'd still love to say something terrible to them before I meet with death.'

'You talk of death like a friend.'

'It helps pass the day.'

'It makes mine longer.'

Lucky considered how anyone could find comfort in death. Though no one could escape it, no one could escape the fear of it either. Every day, she buried morbid thoughts and made light with religious aphorisms whenever death's horns prodded her in conversation. It was wise to fear death, to ward it off with a shaky hand.

'I was the same, but I've changed from months of sitting in here,' Rokeya said. 'Now, I fear something else. Death is not worse than living captive. The soldiers want money, medals and trophies, things that can be lost, stolen, burnt and aged. I want something that will travel with me beyond death—freedom. And I won't wait for death to get it.'

Dumbfounded by the wisdom of this young girl, who moved with such certainty and conviction, Lucky grew ashamed of her own cowardice.

'Lychee Bhai is here,' Rabia hissed from the window. A man with a large cart entered the courtyard, his orange beard shining like a tomato in a cauliflower field. 'A fat man of our own blood.'

'He doesn't look fat to me,' Lucky remarked, frowning at the small figure weaving between the soldiers. Shorter and thinner than Lucky, with wrists the same width as her son's, he looked to be malnourished.

'He's not fat in the stomach like hero over there.' Rabia tilted her head towards the Fat Man as he sped to save a box of mangoes from toppling off Lychee Bhai's cart. 'Ours is fat with the possessions of others.'

'A glutton for gold,' Mohini chimed in.

'Our fat man, their fat man, they're all the same,' Rokeya said. 'He'd rather keep his farm than keep his freedom. And if he's lucky he might get to keep his neighbour's farm too.'

Lychee Bhai's laugh echoed across the courtyard. Soldiers swarmed around him, taking down the crates and bags that filled his cart. Major Moustache laughed with him, blowing cigar smoke into his face.

'Still, that fat bastard has his uses. He tells us of the outside,' Rabia muttered, squinting at his small frame lost within the crowd.

'Is he trustworthy?' Lucky asked.

'No razakar is trustworthy, even if he dresses like a mullah. His arrow moves with the tide of the winning side.'

When Major Moustache was called away and the hungry soldiers had their backs to him, Lychee Bhai lit a foreign cigarette and walked towards them. He stood a few feet away and angled his body to look across the forest on the western side of the camp.

'Punjabis are being pushed back by the Indians and Mukti Bahini,' he said, exhaling a long pillar of smoke.

Rabia and Lucky, who sat closest to the window, leaned in. The others remained where they were. Mohini sat in front of the Slightly Cross-Eyed Soldier telling him a story loud enough to drown out their voices. The Slightly Cross-Eyed Soldier listened to her intently, though none of them knew if he understood a word she said.

'Mukti joddhas are imprisoned here.' Lucky's voice was barely above a whisper, but Lychee Bhai's cigarette stilled in his mouth, so she knew he heard her. 'If they should escape, would you give them safe passage out of the district?'

He exhaled heavily, watching the soldiers open the last of the lychee crates. Suddenly, he was exhausted. His feet hurt and his back ached from days spent bent over packing crates alone, the sun burning his forehead and the bald patch on his head growing bigger at a speed that felt providential. For a moment, Lucky thought he would not answer.

'If they fail, no one will know what happened to these men. The Punjabis won't talk, I can't talk, and neither can you,' he said, his lips barely moving so the cigarette remained still in his mouth. 'Will you condemn them to an unmarked grave, never to be found again?'

Lucky could not reply. Death waited for the mukti joddhas if they escaped and came back for the women, and death waited for them if they tried to escape but did not succeed. Either way, the women were asking them to risk their lives. Shame held her lips closed.

'You think truth is so cheap it's worth silencing for as little as a few women's reputations?' Rabia snapped. She gripped the bars with her hand and seethed at him through the gaps.

Lychee Bhai turned, looking at the women inside the room for the first time. He inspected their limbs, the holes and cracks in the wall, his eyes flitting everywhere except their faces, as though he had been told he would not have to help them if he did not meet their empty gazes, see their bruises or watch their tears soak the soil. The sound of the soldiers loading empty crates back into the cart jolted him from his ruminations and he turned to Lucky, winked and walked away, neither accepting nor rejecting her request.

On the windowsill, a dead spider lay on its back, its legs bent inward like the skeleton of a naked dandelion.

That evening, Suhana delivered their dinner with a swollen mouth and nose. She looked Rokeya in the eyes and tilted her head in a slight nod, her jaw too bruised to fall any further. It was all the confirmation the women needed. They would move forward with their plan, with or without Lychee Bhai.

'You don't have to do this,' Mohini said to Lucky as night fell. 'You might regret it.'

'I regret too much of my life already,' Lucky replied. She had had enough of sitting on the sidelines of her life while others told her what to do, what to think and how to feel and called it fate. If her life was to be gambled on one night, she would stick her hand into the fire and foil the devil's plan herself.

Behind her, Jamila was sleeping. Every day, Lucky noticed her sister's voice growing smaller and smaller. Her look of care for Lucky was replaced with a resigned blankness, as if she had foreseen their demise in the forest when Lucky had pleaded with her. Guilt caused Lucky to rise early most mornings and retch into the waste bucket wishing she had listened to Jamila and turned around. Now was her chance to join hands with women wiser and braver than herself to atone for her mistake.

At midnight, when some soldiers had gone to bed and others were dozing at the entrances, Rokeya, Mohini and Lucky returned to the window. Mohini whistled. The Fat Man was the first to look back. Beside him, two drunken smiles peered up at them.

Each night, as Major Moustache retired with his darlings, the young soldiers who rarely left the camp sneaked drinks into the courtyard and made merry of the long, quiet evenings when nothing happened. No war and no Major could dampen the call to live out their youth in reckless stupor.

Mohini's sultry whistle sailed through the air until it tickled the chins of the lively young soldiers, pulling them from their guarding posts and across the courtyard towards them. Rokeya smiled at the Fat Man and trailed her fingers across the bars. He rose abruptly, knocking his chair to the ground, and stumbled towards them, his belly flopping in exaggerated waves. Lucky dug her fingernails into her cold palm to keep herself in place.

'That damned halfwit,' Rabia cursed behind them.

Drunk and flattered, three soldiers stood at the window looking in, their foreheads resting on the bars.

'Hello, ladies,' the Fat Man said with his small eyes fixed on Mohini's chest. His juniors panted behind him like stray dogs on a molten day. 'What can we do for you tonight?'

Lucky glanced back at the Slightly Cross-Eyed Soldier, who watched them cautiously with one eye fixed on Rokeya and the other on the Fat Man. *To the Most Merciful, the Most High, grant us success,* she repeated again and again, her tongue moving fervently between her closed lips. Beside her, Rokeya, Mohini and the soldiers laughed in whispers. The Fat Man rubbed a lock of Mohini's hair between his fat fingers in promise. Jamila woke at the commotion, her eyes widening at Lucky's hesitant frame trembling beside them. Lucky turned away when she caught her eye, determined not to let anything undo her resolve. Pushing down the disgust lodged in her throat, she leaned towards the soldiers.

And forgive us for what we are about to do.

On the other side of the bars, Lieutenant Patches lowered his comb and watched her stroke her arm in a gesture of comfort. His gaze trailed up her face slowly and unsteadily until they were eye to eye. Lucky smiled.

The Fat Man and his juniors entered, closing the door behind them. The Slightly Cross-Eyed Soldier closed his eyes, and Lucky saw the space between his cap and hairline furrow with tension.

As the soldiers took their fill, Lucky heard a faint knock on the bars above her head.

Knock.

Knock.

One knock meant failure, two knocks, success.

The Mukti Bahini were free.

Lucky turned quickly to her sister across the floor. Jamila's face was ashen. Saliva dripped down her chin from lips swollen too tight on her face. Her thin green blouse was open, revealing a flush chest, bloody and bitten, glistening with moisture not her own. Her saree lay in a pile at her feet. As their eyes met for a moment, Jamila's lips lifted like parchment crumbled under the weight of time, and she mouthed something to Lucky before her face was grabbed to look into the drunken eyes above her. *Sabr.*

Show sabr to him, moyna, Ammu said to Lucky the night before her wedding. Ammu promised by the twilight, by all that was covered by the night, by the full moon and all that glistened under its reflection, that man—father, husband, son or stranger—could never truly understand a woman, never truly make a woman happy nor understand the pain he caused her. So, she should show beautiful patience worthy of reward. Like a barren land waiting for rainfall. Like a lone cloud waiting for companions. Like a sick man waiting for a cure.

Lucky closed her eyes.

Midnight was a valley between two mountains. The soldier's heavy hands made a teacher of the night, its shadow luring Lucky into the darkest parts of herself until her pupils grew wide and slow and the thump, thump, thump of flesh on flesh was all she tasted.

Goosebumps came from a coldness within, and she traced the ridges as they formed in relief. It was a reliable friend, her scaly skin, a certainty that her body still responded to her, unlike her eyes which had forgotten her. When wakeful sleep reached up to greet her again, it pulled her by her hair into herself and her shivering body surrendered to the slow, beating heart of the deep ocean. There, pain did not press down on her chest but swayed like smoke on a blustery day. There she inhaled crisp air like the crunchy, open leaves outside. There she roamed where the sun never rose, nor the moon set, where shadows walked without fear of erasure, and jasmines never whittled to the ground. A place where time had no place. It was there she touched the wall she had built around her heart. She sat with it pressed against her back, and each night she turned to feel it with her fingers until the warmth of her fingertips melted small craters into its chest. Each night she had to claw an opening that she could crawl through to the other side of what she had become, to swim back into the light where wakefulness was suspended in deceitful slumber.

Lucky woke to a soft hand on her shoulder and the scalding sound of a furious rain. She felt damp ground beneath her and realised her petticoat was missing. Above her, Rabia searched her face until she saw recognition.

'I'm okay,' Lucky whispered, pushing her hand against her heaving chest. Jamila's face rested in the crook of her neck, and she held still so as not to wake her.

'You were crying in your sleep.'

She touched her face, surprised her fingers came back wet. 'Oh.'

'It had to be done.'

In another life, Rabia's candour made her bad company, but in the room her sure words were strength, kindness. She spoke without decoration or charm so their actions were neither scorned nor studied. To Lucky she was hope, hate, freedom. Kindled by evil and sealed by sorrow, a deformed but tender sisterhood tied the two women together, and they knew it would remain with them long after they parted ways.

'Tonight, what I've done, I've done by my own hands,' Lucky said.

'And you're a better woman than me for doing it.'

'I have sinned.'

What that word meant in the room, neither of them knew. Still, it felt dirty, wicked, like damnation.

'Don't be so quick to join the devil in dance over one small choice,' Rabia told her.

Lucky trembled. 'I held his hand willingly.'

Rabia sighed. 'You mustn't punish yourself with regret, it lingers too long in the heart and torments the soul. Ask for forgiveness and learn to release the memory.'

Lucky traced her fingers along Jamila's arm to feel the bumpy shield covering her beating veins. She cupped her hands in prayer and asked the angels' pens to stand still. Outside, the jasmines opened their petals in bloom as she fell into another deep sleep.

12. SOUL WHISPERS

Before the Fat Man became a soldier, he had been a bus conductor so he could touch money all day. The smoothness of the paper and the coolness of the coin made him forget the lingering anxieties of a poor childhood, of days with no light and no food, crying siblings and the heavy hands of strange men. As a bus conductor, the Fat Man made enough to make a home. There was light inside when the streets turned dark, lunch and dinner on the table, and no strange men in sight. But the Fat Man was a poor man's son and they never let him forget it. The fathers of brides complained that the Fat Man was still too poor and too fat for their daughters. Back-alley encounters became routine for him, until his face, soured by the unfairness of life, left a permanent pinched mark between his brows. A face only God could love. Now fathers of brides rejected him not only because he was too poor and too fat, but also because his pinched face looked too bad-tempered, like the face of a man who would lay hands on his wife. So, tired of those who claimed they could read his temperament in his features, he joined the army, where the lines on his face rewarded him, no one called him the son of a poor man, and he no longer paid for women with coins.

Now, the Fat Man ran between the houses in the camp, throwing himself into every bush and body of water, forgoing breakfast, lunch and dinner to look for the mukti joddhas, and meeting the furious Major's baton every time he crossed his path empty-handed. If he didn't find the prisoners by tonight, the Major vowed to shoot the fat pig himself.

'There he goes, pockets jingling like a young bride's anklets on her wedding night,' Rabia said, looking out the window to the Fat Man, who was eyeing Suhana on her way to the room. 'He'll finish half the plate before she can bring it in, rakkhosh.'

The women lay on the ground facing each other, talking amongst themselves, their soft brown eyes changing like autumn leaves under the afternoon sun. Others who hadn't prayed for months had been kneeling in sujood since morning. Victory was theirs. The soldiers had woken to an empty cell, blindfolds and rope ties strewn across the floor. Major Moustache had beaten the two young soldiers unconscious and threatened to kill the Fat Man for letting them escape under his watch. But the mukti joddhas were gone. Help would come for the women. All they had to do was wait.

'Hopefully they've made it out of the district,' Rokeya said, cupping her hands in supplication.

'Inshallah,' the women chimed.

The Fat Man stumbled over his boots, pushing another soldier off balance. The women had never seen such fear across a soldier's face.

'Do you really think the Major will kill him?' Lucky asked.

'Yes,' Mohini said, motioning to the Fat Man. 'He's no soldier, he's a fool looking for acceptance from a uniform. Half of my customers are men like him. They want to be touched lovingly by a woman, but it hasn't been written for them, so they come to us to pretend. They don't know how to love so they're harsh. Their hard hearts only show these men what they don't have, whispering reminders to them every day.'

'The other half?'

'The other half are dogs.'

Lucky thought of what the Fat Man did to Jamila. 'Good, I hope he's killed.'

'I won't be crying.'

'He's running so fast... Maybe the elders were right, and you can feel when death comes for you.'

'They were. I've known people who had that feeling before they died. Sometimes weeks, months before.'

'Who were they?'

'Other working girls. We spoke about death often, you have to, to stay safe. To protect each other. Some said it was an overwhelming feeling of peace, others that it was an increasing feeling of terror. And then they were gone.'

Lucky shuddered at the implication. 'Was their manner of death reflective of how they felt?

'Something like that.'

'I see.'

Lucky traced the silver-brown stretch marks around her underbelly she had once despised. They had grown despite all the oils she had rubbed along her pregnant stomach and the pastes other neighbourhood mothers had gifted her. She thanked God for never letting them fade like she had wished, so she could look down at them now, whenever she wanted, and remember her son, whose mother was now gripped with the sensation of terror creeping after her.

'When I began to work, my mother told me, *my soul whispered of a danger that wasn't there. All these years I thought it was for me, but now I know it was for you.* My Nanaji split my Naniji's face open if she didn't have dinner ready when he came home, and he always came home at a different time. Our neighbours saved her from an early grave many times. My Ammi feared my Baba would do the same to her but he never did. She worried the joy out of her life with the fear of what she knew. Every man was her father or had a part of him in them.'

'She saw it everywhere she looked,' Lucky nodded, thinking of how Ammu never married again after Abbu's death.

'A person can feel their destiny long before it happens. Mothers feel it for their children, but they don't know how to stop it, so they become harsh. My mother was right, here I am, but still, can you believe, even now, my soul whispers don't speak of death?'

She could believe it. A smile lifted Lucky's cracked lips, tearing into her bottom lip until a patch of red stood exposed to the chilly air. They would not have been friends before the war. Lucky would have avoided Mohini at all costs, turned away in disgust, called her immoral, disgraced, a seductress, a husband thief. Yet in that same transaction that seemed to rob everyone else, Mohini carried with her the strength of a woman.

The Fat Man tapped his baton on the bars of the window. 'Tonight, we have visitors. High profile. Get them ready,' he said to the Slightly Cross-Eyed Soldier.

'Higher profile than you, Khan Shaheb?' Rabia turned to the Fat Man. 'We brush our hair and wear sequins for them but for you dirty knots and tattered clothes are enough. Then you must be the lowest rank? A doorman. A cockroach that scurried its way into a uniform.'

The Fat Man's fat cheeks tightened around his thin lips so hard and fast Lucky moved back, worried they would burst and his innards would cover her. Pushing his fat hand through the bars, he grabbed Rabia's hair and raised her until they were eye level.

'You're here because your mother's a whore and your father's a traitor. Nothing more than an organ to be used. Everyone has their place in this world and in their place whores will stay. At the bottom. The filth of society. Mice that scurried their way onto quicksand.'

The Slightly Cross-Eyed Soldier wove between the women to the window. 'They'll be ready,' he said. The Fat Man nodded, dropping Rabia to the floor. He spat into the room, splattering her face and neck before he left. Rabia wiped her face with the head of her saree and lay between Lucky and Mohini with a satisfied smile.

The Slightly Cross-Eyed Soldier dragged a box into the centre of the room. Inside were folded sarees and shalwar kameez. Pieces of all colours, with flowers, leaves and geometric patterns in gold and silver threading, a few even displaying shining sequins. Major Moustache's box of delights. Handpicked from bazaars, women's wardrobes and still warm bodies used and shot, his curated collection housed all that would look beautiful on his darlings.

When the Major hosted high-ranking officers, the Slightly Cross-Eyed Soldier would bring in buckets of water and a bar of soap for the women to clean with. Once they were dressed, one by one, each woman sat at the Slightly Cross-Eyed Soldier's feet while he brushed the knots out of their roughly cut hair. Major Moustache would walk past the room while the Slightly Cross-Eyed Soldier worked, humming his approval or grunting so the Slightly Cross-Eyed Soldier would have to start over again. Sometimes, he stopped by the window and told the women to swap clothes, so they each wore the dress that complemented their complexion best. Only when the Major endorsed them with a nod and a curt 'gorgeous' did the Slightly Cross-Eyed Soldier release the tension from his shoulders that held the comb in place, and the women begin to tremble in anticipation of what was to come.

The Slightly Cross-Eyed Soldier's fingers were gentle. He took his time unwinding each knot so not a strand fell out. When the comb's teeth scratched lightly against their necks, he pulled away apologetically and made the next stroke even softer, so it felt like clouds touched their hair. Their own mothers had never brushed their hair so lovingly. His eyes glazed over with such deep focus when he held that comb, Lucky knew he no longer heard the planes searing the skies overhead or felt his uniform brush his skin. What unsettled her was that while one eye rested on the head of the woman in front of him, working diligently, the other rested on her. Did that eye see her or was it designed to deceive, feigning omniscience to keep her on edge? Or was it the opposite, was he focused on her intently and moving his hands in absentminded motions? Uncertainty lined her gurgling stomach with acidic anger.

'Not me,' Lucky said, slapping his hand away from her head. Above her, the Slightly Cross-Eyed Soldier's eyes widened as he moved back, the comb hovering above her head in surrender.

Lucky moved towards Jamila and sat behind her, spreading her legs on either side of her sister's body, and pulled her towards her chest. She rested her chin on her shoulder and waited for Jamila's heartbeat to synchronise with her own.

'We'll be home soon, and we'll be happy again,' she whispered into Jamila's hair, its silky weight heavy on her eyelids. 'When we return, we'll find that fiancé of yours and have him dig out a mountain of gold for your wedding. Just wait a little longer, we're almost there.'

Jamila released her weight onto Lucky's chest. She hesitated in her reply, stopping and starting several times before her words could reach the tip of her tongue. The sound of boots and the door opening granted her the final dose of courage she needed to speak the words aloud. 'Let's live however we can,' she told Lucky, 'even if we must betray our souls to stay alive.'

'Ammu told me the only reason people don't make it to heaven is because they don't ask for forgiveness enough.'

'Don't say it so loud!' Rabia hissed at Noori. 'The Khans might learn something and avoid hell altogether.'

The women doubted that was possible.

Lucky could remember the first time she asked for forgiveness. It closely followed the first time she thought of forgiveness. It wasn't a pleasant revelation. Forgiveness confronted her with a mother's loving rage, to which she had no choice but to submit.

Mr Ahmed's corner shop was called My Ahmed. The sign maker was a poor man who had never seen English letters before. Too embarrassed to correct him, Mr Ahmed hung the misspelt sign above his shop for the next twenty years until the man died.

My Ahmed sold sweets, pens and hair clips. Lucky and Jamila saved every last rupee from their birthday money, Eid money and lunch money to spend in My Ahmed, and had fast fingers for the times when they fell short. When metallic pink hairbands fringed with glitter baubles arrived from India, the girls slipped a couple into their pockets. The day Ammu found their stash of stolen goods, the two sisters got a thrashing. Within the hour, Ammu had marched them both, tears of embarrassment on their cheeks, their faces still pink from punishment for the world to see, to the front of My Ahmed to apologise.

'God won't forgive you until you're forgiven by those you wronged first,' Ammu threatened when they returned home. 'And people aren't so generous, so don't go around doing things you need to be forgiven for.'

Now Ammu's warning swam side by side with Rabia's words as Lucky listened to her argue with Noori about the mercies of God. Noori's soft face, which held all the roundness of a child whose fat had yet to melt, now twisted and turned and tightened her jaw as she argued. Rabia furrowed her brow and shook her head. She would never forgive those who wronged her so God would not forgive them either. He had made the promise, signed the universal law, like the law that held the clouds high up in the sky and not brushing her toes as she walked, and she would ensure it would be upheld by doing her part to never forgive.

'Let them believe they're already in paradise,' Lucky agreed. 'Not every enemy should be forgiven, and for some, justice should be just as merciless as the hands of the unjust.'

Mohini looked at her from her upside-down position on the floor. 'It's true that not every enemy *needs* be forgiven, but the person who forgives is better for doing so. Even if it has no worldly benefit, she releases a weight off her heart, and that's worth forgiving for.' She paused between words to watch Lucky's reaction, firm in her opinion but wishing not to offend.

'My father forgave evil as it was being done to him,' Lucky said, her lungs tightening with equal measures of sadness and spite. 'Not like the rest of us after deep thought and wrestling with our emotions, but in real time. He forgave easily and smiled today with yesterday's enemy, so, naturally, people continued to wrong him. I hated him for making our lives difficult. On miserable days that bring back those memories, I still do. The cruelty of forgiveness can live beyond the grave.'

She felt Jamila's curious eyes on her. Jamila had never met Abbu. He died before they took her in. And when she asked about him, Ammu only smiled and Lucky changed the subject.

'Maybe he saw value in forgiveness where you didn't.'

Lucky turned to her sister in surprise. Jamila had never pried into Abbu's story, so she didn't expect her to ever defend him.

'What do you mean?'

'He had a greater responsibility to forgive the people in his life than you did.'

'At the cost of his wife and daughter?'

'Some men aren't made for family but for community. A man like that wants to walk beyond his small house and his small family through the neighbourhood with his head held high. When he treads on others' toes he asks to be forgiven, and in return forgives readily the greatest offences. He's happy to trade peace for insults and betrayals as long as he's included in their company.'

'Men like that aren't fit to be called husbands or fathers.'

'Maybe they're not, they would rather be men than family men, and when forgiveness is free for everyone but costly to you, it feels like injustice, doesn't it? Like an evil. But when it's directed your way above everybody else, doesn't it feel great?'

The women listened in silence. Lucky knew there was truth to what Jamila said, and she knew she would reject that truth in favour of her anger, which still simmered under her relationship with Abbu over a decade after his death.

'We forgive each other easily,' Jamila stated.

'We do.'

'That's between women,' Chanda interjected. 'Men aren't so forgiving of women.'

'The good ones are. My husband forgives easily, he's kind when I wrong him, and quick to forget my insults. He's maintained our marriage better than I have all these years, and I'm thankful for it. I miss him the most,' Lucky admitted.

'Have you told him that?' Mohini asked.

'He knows.'

'People don't just know.'

Thinking about it now, Lucky couldn't remember the last time she had thanked her husband, not even in the countless letters they had exchanged over the years they had been apart. How would he know how greatly his words affected her, how she could feel his adoration through the pages, all while she kept hers locked safely in her chest, revealing only careful words of support. She kept a happy home, raised their son and satisfied a demanding mother-in-law, but did he know that she did it all for him? In her efforts to give him everything, she forgot to show him her love. Her chest burned with remorse. Should she only realise this now in the face of death? With no chance to make amends?

Mohini squeezed her hand, noticing her silence. 'Tell him how you feel once we leave. Show him too, or you'll both miss the chance to feel alive.'

'What do we need men to forgive us for?' Rabia demanded. 'If I'm destined for hell, it'll be of my own doing. I won't be going there for anyone else, ha! There isn't a single person in the world worth burning for, and in this war, there isn't a single person we should be seeking forgiveness from.'

'I'd like forgiveness for myself, for everything I've done wrong in my past,' Lucky said. 'There's so much I want to change, so much I want to do now. And I'm ashamed of how little I've considered God, how I've never included him in anything I do. If I live to see beyond these walls again, I'll make room for him in my life.'

Rokeya nodded. 'I think we can all agree with that.'

'It's easy to replace God with life, and when that goes on for too long, forget him entirely,' Sumayyah reflected in the dreamy voice of a preacher. Her father was an imam, who had taught his children to memorise the entire Quran. Throughout the day, Sumayyah's low, melodic recitation murmured across the room. Sometimes the conviction in her tone irritated Lucky, other times it put her at ease. For those women who no longer spoke, ate, slept or hoped, the drumming of Sumayyah's voice in their ears was the only sign they were still alive.

The soldiers hated Sumayyah. She read each surah with gusto and made a show of counting zikr on each of her knuckles as they took her away. Covering her mouth with their hands, they forced themselves to forget themselves and the reminders in her recitation. When she returned black and purple, she recited to herself in whispers, blew on her hands, placed them over her eyes and ran them over her body. Then, she walked around the room blowing over the faces of the women whose empty eyes were no longer of this world.

'Baba told me, the prayer of the oppressed races up to God like lightning,' Sumayyah said.

Lucky considered her own prayers. She felt her heart harden with each passing day, her faith threatening to leave her like candlelight on a windy night. She doubted her prayers had even the power to crawl beyond her breath, let alone up to the skies.

'You want us to prostrate and do puja here, in this filth? While *we* are filthy?' Chanda challenged. 'Why? To insult God?'

'All the land we fight over belongs to God, so every place is fit for prayer,' Rokeya said. 'He won't turn from us for our position.'

'Maybe we sit in the greatest position of them all... right here in this filth,' Mohini considered. The women looked to her in confusion.

'The believer is said to be able to find a part of paradise on earth,' Jamila remembered. 'Well, the only paradise we'll find in here is in prayer. It's how we fight pain and shed it like bark off a dry tree. In this filthy room, we have nothing but time to plead for victory and mercy, and whose prayers should count as greater than ours? Maybe that's the paradise of this world, and if we don't find it here, we won't find it anywhere.'

Sumayyah nodded eagerly. 'The Prophet, peace be upon him, told us our own actions don't take us to heaven, only God's mercy does. He would say this not to make us feel small or scare us, but to comfort us and take away the anxiety of failure,' she recalled, her voice far away as if she were reading one of her father's khutbahs.

Rokeya hummed in agreement. 'We may sit in filth but we're not filthy. In this prison we can pray with or without moving our lips, sitting or lying down, in any language we want.'

'It feels wrong,' Noori sighed. 'We bleed from so many places and can't wash ourselves. I don't even feel human.'

'We're human by our souls, not by our bodies,' Jamila said. She wrapped her arms around Lucky's shoulders. 'We don't need to be pristine to have an audience with God.' Jamila's arms had grown thin, and she slept day and night to appease how weak her body had become, only rising when a soldier shook her awake to take her or when Lucky had the will to speak a few words to her. Now her forearm rested under Lucky's chin, which had grown pointy, their bones kissing under thin layers of skin.

A chorus of hums echoed across the room in agreement. The Slightly Cross-Eyed Soldier moved his weight from one leg to the other.

Mohini clapped her hands. 'When we leave, let's leave behind all the pain, all the parts that remind and can't forgive, let's leave it all behind so tomorrow's eyes don't hold the sadness of yesterday.'

That night, the Fat Man lived. When the wind was curiously quiet and the air heavy on the women's shoulders, when no soldiers came to visit, twelve shots rang out with practised rhythm. The Shaytan had found the fugitives crossing the river to the next town by foot. The next day, when the visitors asked Major Moustache about the incident, he confirmed part of it and said nothing about the rest. Like the words of a killer who didn't know why he killed.

In the morning, the women rushed to the window to see Suhana facing them alone in the courtyard, holding an empty plate, food splattered the floor, staring back at them with terror. The Slow-Smiling Soldier stood behind her, eyes bright with excitement, fingers twitching with anticipation.

'No more honeys and darlings now, churails,' he said, winking at them huddled behind the bars. He wrapped his arms around Suhana's waist and breathed into her hair, which trembled beneath his lips.

Those already empty-eyed and numb cried and pleaded again like they did the first day, their pain doubled for the men who were killed, who held in their hands the promise that the women would return to their children. Now their last hopes lay face down in a river, floating downstream, heads seeping into the beloved land, not knowing why they had been killed.

Lucky looked back accusingly at the Slightly Cross-Eyed Soldier. His knees jumped as they listened to marching steps approach them. Catching Lucky's eye, he looked back at her with a plea.

Rokeya released a moaning sob. Lucky's head grew heavy, pulling her down to rest against the wall, her chest caving in as she struggled to swallow her breaths.

The mukti joddhas were dead.

Now, it was their turn.

Soldiers marched into the room, their eyes more venomous than she had ever seen. Lucky whispered the shahada. *Ashhadu an la ilaha illallah wa ashhadu anna muhammadan rasulullah.* She reached for Jamila, gripping her fingers so hard they cracked in her hands.

'Say it!' she cried, shaking her until she saw Jamila mouth the words.

So they would die believers.

13. SEALED HEARTS

The trees wept all night and the leaves turned inward, lowering their gaze to the ground, no longer bearing witness to searching eyes. Long, black rope swayed from a prostrating branch like autumn leaves. At its end, something stiff swung from a tree. Its limbs lurched with the violent wind, waving at the women who peered out. Slowly, it unravelled and fell.

Like a fat hog plum.

With a silent thud, the young fighter crumpled to the ground.

The clanging of metal on the visiting major's chest could be heard approaching them over the torrent and the women's frightful cries. With clothes stained with blood, his men entered with varying degrees of limp in their step. Injured and angry, they led the women out, one by one, some by the neck, some by the hand, some gently, some roughly, all weeping.

Major Moustache leaned against the doorway and told the Slightly Cross-Eyed Soldier, whose head hung and whose eyes stayed downcast, 'Come, watch. Are you not a man?'

Early the next morning, the Slightly Cross-Eyed Soldier returned, headed straight for the waste bucket, and was sick on top of their sick, his stomach unable to reason away what his heart could. Lucky noticed a faint bruise kissing his neck like the one that graced her own. A gripping hand, tightened until disobedience became obedience. She touched her stinging bruise and wondered what kept the Slightly Cross-Eyed Soldier pinned to his chair.

Mohini winced as she sat up, counting the heads in the room. 'Are we still alive?'

'Just about,' Lucky murmured.

'It's a miracle we're not dead.'

'I'd have preferred it,' Chanda retorted.

'Has anyone seen Suhana this morning?'

'No.'

Soldiers paced the courtyard, on edge. The youngsters sat in a corner, surrounding a radio. Every so often, one jumped up and cursed. It went on for hours until another kicked the radio against the wall and it broke. No one protested. They were thankful for the silence. Razakars came in and out, covering their mouths when they whispered, so the women couldn't make out their words. They had been asked to stay in the camp as reinforcements. The mukti joddhas' escape two nights before had rattled the soldiers, and their riverside execution was no comfort. They had got too close to base. Found a way to escape. Almost got away. The soldiers were sure more would be coming.

As the bucket's swishing settled, Lucky felt eyes on her. A razakar peered into the room. He leered at their bare limbs, unaffected by the bruises and cuts that lined their skin like spreading mould. Lucky covered her face in fear they might cross paths again later.

The women grew silent. Chanda stared at the razakar with purple-rimmed eyes. Empty and bloodshot. Lucky noticed a perfect line around her wrist, etching charcoal on Chanda's sandy skin. Something about it piqued her interest.

'Where did this mark come from?'

Chanda raised her eyebrow. 'I'm covered in bruises, and this is what you want to know about?' she laughed. It echoed, distant and hollowed. A ringing in Lucky's ear remained from the night before. 'You really want to know the secrets of my heart?'

'Yes.' Lucky's returning smile stretched her face until it pulsed hot, tearing open her split lip, its thin healing layer too fragile to hold her together. 'I might get to know something of mine.'

The line on Chanda's wrist darkened around the sides. Under the changing shadows of the evening, the ridges and hills of a deep dent rose and fell on her scarred skin. In the middle of her wrist, the line was fainter; its cracks mimicked the starved soil of a rainless summer.

'You're right, there's no better time.'

Jamila turned in her sleep, resting her head on Lucky's leg. Her lips remained locked like a stone door. Lucky spent the morning pressing ruti and daal into her mouth, pleading with her to swallow, but Jamila would not eat. Lucky pressed her thumb into Jamila's wrist to keep count of her heartbeat and waited for Chanda to speak.

'These marks come from a single red elastic band that sat on my wrist for five years. It came wrapped around a bundle of coriander.' Chanda enjoyed the bewildered movements in Lucky's brows. 'In the middle of the bazaar, its redness spoke to me, so I kept it. It felt more precious to me than any gold bangle. And it came to mean to me... something more. It was a deterrent. I pulled back the elastic and let it sting my skin whenever I had a bad thought, whenever I felt envy, hatred, selfishness. It stung me back to a moment before my desires devoured my will.'

'Where is it now?'

'It snapped the day I came here.'

Under the darkening sky, Lucky saw the skin beneath the cracks in the centre of Chanda's wrist were dented more deeply than she had thought, as if the bone had eroded, like a rock under the ocean, against the sting of the elastic band. The charred remains of her heart's efforts to ascend beyond her faults and flaws were all that remained on her skin.

'They say a girl who doesn't cry during her wedding biday will cause problems for her in-laws,' Chanda resumed, mischief wavering on her lips as she leaned in. 'I didn't cry. I was glad to leave, but I was also afraid, and right to be.'

The moment she married, Chanda felt her mother's insanity rise within her. All of her brothers and sisters were selfish people.

Her mother cared only about herself, and her father wanted peace, so he grew silent and docile as he aged. In the middle, they all suffered. For years Chanda did not marry, and once she grew past the age of being desired, people whispered that an evil wind had blown over her. 'Really, I feared I would treat my husband how she treated my father. My mother's family had bad blood, everyone said so. And half of that blood fills my veins.'

Eventually, the selfish spell of loneliness outweighed Chanda's desire to save others from herself, and she married. She feigned being obedient and dutiful, bashful and well-mannered to be a good wife.

'Did it work?'

'For a while, then I had children and realised I really was my mother's daughter.'

Love. Motherly instinct. She searched for these things in her heart, then in her head, but could find them nowhere. Her heart was as empty as it was before her children arrived. The only regard she had for her children was for their sweet smell; she could hide her face in their hair to avoid the stench that came from her husband. He had taken notice of her crinkled nose whenever he approached her. And she didn't want that ire to settle into his hands.

'When they disobeyed me, I felt my mother's hands crawl up my throat. I saw through her eyes but bit my tongue so I wouldn't speak through her lips. But I couldn't outrun her forever, and at some point, I accepted that I was destined to perform being human.'

'You're too harsh on yourself,' Lucky said softly, her thoughts wandering to Abbu's anger, Ammu's acceptance, how young and alone they were when they had her. 'A young girl taught nothing of the world shouldn't expect to know it.'

'I learnt that later in life,' Chanda nodded. 'I learnt that by pushing down her hate, I pushed down everything else too, things that were mine to have… like happiness, kindness, laughter, it was all there waiting for me to find it.'

'Happiness has a way of hiding itself between the disagreements.'

'And love too.'

'Yes,' Lucky whispered.

'Even here, we love, I see it between us,' Chanda professed. 'All these years, I didn't know that I thought of my children the way you think of yours, care for them like you do and in ways that are my way.'

'We love differently so our children grow to become different from one another, that's God's will.' Lucky's words fell heavy on their chests in hard, small drops like hail on a tin roof. A silent hum embraced the air, the river stilled and the wind whispered, as the night creatures burrowed, following in silent step.

Chanda gazed ahead at the jasmines outside the window. 'I touched their feet and asked for mercy. It's my greatest regret. Still, they killed my husband and beat my mother-in-law, who covered him with her body. They pulled me from the room and unwrapped my saree. I wasn't wearing a blouse. I was still breastfeeding. I asked if they had no mothers or sisters of their own. They understood what I said, how could they not? Right there, in front of the door, they took from me...' Chanda paused for a moment, reliving the memory, before shaking her head to cast it away. 'Fear is human. It has eyes, ears, a mouth and a nose. It grips my heart and blinds me, so even now I can't remember how many they were.'

'It's a mercy you don't.'

'I guess so.'

'Thinking of that time... won't help.'

'It won't, but now I worry that if my fear ever left me I might betray myself. And that red band will be commanded to sting me for eternity.'

Straining her eyes against the blackness of the night, Lucky saw Chanda had turned away, her back a shield from further questions, marked with wounds that shone like insults under the faint, cloudy moonlight. Lucky moved closer and lay her cheek against Chanda's, willing her own warmth to heal her.

'Let them break your heart today, Chanda, so long as it remains whole on that day where God will break their hearts before us all.'

Her cheek burned hot against Chanda's fevered skin until it throbbed like she had been slapped. As the heat lulled her to sleep, memories of Ammu welcomed her.

The first time Ammu slapped Lucky she was five years old. Ammu's red face hovered above clattering, boiling pots and her hands rushed under the merciless clock. Lucky spotted a yellow cloth on the kitchen shelf. A perfect dress for her doll. Ammu's back twitched like waves on a stepped puddle, and Lucky thought it best not to disrupt her, so she reached up on tippy toes. Between pinching fingers and wiggling knees, a bowl was elbowed, and a waterfall of rice and cinnamon sticks tumbled down her chest and into trouble at her feet.

Ammu turned with a gasp. A frozen Lucky watched her mouth scrunch inward and harden. Ammu had lost her patience. She grabbed Lucky by the wrist, pulling her forward, and slapped her hard across the face.

It was quick, so quick that Lucky stood expressionless for a long while before she remembered to cry. The kitchen and all its bubbling bowls rang in her ears. Suddenly, her heart was on her face for everyone to see. It shrivelled in on itself with a stinging humiliation and gathered fiery tears. Above her, Ammu heaved, turned back to the bowls and left her still frozen.

In an instant, Lucky knew what the heart was. It was a house. A house that held the most noble part of her; its essence radiated into each room and its temperament was like that of a feather blown about on a windy day. It felt but also thought. The heart pondered. It burned with desire and inflamed itself with intention. It did not rest in wakefulness or in sleep, it burned like a hearth fire. Both goodness and evil lived within it, she was sure of it.

From that day on, she knew she had to protect her heart. Give it her attention so others could not pierce it. Live her days with one eye on the world and the other on her heart. Control it. For a heart without control was a house without walls. Defenceless.

From that day on, she did not show too much excitement, or too much sadness. She never cried again in front of anyone, not Ammu, Jamila or Waleed. To cry in front of others was to submit to a humiliating weakness. A bright stain on her front door. And it was not polite to invite people into a dirty house.

The door of the room swung open, and the women scurried into the corners of the room as Major Moustache came in. Lost in her memories that shone real in front of her, Lucky remained in the middle, her eyes fixated on the door, dreaming through him. When his palm struck her cheek, the sound booming across the room, her head turned to the side but her body remained frozen straight, facing Ammu.

'You dare to look me directly in the eyes, whore?' Major Moustache taunted, crouching in front of her as she struggled to catch her breath. Turning her face back to him, she peered into his eyes through her hair.

'You're brave now that you've killed your own brothers, eh?' Major Moustache whispered, blowing hot, putrid breath into her face. 'I know you little mice were involved. Those sister-fuckers didn't run without help. Who was it? Are you the mighty military strategist in this den of whores?'

Major Moustache prodded her forehead with each question. She held her neck stiff so it wouldn't fold, her eyes never leaving his. When she didn't answer, he gripped her chin and peered into her pupils, their noses almost touching. After a moment, he laughed, spittle flying in her face. He stood and clapped, the force of his hands rebounding across the room.

'I'll admit, it was a surprise. A good effort! Maybe Bengali women are worth more than what's between their legs,' he winked at Lucky, his claps becoming louder. 'Little Mouse, when this is over, I might just take you back with me in a cage.'

The women remained silent. Major Moustache scrutinised them until he came across Sumayyah and Noori, who lay on the floor asleep. He shoved his boot into their stomachs and when they didn't move, he gestured for Mohini to wake them. Mohini rose to her knees.

'Speak.'

'Khan Shaheb, we couldn't wake them since this morning. They're feverish and continue to bleed from their womanhood. If you could send someone to see them...' she pleaded.

He had heard enough. With one last glance over the girls, Major Moustache walked out.

When Lucky pulled her hand away from her face, small, crusted fragments lay broken on her palm. Droplets of blood that had seeped from her ear into her hair and face had hardened into a thin layer of crust and sat powdered across her hand. A crescent-shaped scab she had noticed the morning before in the reflection of the water bucket had fallen off her chin to reveal a raw pinkness underneath. A morbid night sky lay in her palm, scattered between the red dust. *Even here there is room to heal,* she thought, rubbing at the fading scar on her chin.

'Change the cloth between their legs, and wrap it tighter,' Jamila said, removing her blouse and handing it to Mohini, who hovered over the girls. She lifted her petticoat over her breasts to make a small dress from her armpits to her knees. 'He won't send anyone.'

When she sat back down, Jamila touched Lucky's cheek with such grief burrowed in her eyes, it alone made Lucky cry. Untrue words graced Lucky's tongue and trickled to her lips. Digging her nails into her palm, she raised misty eyes to her sister before opening the door to her sealed heart.

'It hurts. My mouth is split open inside,' she whispered, tasting the blood swirling around her tongue. 'I want to sleep a long sleep and wake up having forgotten it all. If that was possible, I could bear it for another night.'

Jamila pulled her to her chest. For the first time in years, Lucky took comfort in someone else's embrace. She had forgotten its warmth. Its tender acceptance. Under the soothing wave of Jamila's gentle rocking, she replayed how Major Moustache had looked over Sumayyah and Noori as he left. His was a heart surrounded by a blanket of black ice. Only hellfire could melt hard hearts like his.

Yet, a small part of her recognised his frosty gaze. It appeared on her face too. On her mouth which rested so straight it looked like it could never bend upward in a smile without breaking. Yes, she knew what it was to have a hard heart. Even now, her son was wrapped tightly inside her chest. Her love for him, so large, so thick, lay buried deep beyond his reach, so he had no choice but to wander around her all day, trying and failing to touch it. He would remember her by one word. *Later!* What he saw of her love was a reflection of the stars on a lake, not the stars in the sky. Hard love. Years of caution had built chains around her heart so no one could come close enough to hurt her, or close enough to love her. Her vigilance turned into loneliness which turned into a mask of disinterest towards the world. Tears seeped into Jamila's petticoat, as Lucky feared one day her family would stop waiting for her.

Snakes circled her bedroom window. Slithering bodies wound in and out of each other until only tiny triangles gave passage to sunlight. Before the pinpricks of light could vanish, she fell to her hands and knees searching desperately for a weapon, a shield, something she could use to push them away with. The hissing grew louder. The jagged edges of a rock hit her knuckles. One from her son's collection of oddly shaped stones that he hid around the house. Rock in hand, she whispered a prayer for Rayan before throwing it with all her might, pushing the hissing snakes out and letting sunlight back in.

Clouds spun under her closed eyelids. She woke to find a skirt twirling above her head as one of the women made her way out of the room. They didn't know her name and she never spoke, only sang, so they couldn't ask her. They called her Dancingji, dancing aunty. The soldiers called her the Madwoman. Each morning, Dancingji woke them with her sultry voice and the swirling of her saree.

'She's talented,' Mohini observed. 'Was she was taught professionally? Is she a working woman, a student of the art, or just someone who loves to dance?'

'She was dancing when I got here and she'll be dancing on my grave when I leave,' Chanda said. 'They've stripped her of all dignity, and now her mind's gone to a different place.'

'To a more peaceful place. There's still dignity there,' Lucky said.

'I wonder if she's really mad. She could be laughing at us in secret, performing some magical dance of spite to curse us all for eternity,' Jamila speculated.

The soldiers enjoyed Dancingji's madness when they were in a celebratory mood. When a group of mukti joddhas were killed or gold and jewels were pillaged, they gathered in the courtyard and asked Dancingji to perform for them. They clapped as she swirled around the veranda, her saree unravelling in the wind, cheered, jeered, whistled and whooped and threw chewed pomegranate seeds at her in recognition of her talents. The perfect end to an evening of fun and laughter before a hearty meal and night conquest.

Usually, the soldiers kept a distance, throwing things at Dancingji if she made a grab for them through the window or serenaded him, fearing she was not mad but possessed. Some feared her touch would possess them too, that they would wake in the dead of night, pulled to their feet by some seductive sorceress, walk to the courtyard and begin dancing too. But by night, they braved their fears and dared each other to lead her out of the room.

Possessed or not, Major Moustache loved his live performance. Other Majors and Minors were welcomed to the camp by Dancingji's one-woman show. She was a summer breeze when she danced. With each turn, her eyes fluttered and laughter appeared on her mouth. Lips lifted in a dreamy smile, brows rested and talented tongue hit each note. Her slender bronze limbs shone against her bright dress, adorned with bells and jingling bobbles, a gift from the Major specially for her. She was his entertainment, her madness his joy, and so she lived.

The Slightly Cross-Eyed Soldier woke Dancingji as the sun rose and sent her out, so instead of the rooster's call, the sound of her bells and sweet song woke them.

'What a pleasant way to begin the day!' the Major cheered, kissing Dancingji's cheek. An intimate kiss, lingering like a husband on his wife's mouth. Lucky wondered if Waleed's letters were piling up somewhere in the world waiting for her.

'Those shameless bastards,' Rabia muttered, shaking the bars of the window. They stood firm and unmoving against her grip, so she only shook herself. 'I hate the ones who talk to us lovingly even more than the ones who bark at us like dogs. At least they're not liars.'

'Do you really think dignity remains even in undignified places?' Chanda asked Lucky. She tilted her head towards a soldier who stuck a couple of rupees into Dancingji's blouse. Small glass sequins on her skirt sparkled towards them under the sun.

'I do, and she's in a more dignified place than we are, wherever she is. Who knows why she dances? For herself? Them? Us? What I'm afraid of is one day she may come to regret this moment and stop dancing altogether,' Lucky said, as the shadows from Dancingji's saree passed over her face to the beat of Suhana's screams in the distance.

14. FOREFATHERS

'Delivery,' the Slow-Smiling Soldier said, holding Suhana by the waist.

Suhana's face was a purple patchwork. Charred bruises around her eyes and nose clogged her airways so that a strange whistling sound came from her throat. Saliva and blood dripped from her mouth, which was cut open. Two of her fingers tilted in strange angles. Blindly she held her arms out in front of her before falling into the room.

Lucky and Jamila crawled to her when the Slow-Smiling Soldier left. Cradling her twisted arms, they guided her to the water bucket. They had heard her screams since noon the previous day. Heat stung Lucky's eyes and threatened to spill over at the memory of it.

'Water, drink up…' Lucky placed a cup under Suhana's lips.

'No.' Suhana's voice was strained and scratchy, and sobs lined her tongue. 'Let me die without pain.'

The women gathered around, piling their clothes to create a pillow for her to rest her arms. They used their hands to fan her skin and blew on her face and head to cool the swelling.

Rokeya kneeled before her, her lips quivering with repentance. 'Forgive me, Apa. You warned us this would happen and we didn't listen.'

Suhana stroked Rokeya's face with broken fingers, quietening her cries. 'I'd rather die like this than die serving dogs.'

'Don't talk of death,' Lucky hushed, resting her cool palms against Suhana's cheeks. 'You took a great risk for us and we're grateful to you. Rest now, God will show us mercy.'

Suhana's lips separated with a dry, tearing sound. 'I know I'm not liked. I walk freely while you're locked away. I wear gold and serve you food shamelessly despite my sins. But shameless as I am, I still want at least one person to know I'm no traitor, colluder, whore or coward before I die. When the world calls me names, I want someone to remember me in the way that history will deny.'

'That's not true,' Jamila objected, wiping Suhana's face with a wet cloth. 'You feed us, make sure we're warm. We pray each night that you'll return to us in the morning. And we wonder what you must endure to give us these comforts.'

A quiet smile made its way onto Suhana's face, a shy glow of acknowledgment.

'Will you listen to the story of how I came here?'

'We'd be honoured,' Mohini said.

Suhana closed her eyes. 'My husband is older than me,' she began. 'We were told he was a pious man, but people gossiped that he loved women. I still married him because we were poor.' She paused, breathing in low gasps. 'I shuddered when he approached me and he resented me for making him wait. After a while, he no longer came. They said he was God-fearing, but there was no god in our marriage. I suspect he visited other women, why wouldn't he? I had a weak body that couldn't hold a son. And out of spite, I asked God not to burden me with his child, so maybe then he would return me to my parents. But after a few years we had a daughter. My mother-in-law never let me forget that having a son would have changed her son's ways.'

The women could hear Suhana's chest rattle in her body as she used all her strength to speak, and it frightened them. It moved to a strange rhythm and creaked when she fell silent. Beside Suhana, a girl traced the wedding henna which had still not faded from her palms.

Suhana's husband was a fisherman who had a boat of his own. Early on, the Mukti Bahini used the boat to go back and forth between enemy lines. They slept on the boat at night when the army patrolled the area and flipped it on its mouth to hide under it in the day, their heads bobbing above water, to ambush lost officers. On a quiet day when the Mukti Bahini went to train in the neighbouring village and did not use the boat, and all the men of Suhana's village went fishing, soldiers came.

The soldiers did not enter the village first—the razakars did. When the villagers saw them approaching from a distance, they took shelter in the mosque. If they were found together under God's roof, surely they would be shown mercy.

The razakars lined the women out front ready for the soldiers to arrive. Suhana's maid who did not yet have breasts stood next to her in line. As the sound of the army trucks came towards them, Suhana saw her husband's boat come to the bank. The yellow bamboo basket she wove for him sat at the helm so the villagers would have a clear view of the day's catch and could prepare his praises. She had spent a long time painting that basket, on those miserable nights after she had failed to conceive another month.

The look on his face when he was close enough to see what was happening was one she would never forget. She saw the lotus flowers and their large green pads making way for him. A yellow basket full of wriggling fish taking their last breath, dinner for the Mukti Bahini who would soon return. And her husband's cold eyes. His staff struck the river bottom, stopping the boat just as the soldiers stepped out of their trucks and touched Suhana's face. His hands gripped the oar when his baby began to scream. The boat turned and left as the village went up in flames, until smoke covered the lotus flowers and their parting pads, the tails of tengra fish in the yellow basket waving goodbye.

'That's the heart of a man who does not love you,' Suhana said.

The weight of a familiar sadness bowed their heads. They all knew a worthless husband. Some were their own. Men who married because they needed a woman to care for them or their mothers, to give them children, to warm their beds and make them meals, to wash their clothes and bear their beatings, for any reason but to know and love them or to be known and loved in return.

Suhana remained quiet for some time. After the pulsing in her swollen eyes calmed, she continued.

'After that, I didn't have the courage to flee. I stood there with my baby and my mother-in-law stood beside me. Maybe she stayed with me because her son didn't, but she stayed with me until the end. She was a woman after all, she felt what I felt, perhaps this was her apology. Or maybe she was shocked that her beloved son would leave her too. Children don't love their parents as much as their parents love them. So, when they turned their rifles on her, I forgave her for everything.'

Lucky thought of her own mother-in-law, meddlesome and particular about everything but never one to cause trouble in their marriage. If anything, her mother-in-law took her side in a disagreement. With no daughter of her own, her mother-in-law became her shadow, prattling alongside her all day.

Suhana took a deep breath. 'Then my life changed.'

A soldier had pulled her into his truck. She screamed when he touched her with the same hand that a moment ago had pressed the trigger that killed her mother-in-law and baby. In a gentle voice, full of affection, he said, 'Don't be afraid. We'll treat you well.'

It was the Slow-Smiling Soldier. He wanted her for himself, and he planned all the ways he would have her on the way to the camp, but when Major Moustache saw her, he had to give her up. The Major had a particular taste, and he didn't share. The Major drove her around the different towns and villages they conquered, pointing to the places he personally set alight, and gifted his Suhana-rani bloodstained treasures which she accepted with a smile.

On one trip, they came across a group of boys, babies without parents. Feeling generous, the Major held out sweets for them.

Their rumbling stomachs betrayed their hostile glares, and they stood in doubt looking at each other. It sickened her to see her children like this.

'Take it, it's tasty,' she encouraged them.

Terrified, the oldest boy recoiled from her outstretched hand, and his mind whirred before he gasped, 'Bengali!'

He turned to the others, pushing them back. 'Don't talk to her, she's a... prostitute!'

She knew he called her that because his child's mind struggled to form the word 'traitor'. He was too scared. Too young to know its meaning. A Bengali woman sitting next to a soldier smiling had obviously sold herself to the enemy. She was a soldiers' whore. As the boys ran away, the Major laughed, not understanding the child's expression.

'I felt that if someone had thrown hot coals on my body, it would have been kinder. When the Major saw my face, he knew the child had said something. He turned the car after them, but I caught his arm and joked to calm him down... The disgust in that child's eyes still haunts me to this day.'

The women were lost in their thoughts. Had they been in the child's position, would they have said the same? Or would they have understood that to live, sometimes you had to die inside? Jamila rolled her earring. Behind them, the Slightly Cross-Eyed Soldier shifted restlessly in his seat.

'A woman's dilemma is that she must always consider what she should say and what she should shield,' Lucky said. 'You're no traitor for keeping your silence.'

'It had to be done,' Mohini murmured.

The women hummed in agreement.

'Somewhere, someone has a drop of my blood in them. I don't want them to be shamed by stories of me, and my forefathers and my descendants disgraced, but I know no one will defend me once we leave. I only tell you this so you don't hate me for my cowardice when really my feet that walk freely through the camp are shackled more tightly than yours.'

'People must hear your story,' Rokeya said firmly. 'What they've done to you, how they did it. It's important.'

'What good is a story when you disgust people with your words?'

The room exhaled with a deep sadness.

'When women become wise, the world calls them whore,' Mohini whispered.

'Or mad,' Rabia said.

'But if we don't take charge of our lives, others do it for us,' Lucky said. 'There's no winning.'

'Victory is different to different people,' Jamila replied. 'Some want to be heard, others forgotten, others remembered, others hidden, so they may find peace. Only fools travel in search of one answer for all people. And the world looks at us all as one.'

Suhana had already fallen into a deep sleep, her rattling chest quieting under their care. The younger girls huddled around her, praying their warmth would heal her faster.

One by one, they stopped bleeding. Some grew early on, some grew later on, some were left to grow, to purify the land. Bellies continued to grow and grow and grow, seeds left in safe lodgings, for their destruction. Some, like the Major's women, were made to swallow a coloured liquid to cremate their insides, saving them from an unwelcome alliance. Those yet to grow were used even as they bled. Bleeding. Bloating. It made no difference to marching men.

Sometimes Lucky prayed against her stomach, which burned like the blazing sun outside. Others prayed for their hunger to scorch the stalk inside. Lucky imagined her tears turning into clouds under the searing heat and drifting across the room until they landed in another pair of eyes.

Outside, the Slow-Smiling Soldier led the Friday prayer.

'I've missed a cycle,' Mohini said matter-of-factly. Her eyes held mischief awaiting Lucky's reaction, but behind her playful goading, Lucky saw fear.

In the distance, gunfire screeched in an alien tongue.

'It doesn't mean anything.'

'This is the first time. It never happened when I worked.'

Before her was Mohini's bare stomach, still flat, caving inward, barren of food for days.

'When women think too much, they miss a cycle.'

'Then all the women of this land would be barren together. Sometimes the simple answer is the right one.'

Lucky trembled with rage. She pictured one of the soldiers being welcomed home with loving embraces. Regarded with admiration and given tributes for delivering the disbelievers from damnation. All this, after he had gouged out their souls. Gorged on its embers. Gutted the rest of them over a burning fire. Would his wife suspect what he had done, notice a difference in her husband's touch? Would she, knowing his secret, keep quiet to protect her family, just as Lucky would protect hers? Would these seeds that sprouted in their stomachs prod him as he played with his lawful children, weigh on his thoughts as he aged, if only with curiosity, or would those worries be left behind with the bullets lodged deep inside their enemies? Lucky prayed these bloated bellies would forever haunt the men who planted their seed there, like they would forever haunt the women who carried it.

'Memories of us will torture them,' she said defiantly.

'No, they won't,' Mohini replied. 'They'll lock their eyes and ears in a safe place and sleep peacefully next to wives who prayed for their safe return.'

'Even the ones who won't get nightmares will remember.'

'And then they'll forget all over again. These men sit comfortably in their wickedness. You think they'll ever want to change their ways? Remember and repent? They don't want to know all the harm they've done, they deny it, call you a liar, because they couldn't squeeze a drop of human blood from their hollowed hearts if they tried, let alone do enough good to make up for their wrongs. But the more they distract themselves, the more joyous they become, the deeper the divine destroyer digs a ditch for their ruin. Call it karma or call it hell, their suffering will be eternal.'

Mohini always surprised Lucky. One moment she was sunlight drying petals after a rainy night, the next she was the blizzard that bent the stalk till the petals touched the ground, scraping off their splendid colour. Yet, Lucky felt both were right. While she struggled to measure the weight of the swinging pendulum, others saw its numbers clearly. They knew what to do, say and feel at the right moment while she ran behind them with failing vision.

'Believe me, it's better for us if they forget,' Mohini said, tracing small circles along her midriff.

The blazing sun turned the sky a molten brass but there was a dark, musty greyness to the room. A grey smokeless fire, its fuel people and stone, stoked a phoenix in their stomachs that stripped away the inner lining, only to renew and repeat itself every sunset. Lucky and Jamila lay beside each other listening to the acid rumbling of their stomachs as the sun went down. When the colours lost their lustre, Jamila turned to Lucky and asked, 'Boro Apa, do you remember Chowdhury Shaheb?'

'Alma Aunty's father. He was a great man.'

'I'm glad he didn't live to see this. He's one man I would hate to see fall.'

Chowdhury Shaheb was a busy man, and like most busy men, he died young because his heart could not serve how busy he was. A successful and generous businessman, Chowdhury Shaheb never sat at a table for lunch or dinner without three destitute men he had invited along the way to eat with him. His two wives, equally as generous as him, never wore the same saree twice. When women and girls spread their hands out to them, they'd unravel their sarees there and then and give them away.

Chowdhury Shaheb's lands flourished. His workers were pleased with him and his sons and daughters adored him. But as a God-fearing man, he feared his blessings and chose his words carefully concerning them. When asked how many children he had, he answered that God had loaned him twelve. When his townspeople congratulated him on his success, his family, his money and his land, he trembled and gave away bags of rice from his fields to the villagers to prevent ill from befalling him. And it never did. But over this pleasant and peaceful life, a restless wind began to blow.

On a warm, dry day, the bakery at the end of the road blazed with a fire so high the whole town could see it. It burned towards Chowdhury Shaheb's house, which had a general store at the front. Chowdhury Shaheb, ever a practical man, thought of all the documents, gold and money he held in safekeeping for his family and trusting neighbours. His chest pulsed with calculations.

Shopkeepers ran in and out of stores, carrying in buckets of water to douse what they had lost and carrying out valuable items. When Ammu's friend Alma Aunty found out about the fire from the local authority announcement, she ran straight to her father's shop, only to find him missing.

'Where's Abba?' she panted.

'I saw him go round the back,' said the shopkeeper, his face blacked with smoke, sweat seeping through his charred shirt. 'Chowdhury Shaheb's been gone for a while.'

A small shack stood in the middle of an opening, its door slightly ajar. Hovering around the toilet door, Alma Aunty called out to her father. In the distance, the fire gasped, pulling the winds towards their house.

When she heard no answer, she pushed the door to see her father sitting on the toilet, fully clothed, bodna filled to the top at his side, dazed.

'Abba, why are you sitting here? We need to move. The house...' She shook his shoulders, frightened by the absent look on her father's face. 'Do you need the toilet?'

When Alma Aunty shook him again, he looked up and only smiled at her. 'Yes... let's get going,' he said, as if nothing unusual had happened, and they ran back to their road.

The fire stopped twenty houses short of Chowdhury Shaheb's. No one had died and for Chowdhury Shaheb, nothing was lost. But from that day on, he felt a pulsing come and go in his chest. He became quiet, worried others would find out something was wrong. Eventually, his wife told him to see a doctor. A bus filled with his two wives, twelve children, a couple of sons-in-law, a handful of employees and Ammu, Lucky and Jamila made its way to Dhaka.

'One of the valves is weak,' the doctor said.

'Valves?' Lucky asked, listening to Ammu tell the story years later. Jamila sat beside her with a puzzled look on her face. They had been too young to remember the details.

'Little rooms in the heart. There are four of them, and we need all four to live well. I thought it was bulb, like the bulbs that give light,' Ammu laughed, pointing to the ceiling. 'I wondered why they didn't hurry and replace it! For years after his death, every time the light flickered, I remembered him. It felt important. A sign of something good to come.'

Now, Lucky thought of the goodness of Chowdhury Shaheb's heart. After Abbu died, Lucky's uncles and cousins had tried to take his land and bribed his employees to stop working so Ammu would turn to them for help. Though she understood what was being done to her, Ammu was powerless to act otherwise. It was but the grace of a good man, Chowdhury Shaheb, that saved her and her family.

'Men like Chowdhury Shaheb build and protect,' Lucky said to Jamila. 'He helped with our fields after Abbu died and made sure we never went hungry, and he had his sons guard our house whenever there was a disturbance. Hundreds of people came to his funeral and stood in line for prayer. Now his children do as he did, that's the power of a good man.'

Ammu always told Chowdhury Shaheb's story when she was in a good mood. His spirit was the one they would disappoint if they stole sweets from the market. His character was the one by which they measured all men. The sisters had heard

Chowdhury Shaheb's story so many times they could recount each word and see each expression as if recalling their own memories.

'He gave us sweets and money whenever he saw us,' Jamila reminisced. 'Ammu always thought we stole them.'

'She'd have strangled us if she knew he gave us that much money.'

Lucky married Waleed because he had the same generous spirit she had seen in Chowdhury Shaheb as a child. She wanted her children to inherit the goodness of a father with those characteristics, and she watched with pleasure as Waleed's mannerisms bloomed in their son, his relaxed demeanour, his friendliness and courage to laugh boldly, he had it all. Lucky pitied the soldiers' children whose fathers would return to them one day. And she wondered if those children, born from women who sat in rooms like theirs, would carry with them their father's flaws.

'For all the devils and cowards that walk among us, there are all those who are good, spread far and wide throughout the land. They'll help us be reborn from our mistakes,' Jamila said.

'Men like Chowdhury Shaheb and his children will rebuild the nation again,' Lucky agreed. 'And so will we.'

15. THE COLOUR OF GOD

'D'you fools think you'll see heaven? Return to your wives and children, eat mishti with them? Fire waits at the soles of your feet, you bastards!'

A baton made its way through the window, narrowly missing Rabia's head. Her hair was a bulbul's nest, and the women wondered how it got shorter each time she returned to the room. Meanwhile, Rabia looked at the girls who hadn't yet started their menses, who held rags between their legs soaked in a different kind of blood.

Night fell and candlelight enhanced her jagged locks. A faint glow pulsed around the room, until elbows, knees, breasts and buttocks formed dark hilltops in the dimness, noses both sharp and round, hollowed cheeks and knotted hair becoming clear with the squinting of their eyes. Rabia sat in her spot under the window and looked out. The soldiers and officers outside held lamps to see each other, only extinguishing the light when they entered the room. The women needn't know whom they served, only that it was their place to serve. Rabia shook the bars of the window and when that did nothing, she pulled at her short clumps of hair until tiny strands blew away in the breeze and settled in theirs.

'Damned churail,' Lieutenant Patches cursed, looking into the room with bared teeth. 'We shouldn't have brought this one here.'

He turned his back, heading towards the kitchen. Armed with Rokeya's translation, Rabia sprang to her feet, rattling the bars of the window.

'No, you shouldn't have, you coward! I'll make sure you choke on that comb if it's the last thing I do!'

'If he returns and makes Suhana translate, he might stick that comb in your eye,' Mohini said, amusement lining her voice.

'I'll pull it out and stick it up his nose, so he can whistle a tune for that lover's quarrel on his face. A song to rival Tagore's.'

Beside her Noori and Sumayyah cackled faintly, clutching their empty stomachs. The Slightly Cross-Eyed Soldier kept his twitching face still, his mouth threatening to soften its straight line.

Major Moustache and the Shaytan had been gone for days, leaving the Slow-Smiling Soldier in charge of the camp. Like the women, the soldiers watched him with cautious brows and tight lips, worried they might invite his eerie attention. All were apprehensive, except Rabia.

Rabia fancied herself a poet. Her countless hours in the room were spent formulating rhymes, perfecting each cursing couplet and cutting the fat around its edges to puncture her target fatally. If she could gather a snigger in her chest and have it bubble out of her of its own volition when she delivered her lines to a confused Khan, earning a chuckle or two from the room behind her, she had succeeded. If the Khan's brows leapt in shock and the girls rolled over snorting, the day became glorious. If they hit her before she could finish her lines and she could not rise again that evening, she would try again with words more obscene when the sun rose.

Rabia would make her own fun, no matter the circumstances. When soldiers rolled into her village, she laughed aloud so her weaning daughter could sense her mother's joy on her lips, feel her rumbling chest against her face instead of the rumbling ground beneath their feet. She had been called insolent, shameless, sinful for laughing in the face of death. It didn't surprise her. Only a fool would rely on those who couldn't laugh during good times to laugh during the bad.

Nose resting between the bars, Rabia scanned the courtyard and threw jabs at the Slow-Smiling Soldier when he walked past. At first, he enjoyed it. He threw playful glares back at her and thrummed his fingers against his thighs as he approached, beckoning her ire. But as days went by and Major Moustache and the Shaytan did not return with their treasures, and Lychee Bhai did not arrive with his lychees, the Slow-Smiling Soldier's slow smile took on a sinister edge. While the women shrank themselves into the walls, pulling others with them when he peeped into the room, Rabia saw the Slow-Smiling Soldier's troubles as a sign of fortune's favour and taunted him all the harder for it.

'Black bitch,' he sneered.

Rabia, whose skin shone darkest of them all, spat at the soldiers who laughed at her colour but fought each other to taste it. Like her mother she was as dark as a crow, and as vicious as one too. Towards the end of her life, after her family had cut ties with her and she'd lost most of her friends, Rabia's mother had told her daughter to be patient with those who slighted her and she'd become beautiful. *Even dark girls like us,* she said, *because beautiful people aren't always good, but good people are always beautiful.*

But Rabia didn't want to be beautiful or good. She wanted to be free.

'Khobis! Is that all you've got?' she yelled back.

Like most women, Rabia hadn't noticed her beauty fading until her husband began to look elsewhere. She had been unaware of how her body creased with years of sweat and tears. How her tired soul had leaked from her eyes until they became hollow, and bags stretched and formed to hold them up, how it leaked from her plump fingertips until they shrivelled and hardened with struggle, leaked from the roots of her hair until it lost its lustre and lay greying and limp on her shoulders, leaked from her spine and into her chest, until the weight of her duties had made her bow her head to those who took from her, little by little, until she was ready to enter her grave. How infantile those reasons now seemed under a bombarded sky.

She looked toward the Slightly Cross-Eyed Soldier's rifle, frowning at the terrible image her mind threatened to conjure. She couldn't imagine turning a gun on herself, though she had been cutting herself in smaller ways for years so that she was already covered in scars that stretched into different shapes, lightening but never fading away, as she grew. She made note of them. A branch. A bow. A witch's wand.

'It's dangerous to poke at them now,' Lucky warned her.

'She's right,' Jamila said, sitting under the window to watch the guards watching them. 'Let them be, and let there be something left of you to be freed. There's nothing wrong with surrendering in the moment to win in the end.'

Rabia did not respond. Her eyes were fixed far away, and her silence ticked loudly in the women's chests.

One rainy day, Rabia returned with bruises lining her skin and bleeding teeth marks on the back of her neck. She grabbed the metal water bucket from the middle of the room and bashed it against the bars of the window until the entire camp shook.

Lucky scrambled towards her, her weak legs buckling beneath her. Rabia pushed her away with a strength that did not match their endless days of hunger. Rage lit her eyes. The women rushed to grab her, pulling her from the window by her arms, legs, waist and petticoat, but midnight's shadow had cast its veil over Rabia's heart, and she would move forward.

Bang.

Bang.

Bang.

The bucket sang throughout the camp.

She would make them rise.

The Slightly Cross-Eyed Soldier leapt up from behind them, pushing the women away and wrestling the bucket from Rabia's grip, but the Slow-Smiling Soldier had already walked in.

'You're really asking to be killed,' he said. A small knife swung lazily in his hand. His signature slow smile was missing.

'*You* should worry about dying,' Rabia spat, seeing the shape of his words on his face. 'How will *you* answer for what *you've* done?'

He looked at her quietly, scanning her eyes, her nose, then resting his gaze on her lips.

'I understand you just fine, whore,' he said in a low voice. He smiled slowly, but his slow smile did not reach his eyes. Its coolness froze the women in place. It was bitter and smelt of iron. A warning that reverberated along the walls of their wombs.

The Slightly Cross-Eyed Soldier moved to grab Rabia but one sharp look from the Slow-Smiling Soldier stopped him in his tracks, so his hands hung mid-air like shade-giving palm leaves behind her. Gripping her chin until his finger burned red on her skin, the Slow-Smiling Soldier shook Rabia's face. Her neck cracked angrily against the charged air. She grabbed his wrist, her mouth a snarled line. The ping, ping, ping of her hair tearing from her scalp squeezed the air so tight that in the corners of the room, the ants stopped marching.

'I'll send you to hell faster than any angel can.'

'You're just a man,' she whispered.

Loosening his grip on her hair, his slow hand slithered down her neck and pressed inward. She pushed against his chest, her clenched teeth fighting to keep in her skin's scream. Each pound of her palm jolted straight to his brain, and for the Slow-Smiling Soldier, who already had a headache, it confirmed that he had had enough. Raising his left hand, he swiped at Rabia's midriff to ease its pounding.

It was so quick Lucky missed it, though she was looking right at them.

The Slow-Smiling Soldier watched Rabia's eyes widen. He felt her chest cave in, her palms loosen in his hold, and breathed in what she breathed out, her warm whisper lining the inside of his nose and mouth. He watched the confusion in her eyes turn to disbelief as shock turned to pain. Yes, this was how they all looked, dumb and inconsolable; no one ever believed they were going to die. Her grip on him softened and so did his grip on her, so for a moment it looked as if two lovers held each other, but as clarity wavered in and out of her pulsing pupils, she murmured a few words into his ear, and he realised she would try to shred him with her last breath. It was a shame. She was fun, unlike the others, and he liked the way her tongue poked at him viciously like an accusing finger when she ran her mouth.

He winced as her nails dug into his hand, still around her neck, until they tore deep into his flesh. The slow dribble of his blood down his wrist and into the sleeve of his shirt formed an uncomfortable ring of dampness on his skin, pulling him from his trance. The Slow-Smiling Soldier pushed Rabia away from him, turned, and left, her last words to him, so sure and giddy, still ringing in his ears, posed to haunt him till his last hour. *Thanks, you've made a martyr out of me.*

For a moment, she looked like a cow after it had given birth to a calf, its intestines spilled out onto the ground.

Grotesque wonder flashed briefly in Lucky's mind. For the first time, she saw the presence of every breath in a body, rising and falling like waves on a dark, desolate night. Then, like the tumbling words of a desperate liar, blood bubbled out of Rabia's open stomach, soaking through her yellow petticoat, a midday sun covered by a menacing molten mist. A pear with two handles hung by a bloody thread from the jagged skin of her stomach and her eyes rolled in her head. A moan like Lucky had never heard before came from her mouth. Hellish. It seized their lungs and shot splinters into their souls. Rabia's flailing fingers gripped the edges of the Slightly Cross-Eyed Soldier's uniform as they both fell to the floor.

Crawling towards her, fingers fluttered around her spilling body. Strange noises came from Lucky's throat. The younger girls passed out, never having thought a day would come when they would see what they looked like from the inside. Rabia gritted her teeth until the grinding sounded like it would break her jaw.

'Clothes! Put pressure on her stomach!' Lucky shouted, redness spreading across her arms and legs. Milk-thick tears clouded her vision so she could not see Rabia below her, only feel horror's warmth on her fingers.

The women stripped off their blouses and petticoats and knelt naked around her, pressing onto her stomach, covering her insides hastily like jealous lovers, pushing back her womb and the pulsing, bulbous, smooth, slithering tubes that unfolded around them and coated their dirty, shaking hands with varying shades of crimson, until the only sign of her wound was a dark pool around their knees.

Rabia's grip on Lucky's arm loosened, and Lucky saw death climb its way up her body and into her eyes.

'It's done,' Rabia whispered.

'Hush! Focus on breathing,' Lucky sobbed.

Red soaked its way into the mud and made a line for the small pink flower in the concrete. The Slightly Cross-Eyed Soldier stood by them, unmoving, bile rising to his throat.

'Let me speak,' Rabia breathed.

Lucky pressed Rabia's palm to her face, her tears drawing clear lines along her friend's bloodied arm. Grief's shaky breath made Rabia smile.

'I worked as a seamstress to help my husband,' she began, as her throat gurgled. 'I spent whole days winding thread onto bobbins, watching it go round and round, so one day I might stitch together something beautiful. I was a seamstress, but I couldn't stitch my Rubi back together, and today I can't stitch myself back together.'

Lucky pushed Rabia's hand harder into her face and wept, her body heaving with an ancient grief. Her gasping mouth tasted the red warmth of Rabia's skin, until the bones of Rabia's fingers clanged in protest against the bones of Lucky's eye sockets, willing their souls to somehow merge together so she could stay.

'Why do you cry more for me than for yourself?' Rabia's tongue was heavy in her mouth, and she no longer felt her legs.

A chorus of cries was all the women could respond with.

'My insides are still sore from giving birth. It calls to me. I want to see my Rubi again, maybe that's why I spat at them. I want to see my love without looking up at her from this lonely place.'

Tears seeped from Rabia's closed eyes like an overflowing well covered with a stone lid. Lucky placed her finger on Rabia's cheek and found it cold as ice. *Tears of happiness are cold, tears of grief hot,* Ammu told Lucky and Jamila as young girls when they fought. She would place their hands over the other's face so each could feel the heat of her sister's tears.

A heavy gurgling sound like a city road drain swallowing up the last of the monsoon floods rushed out of her mouth. Lucky cupped her hands under Rabia's chin as she coughed up chunks of herself. Ruby red swam smoothly into her open palms, the warmest touch Lucky had felt in a long time.

'Don't leave,' Lucky pleaded. Rabia's eyelids drooped in a melted way and fixed on a point in the corner of the room behind Lucky. Lucky was afraid that if she looked back, she would see the angel of death standing among them.

'Say it now,' Sumayyah urged, rubbing her fingers across Rabia's lips.

In a moment of courage, fuelled by anger and defiance against the heavens, Lucky turned to look behind her, red spilling out from her hands onto the floor, but saw nothing.

With her eyes closed, Rabia smiled. 'I see you free. I won't live to see our victory, but it's enough that I can see that day for you. Forgive me, I couldn't listen to you all, my heart wouldn't allow it.'

Chanda and Noori massaged her hands and feet, willing them to come back to life.

'La ilaha illallah,' Rabia said, her faint voice disappearing from under them.

Warm air released from her lips. Her face smoothed and her hand became heavy in theirs.

No one moved.

Behind them, Noori let out a deep moan, her chest pulling her down until her forehead touched the ground. Teardrops fell like hail, soaking the soil beneath them. Jamila thumped her forehead against Lucky's back and wept. Mohini pulled her wet hands away from Rabia's stomach and sat back against the wall, resting her hands on her knees, her fingers dripping deep splatter across the ground. Crouched over the waste bucket, Rokeya retched.

For hours, under the torrent, the river sang a eulogy for Rabia, its low rumble serenading her soul out of the camp. Outside, boots marched on. Jasmines peeled into bloom, their orange tongues beckoning sightseers forward for a taste of their fragrance.

'Bury her,' Lucky said to the Slightly Cross-Eyed Soldier. He sat in his chair, head hung, elbows on his knees, rifle flat across the floor at his feet. One eye turned to her, softening with tenderness at how her fingers twitched between fear and fury, while the other remained resolutely fixed on the door.

For days now, Lucky had watched the Slightly Cross-Eyed Soldier try to do his dishonest work with honesty. Somewhere deep inside, under layers of darkness, she pitied him. Unlike the others, he knew he betrayed himself. He was like a snake who bit his own tail and let the venom seep only halfway through his fangs so he lingered on the precipice of life and death. From his seat, in perfect view of their pain, he learnt all about the world and its people, and it aggrieved him. Yet, he remained diligent in his orders, watching them dutifully, making sure the door stayed locked and the women quiet, his face drawn as if his own sister had died.

'Stop shrieking,' the Slow-Smiling Soldier said to Noori as he entered the room, his eyes lingering over the body, his slow smile unusually reserved.

'Bury her,' Lucky repeated.

'What was that? Should we arrange a janaza for her? Take off our boots and caps and pray for her? The bottom of the river is her resting place,' the Slow-Smiling Soldier sneered. Turning to the Slightly Cross-Eyed Soldier, he ordered, 'Leave her as a reminder of what happens when traitors sharpen their tongues. Soon they'll beg me to take her away because of the stench.'

For the first time, the Slow-Smiling Soldier's smile was not convincing. It was drawn with a child's shaky hand, its lines indistinguishable from uncertainty. His rotten eyes widened at the women's doubt. It enraged him.

'Shoot them if they try to wrap the whore,' he commanded, but his words fell flat on their ears.

Lucky and Jamila wiped Rabia's face and hands. Death's last breath was still raised on her lips, and her body was poised with a dignity that barely fit her small frame. When there was no more water, the women wrapped their sarees around her one by one until the blood no longer seeped through. Her face and hands lay bare, covered only with the edges of a blouse, so they would not be killed.

Lucky drew a box into the soil around Rabia's body with her finger. An open grave at their feet. No congregation in white stood around her. No one waited, palms open, ready to wash her. No one stood in prayer to seek forgiveness and request a smooth journey home. Instead, the women sat around the body in their blouses and underskirts, swatting away mice and cockroaches, their mouths trembling against the words that formed their personal prayers for her. The Slightly Cross-Eyed Soldier kept his eyes closed until the end.

'The best die first,' Jamila's hollow voice rang loud in the sunken room. 'It's God's mercy to his favourites. They don't betray their humanity for the small price of survival, so they don't suffer for as long.'

As days went by, Rabia's skin grew waxy. Her hair and nails grew long as if she were living and breathing someplace else, alive and well in her dreams, or, they hoped, a heavenly realm.

The night breeze covered and uncovered her face. Still, she was beautiful. Her skin had taken on a grey hue, like sunshine behind clouds on a misty morning, but the soft warmth of her dark skin made promise of sunrise. The changing colours of her skin were mesmerising as they were excruciating. Lucky watched her from a close distance, afraid that if she touched Rabia's cheek, it would burn her finger.

When Major Moustache returned and saw Rabia's body wrapped tight in the middle of the room, he barked orders for it to be taken out and buried. Mohini was red-eyed, her gentle smile gone. Without it, her face was different. It made the Major uneasy. He threw a new load of clothes in the place where Rabia's body had lain and made the women change and sit fresh and upright in bright pinks, reds and oranges. Then, as the Shaytan marched the soldiers out and led them to an unknown place to bury the body, Major Moustache took his favourite honey away to bring back her smile.

16. THE LAST HOUR

On a day when Lucky could not feel her fingers and death's cool embrace called to her, the Slightly Cross-Eyed Soldier ran in, his crossed eyes restless and his fingers shaking, and began to cry. His khaki uniform was a dirty brown, his gun stained with mud, his helmet missing.

'It's the end! It's over, it's the end,' he said to the men.

Turning to them, his eyes meeting Lucky's, he said, 'Astaghfirullah.' God, forgive me.

A shot rang out.

The women pushed each other into the walls.

His repentance dripped from the roof in heavy droplets. It marked them in splatters, small and large, across their faces and torn sarees.

With the whites of their eyes stretched wide, leering lips now forced straight, the Major and his Minors ran out, clambering over each other, leaving the room unmanned.

Lucky looked back at the Slightly Cross-Eyed Soldier, his lips slightly raised, his eyes empty, as she ran out of the room locking hands with Jamila and another woman whose belly was round and heavy.

Shouting.

Shots.

Silence.

Shots.

Shouting.

In the fields, long black ringlets shimmered silver under pond water, merging with the reflection of a blue, cloudless sky.

An ascension to heaven.

A welcome mercy.

A sick mirage.

The sky which had bled for nine months was scarred by aerial attack, its lines etched permanently into the eyes of those fleeing the room. A scarlet saree lay strewn across the field, unravelled from a woman unknown, now unknowable, later to be hastily buried in an unmarked grave for scattered jasmines to decorate.

The smell of victory scorched her nose, a blend of fresh air, wet grass, damp clothes, decaying carcasses. Half submerged in the shallow end of the river, dirty fingernails still clasping dry ground above, frozen in their body's last breath.

Corpses of men congregated underwater, some lying face forward, others face down. Scattered heads and knees bobbed at the surface thirsty for air among bright pink waterlilies, confusing busy bees into making wrong stops. Hidden among the lifeless limbs of the fallen heroes, the Shaytan floated, nodding in false agreement that he too had been wronged.

A child lay half buried under disturbed soil trampled by unknown feet, limp like the straw toys Ammu made for the girls when they were young. Toys that never sat upright on their own.

Face to the ground, a naked body rested with a bayonet lodged between its slender legs.

Legs brought together again on a day shrouded in white.

Large black birds were pecking at flesh where breasts once were, wings spanning larger than the thin, tired bodies caged in between. As if they were minions of the army, sent to wipe away history, like a flowing stream gathering layers of froth, only to disappear on a thunderous day, taking with it the crimes committed against them.

Women swayed gently from the trees, their sarees crossing and uncrossing with the direction of the wind, like the motion of Ammu's hands as Lucky waited for her long plait to be tied tightly for school.

A young boy lay tangled on the ground, trousers missing, legs parted, just like the women.

The winds swept dry, crisp leaves awry, gliding over Lucky's crumpled saree, over paddy fields and on top of bullets, veiling them from hurried eyes. Over men and women whose dreams they stole in equal measure. Over the Slow-Smiling Soldier, who slept between the jujube and bamboo trees.

Beetles burrowed out of the ground, feasting on women returned to dust. Later to stir, swell and produce every kind of joyous growth from those miserable remains, giving life to dead land and slaking the thirst of jasmines, which would grow anew where their heads once lay.

Some didn't run but wandered out, neither alive nor dead. They gazed at the women who lay on the fields and wondered, were they better off?

A question that lingered until the Certain End came upon them.

Mukti joddhas ran towards them in lungis and dirty white vests, green and red gamchhas tied around their heads, carrying shotguns as tall as themselves, amid soldiers sitting atop tanks, bright red ribbons lining their turbans.

Their radiant faces tinted with mud.

Their excitement so potent it could resurrect those long gone, drawing them out of their graves like plants bursting through soil to rally to the flag.

Where did you come from?

What happened, you say?

Where have you been?

It's time to celebrate!

The Indians came.

Don't you know?

The war is over.

We have won!

Joy Bangla!

Joy…

Those soldiers who scattered across the land pillaging were finally gathered for reckoning. Faces drawn. Empty-eyed. Sweating in accordance with their deeds, as if the sun had been brought close to their heads. For some it came up to their chests, others to their chins, others drowned, their sweat gargling in their mouths and noses. All carrying clay hearts encrusted with what they had done.

'They were like stampeding asses fleeing from a lion when they saw us with the Indians!' the Mukti Bahini said.

Lucky neither saw nor remembered this. For the sisters it was an hour of silence, to embrace and to unravel, to weep and to wail, to die and to reawaken. To place their foreheads, in that last hour, against the ground in thanks.

Now the winds were sent as heralds of glad tidings to fertilise a land reborn.

17. MILK-MOTHERS

The mukti joddhas struggled to keep the joy in their step when they saw them. They had seen thousands of dead bodies, fields that swam with five inches of blood, buried small children without parents and performed rushed prayers for limbs, killed men, dragged their bodies into piles and cheered, but the sight of the dishevelled women, with empty eyes, jagged hair and tattered clothes, who touched their faces to feel if they were dead or alive, made their stomachs churn.

They took them from place to place searching for medical assistance. But the roads were difficult to traverse, the bridges blown up, the hospitals and doctors' offices torched, and the women too weak to travel for too long. It took them days to find a makeshift hospice offering food and medicine, but it was poorly stocked and filled with men and boys who had their limbs torn off in battle. Soon the women had to search for another place to turn. Those whose towns or villages they passed along the way were dropped at their homes. Now, weeks after the war, those who lived furthest from the camp were taken to a centre, where nurses and doctors tended to other women like them, the new government having mobilised some of its resources for their particular afflictions.

Lucky woke to the sound of a girl in labour. A symphony of cries and curses fevered the air, accompanied by the smell and squelching sounds of birth.

No more than twelve or thirteen years old, the girl wept as she pushed. Her sobbing came from a place so deep inside of herself, it pricked the eyes of those around her. Alarmed at the hellish screams, the nurses rushed to soothe her with comforting hands. The bedsheet seeped red with her undersized innards as the bloody mass tore its way out of her body. Slow and jagged. It arrived too early, with a face like a drop of water on a taro leaf. The girl pleaded with the doctor to kill her too while a nurse pulled her lifeless baby away.

Lucky turned away, burying her face in her pillow to hush the horror. Jamila slept opposite her, dead to the anguish, while beside her Mohini sat looking straight towards it. A hard lump pulsed in Lucky's stomach till she retched.

'There's a bowl by your arm,' Mohini motioned.

Only when Lucky was done did she sit up and turn towards the others. Under the light, the horrors glowed.

'How do you feel?' Mohini asked.

'I don't know.'

Mohini nodded. 'I'm more afraid now than I was before.'

Lucky squeezed her trembling hands. 'They'll blame us for what our bodies produce on their own,' she whispered.

Mohini looked out at the devastation before them. 'They say a mother's love is second only to God's love. I wonder if they'll remember any of that now... They'll make us enemies to our children and our children enemies to us, why, even say we're enemies to ourselves if we want to keep them.'

In this room, only the expecting mothers cried. Lucky could feel the weight of their tears for the grand, rageful, sacrificing love that was demanded of them. She thought of neighbours who had nine, ten children, one a year, or every two years if there was a complication, wives whose husbands beat them for the rising expenses, the mother's resentment with no place to escape to except to her children. Decades later the children would realise, too late, that their mother was that dirty-tasting word. Human. By then they would have long struggled with a love tinged with hatred and a hatred tinged with love, wrestling with the soul's plea to fulfil a hallowed bond.

A mother's love disappoints. It sears and scars even small broken hearts that never once felt its beauty but knew they missed out on something mighty. And in this room, a mother was made hard-hearted through no fault of her own. To look upon her belly with eyes filled with scorn for another. A sacred love extinguished at inception.

Maybe we are enemies to our children, Lucky thought.

Another young girl called out for her mother amid a chorus of moans. Unwilling mothers stared empty-eyed at their bloated bellies and what stirred inside, waving up at them. Agonised cries rose from women as rotting foetuses fled their wombs, some naturally flushed out amid the upheaval, others induced by a doctor's prescription. Those were the lucky ones, the women whose bumps were still only a bite. They still had a choice. Yet as the flow of blood between their legs washed away their last hopes of redemption, they all agreed there was no worse affliction than burying a child, formed or forming. By choice, by nature or by design, the heart grew bigger when it tried to grow another.

'What do you want most in this world?' Mohini asked. They lay on their backs now, facing the ceiling, too afraid to watch what was going on around them.

Lucky thought about Rabia's body, buried at the hand of the enemy and now lost forever. Of Zoleyka, who extinguished her heart between her fists. Of Minna and Mihir, the little girl and boy who were loved by many but never made it home.

'Peace.'

The word sent a small shiver through the room. Women turned their heads towards them, surprised to hear talk of peace in such a place. Mohini considered the word for a long time while the whirring of machinery filled the space between them. Anguished prayers from all directions consumed them. Spat at them. Accused them of disbelief for not joining in.

'Peace is good, if you accept it for what it is,' she agreed.

'It's all I've ever wanted,' Lucky said. 'A calm to stop tragedy from taking a seat in my heart.'

Mohini smiled. 'I've had a life of peace, believe it or not. Maybe more than you have. But I've learnt that peace isn't as generous as the absence of bad, nor is it as boring as nothingness. Peace breathes like you and me and holds its hand out in invitation towards a life that's felt, not just lived. I enjoy peace. But I think there are better things.'

'What could be better?'

Mohini's eyes became serious. 'Respect. Above all, for yourself. What good is peace when anger simmers below it ready to boil it into gas?'

The question intruded into Lucky's thoughts like a door slammed open on a windy day, letting in rainwater and muddy leaves. It cooed at her with urgency. It gripped her short hair like a tempered baby's fist. It pointed its earnest new-born stare at her with venom. She turned away from it. She would think about it later.

Outside, a crowd gathered. Men and women, mostly men. They were neither relatives nor friends, nor neighbours nor well-wishers, but passers-by whose curiosity made them forget propriety. Mukti joddhas guarding the gates waved at them to leave, but the crowd grew until the sound of their whispers rose above the machines and guttural moans.

They had come to see the birangona.

It was a kind gesture, a beautiful word which rolled gently but powerfully across the tongue, but it would not save them. Some of those who gathered outside held blankets, food, clothes and toiletries along with tears in their eyes. Others stood on their toes to catch a glimpse of what a birangona looked like, to see for themselves if it was a worthy title.

'My sisters, you have nothing to be ashamed of, you have freed your country like the freedom fighters, and we are grateful to you,' the head doctor announced in the middle of the room, his brows growing graver with each word. 'The president has honoured you as birangona, war heroines, mothers of the nation.' He looked around and cleared his throat as they looked back at him with their empty eyes. 'Rest, eat, the nurses will come to ask for your name and address. Please cooperate and you can go home sooner. Your families are waiting for you.'

Lucky kept her blanket pulled over her face until he left.

The crowd outside grew louder as people inched forward and pushed against the mukti joddhas, some trying to circumvent the guards by taking dirt pathways to get a closer look at the birangona women who lay inside like corpses of their former selves. It wasn't enough that there were still so many women lying across the streets naked and bleeding, disowned and homeless, mad but alive. They wanted names. Clean faces. To see the families from whence these girls came and hear with their own ears fate's torturous whip flagellate them.

It was ancient knowledge that people preferred a woman who could suffer. Families picked a wife not just for her beauty, family, wealth or religion but also for those qualities already forged in her to endure pain. They searched for signals. A blush of shame. A flutter of embarrassment. The angle of her chin to the floor when she addressed a man. A forehead sculpted by willingness to bow at an elder's feet. They searched for new pain. A droplet of blood to prove innocence. A small dowry to prove humility. An untrained tongue to prove peace-loving. Youth and self-loathing to prove mouldability.

Nearby, two nurses spoke in hushed whispers.

'It's better to be rid of it,' one said, looking to the crowd.

'Let the doctors give them that option,' the other cautioned.

A new-born, still splattered in red and white, was taken from his mother before she could close her legs. The nurses fought for a moment. Having been determined healthy, the baby was returned into the arms of his mother. He blinked up at her, roused by all the jostling. Fresh eyes turned upward finally to behold the vision of their first beloved face. The mother turned away from him, weeping. The baby cried. Twin streams of tears which fell for different reasons. Then the baby was wrapped in a blanket, taken away again and rocked to sleep just out of reach.

'Where do they take them?' Lucky asked, her heart thumping in her throat.

Mohini waited for her to stop quivering.

'To another country.'

'God have mercy.'

The rest of the women were pomegranates hanging from a tall summer tree. In varying stages of fruitfulness, they deliberated. A few had heavy husks, red-purple, with no choice but to fall open or be peeled by hungry hands. A few were budding flowers, no great loss to the tree should they tear off from a blustery wind. Most of the women were green, wondering if the seeds were not yet attached to the inner wall. Waiting for the farmer to prod them to find out.

One woman took a nurse aside discreetly and asked for what was inside of her to go from the darkness of its mother's womb straight into the darkness of the earth. Another waved away the doctor and stared into the sky, still choosing. They imagined their babies, once birthed, pulled from their own empty breasts to the full breasts of a milk-mother from a different land. A peaceful land. A safe place to love and be loved. Where enemies and allies remained in the files of the cabinets of military personnel who fantasised about warlike destruction and its aftermath in boardrooms and thought experiments. Or could they be loved enough, mother and child, by their once loving families to remain in their birthland?

'God will have mercy,' Mohini said. 'It's those outside who won't.'

'You seem so sure.'

'There's no right or wrong here.'

Lucky hesitated, following the bruises on her wrists with her finger. 'A woman has two hearts in her body when she's with child. Two souls. One formed, one forming, one in pain, one flourishing, one leading the other into the world. The forming soul isn't tarnished, by love or by hate, it's as pure as any other. But a mother who can't live with herself or with her baby... no one will be satisfied with her either way.'

Mohini mulled over Lucky's words with a sad resignation before she spoke again. It dawned on her that only women who had once been loved could deliberate so easily between truth and falsehood, right and wrong. It was a blessing to have a choice and hope others would partake in its outcome, whatever it might be.

'Last night, I dreamt I gave birth to a daughter. I feel it's a true dream, it was too vivid to come from myself. I think I could love her... Maybe even more than a normal child. She was created in chaos, so she must be loved more. But I know if she were born, she'd be sentenced to a fate far worse than death, that of living humiliation, and would come to despise me because of it.'

'Will you keep it?'

Mohini turned back to the ceiling, signalling the end of her admission. Life forced its way between them, rising like a slender shiver of smoke above a lit fire until it grew fierce and overpowering and settled heavy above their heads. It became important again, who they were, why they were here, where they would return to. Their differences.

Jamila moaned in her sleep. Her face painted in pink, her arms and legs blotchy purple. Like a spring lake with its flowers in full bloom.

Lucky let her sister dream in daylight. Forget. She thought back to the little girl she used to see sleeping under the sweet-shop counter. At some point after Jamila joined their family, Lucky had stopped noticing the children who slept on the streets of the marketplace altogether.

'Have the others gone home?' Lucky asked Mohini.

'Everyone except Suhana.'

'Is she alive?'

'She left with the Khans... as a war prisoner.'

Lucky gaped. 'But why?'

'What's left for her here?' Mohini traced slow lines on the blanket covering her belly. 'And didn't we agree there was no right or wrong?'

Before Lucky could respond, a nurse with a bright, round face came to their bedside.

'Once you've eaten, we'll take a few tests,' she reassured them. Mohini muttered a quiet yes. Lucky said nothing. The nurse placed two plates of daal and rice, a pair of bananas and some juice cartons on their bedside table and rushed away, only to reappear beside them the moment their plates were clean.

'We should contact your family,' the nurse said, pushing her thumbs into Lucky's chest in search of broken bones. 'Calm down, dear, hush now, it's okay, you've survived the worst of the world, there's nothing that you can't handle from here on. Hush, there you go. Now people may not applaud you like they should, but you should know by now not to rely on the good opinion of others.'

The nurse waited for Lucky to calm before pushing her nightdress to her hips. Scratches like a garden filled with wayward weeds spilled from Lucky's belly button to her inner thighs, painting her with thick nails hardened by spite. Blood wiped hurriedly, but not entirely, murmured low on her groin, so a sweep of red remained on her skin in a failed attempt to wash its memory. Despite its raging colours, she could not feel its wrath against her body, its molten testimony silenced by the sudden fears of rejection that gripped her heart.

'What if it's best if I stayed away?' she said. 'Mukti joddhas are respected for surviving, women are shamed for it.'

'Hmm,' the nurse hummed, finding no open tears in need of stitching. 'It may be true that the same scar of honour on a man is a mark of humiliation on a woman. But listen, you walk with no scars on your body, only your heart. Remember, men can only work with what you tell them.'

Lucky flinched as the nurse felt over her womanhood. She rubbed at the bruises that lined her lower belly, making a note in her book, and continued to feel down Lucky's legs, wiping them once she was done. Disinfectant doused the room's despairing cries, until it throbbed raw with a salty grief. And an acceptance which dried over their injuries with the taste of defeat.

'I might hurt my son.'

'Suffering isn't contagious. It won't pass on to others if you don't let it. Feel pain again and again if you must. Even when the body has healed, our minds have a bad habit of wandering back, just don't let it fester old wounds,' the nurse advised, squeezing her hand before walking to Jamila's side.

Jamila stirred awake as a girl of fourteen ran into the arms of her father and two brothers. Their embracing cries touched the room. The siblings held each other close, merging into one another until the girl disappeared between gangly limbs and words of relief. The father stood to the side, deliberating. Jamila watched him breathe in deeply, preparing himself to break her heart. She began to count down. Three. Two. One.

The betrayal unfolded before them like a cheap drama. The father's feet pointed away from his daughter, fleeing from the words he uttered. The boys fought him, but he pushed them aside. Placing a small bag in his daughter's hands, now all the possessions she had in this world, the father pulled the boys away with him with short parting words. The girl's legs gave way under the realisation that love was neither infinite nor unconditional. She had learnt what it meant to be a sinner without sin. A doctor and nurse led her away, their faces creased but professional. They had seen this before. Beside her another weeping father clutched his daughter to his chest. They left hand in hand.

'Even if some people are given a good thing, they wouldn't know what to do with it,' the nurse muttered to Jamila. Lucky observed her sister, whose eyes were still on the wailing girl. Jamila did not twitch when the father walked away, nor tear up when the girl fell to the floor. She only looked on, and it made Lucky worry.

'They're afraid of us,' Mohini said, shaking her head. 'No matter what we do, we'll always remind the nation of what our enemies did to us.'

Lucky waited for the nurse to shuffle around the curtain before rising from her bed. She hugged Mohini tight, trembling against her skeletal frame. Mohini rubbed her back in understanding.

'Goodbye,' Mohini whispered, kissing her cheek.

Across from them, Jamila sat leaning against her pillow. The bruises lining her mouth had faded to a pulsing burnt green. Lucky moved to her bedside and gripped her sister's hands.

'I'm going to Ammu now,' she said, studying their entwined fingers, afraid to raise her eyes any higher. 'Come with me.'

They left before the nurses and doctors noticed. Hand in hand, the two sisters ran down a dark, muddy path behind the centre. Women and children sat in large concrete pipes lined side by side. Fierce, tall eyes watched over them as they pushed their way through fields of wheat and stumbled over shell-pierced mounds, left from when the skies rained down with death.

A man knelt speaking to the corpse of his wife. A thin layer of dirt and stone separated his words from her. He told her of the crimes he had committed for freedom. Before the war, an honest man was one who had done no dishonest deed. After the war the innocent were those whose guilt had not been discovered. Victory Day had come and gone and people searched the streets for the men who passed fighting beside them, the women they could not save, the children they could not carry, the possessions they had stolen from their neighbours that they were too ashamed to return.

Withered corpses of men and boys piled the streets in different stages of decay, their fingers and toes pointing the way. Lucky thanked them, not knowing if they were all friends or if a foe had infiltrated them to claim glory for the last time. The ones with faces inspected Lucky and Jamila as they passed by, their eyes frozen open in surprise that the women had survived. Those with hollows were less judgmental, the skin-and-bone men, uninterested. A meatless man sat beside the pile, his tongue long gone, his fingers contorted in a fist as if to declare that he had fought until the end. Pride kept his spine upright in its regal manner for the living to admire. Lucky could tell he had been handsome from the curls on his head and the proportions of his shrinking nose. The rags that hung from his body told her he had been the son of a wealthy man. A student. A future doctor, lawyer or politician, not old enough to be judged too harshly by the world, not knowing enough of the world to grow old in his own head. His strong jaw and shoulders were locked in combat. A boy-child who overcame fear to enter the afterlife honoured.

The more she walked, the more she learnt to despise the word 'birangona'. Drunk men, weeping at the roadside, standing at the foot of the ashes of their homes, alone and penniless, turned their angry red eyes towards her and said, 'Birangona? Na, barangona.' War heroine? No, prostitute.

Others, their homes destroyed by a furious wind before the war began, when the sky tore apart and fish swam in the roads, warning them of a greater trial to come, taking with it their homes, crops, cattle and poultry, gazed at her with eyes that said, *silence, you had it easier.* Those who remained unscathed, who still had homes and businesses, families and smiles, hung the independence flag from their rooftops and gazed at her torn saree and knotted hair with its short, jagged cut, their eyes watering with the words, *God help you, God help you.*

Lucky strode past those red eyes.

Past the walls of a room where rusted tin panels hung, embroidered with patches of scavenged wood.

Past its four corners, where women sat empty-eyed.

Past its heavy wooden door, guarded by soldiers with rifles as tall as themselves.

Past a time when the trees wept for her, when the winds howled for her, when the rivers sang sombre songs for her.

With stiff fingers, Lucky gripped Jamila's hand, silencing the sea that crashed in her ears, and strode towards a house far away from eyes that appraised honorific titles. A pink house surrounded by singing cuckoos, cauliflower fields and a warm, maternal smile.

18. A SMALL PRICE

When Ammu saw Lucky and Jamila at her doorway, she covered her face and cried. Small bruises and even smaller cuts on their bodies whispered a terrible tale. The whites of their eyes shone darker than their pupils and Ammu knew they had come back dead, the kind of dead only a living woman could be. Dead with wide eyes. Too vacant to be warm, too wide to be cold. An aged stare, grotesque to the innocent, eerie to the suspicious, ghostly to the indifferent, repellent to the happy. It said too much. It spoke of a woman small in her own sight, with a spirit which no longer served her.

Ammu wondered what kind of sinner she must be for this to happen to her daughters. Was it because of what she had done all those years ago, that thing she couldn't tell anyone about? An unforgivable thing she could never seek forgiveness for, that she had done to save herself, the thing that would ask her *why* in another realm, from unformed lips in a bulbous body that never did grow. Ammu trembled at the redistributed reckoning of her sins.

When days passed and the girls had not arrived, Ammu pulled out a prayer mat packed away in the back of her cupboard. A white and green patterned Kaaba greeted her as she angled the mat towards a direction she remembered from many years ago. It was so beautiful she had been terrified to ever use it, fearing that the floor would turn it grey. With her face on the ground, she begged that they be spared. Saved. Anything but that. *My Lord, let me take their sins, and spare them mine.*

Her limbs had forgotten what prayer was. The joy of it was taken from her a long time ago by men who never missed a prayer. Had it ever been sweet like others attested? Faded memories of her youth hinted at a time once when she might have rushed to pray, eager to ask God for more. She liked the look of prayer when old people did it. They performed namaaz slowly, without the hurried movements and the blurred words of the young. They had flowers and minarets sewn into their prayer mats and prolonged their prostration with sincerity. They walked around with a tasbeeh between their fingers made of olive wood or ebony beads, round or thin, its colour darkened and lightened from their fingertips, its tassel bent and frayed over the years. Their lips barely moved when they murmured the Lord's praises and wished for a dignified death. From those bead-pulling elders she learnt the secrets of whispered words. That life and death lay between rhythmic fingers and a waving tongue.

Sunrise simmered under a cloud of darkness as Ammu's secret words brought her daughters back to her door. When Ammu looked at them with eyes heavy in their sockets, Lucky saw that she had become old. Age had collected in her body in an instant. It had grown unnaturally, forced its way out from inside onto the surface so that it looked sickly rather than graceful. Her bones struck strange angles under her clothes and the slope of her mouth told them too much of the grief inside her chest. Lucky wondered when she had last eaten.

Leaving Jamila before Ammu on the prayer mat, Lucky made her way to the kitchen. A layer of dust swirled around her bare feet in protest of her return. Fruit lay rotten in bowls and flies feasted on a plate that had grown yellow and crusted. A spider rested on a web atop the milk pan. Rats had found an entry into the cupboards.

When she returned from the kitchen with a fresh plate of khichuri, she found Ammu hunched over soaking Jamila's back with tears, while Jamila, dry-eyed, rested her head on Ammu's knees.

The first thing Ammu said to the sisters was, 'Never speak of it.'

Lucky's words came out in bursts. 'It's all my fault, Ammu—'

'Where is Rayan?'

'He's at home, we didn't bring him.'

'Oh, alhamdulillah!' Ammu gasped in relief.

'Ammu,' Lucky whimpered. 'I didn't listen and now Jamila...'

Jamila lay quietly on her side on the prayer mat, staring ahead with empty eyes.

'God has delivered you back to the living,' Ammu said sternly. 'You've been strong, the both of you, and now you must be stronger.'

'We are ruined.'

Ammu covered Lucky's mouth and gathered herself. Her eyes thrummed with grief, maternal and vicious.

'Did you leave the day it was over?' she asked finally.

'Yes, when the Mukti Bahini came.'

'Where did you go after?'

'From place to place, then they brought us to a centre.'

'How long were you at the centre?'

'Just a day.'

'When did you leave?'

'Yesterday.'

Ammu counted the days and grew afraid.

'Did anyone see you on your way here?'

'No, we came through the bushes.'

'Did you meet anyone from our district or your husband's?'

'I don't know.'

'Think!'

'They were from other places, from everywhere.'

'Does anyone know your names?'

'No. Yes.'

'Who? Police? Doctors? The Mukti Bahini?'

'Women...'

'How many women?'

'A dozen or so.'

'Who were they?'

Ruby red, thick in her hands, flashed before Lucky's eyes.

'I'll never see them again,' she murmured, looking down at her shaking hands.

Ammu made a noise at the back of her throat, so small and short it made Lucky want to flee.

'And... is anything out of place?'

Lucky felt her chest begin to heave with understanding of the question. She pictured the nurse returning with tests in her hands only to find their beds empty, sadly shaking her head at the frail hearts of two terrified women who had fled, not wanting to know. Ashamed of her actions, premature and cowardly, that she had taken for the both of them, Lucky hesitated.

'We were checked.'

An anxious breath escaped Ammu's nose. Her daughter had a muted look in her eye like a child caught in a half-truth, afraid to face the consequences of rejecting a law of the universe—that if truth is not confessed in one thread of life, it will show up as a spear in another. She passed her trembling fingers over both of her daughters' heads, as if to reassure herself that they were real and not ghosts of her hopeful conjuring. Then she grew silent, the most terrible silence Lucky had ever heard. Jamila closed her eyes and lay deathly still. The world began to bleed through the curtains and owls rushed out of the trees to remind them that wisdom was only accounted for when acted upon. A damp patch of Lucky's tears on Ammu's saree began to dry and return to its original colour, and Lucky watched a tide fast approach her own eyes.

'Soon I won't be here to protect you and you'll both have to walk through life alone. So, you must listen to what has to be done now.'

Lucky's muscles stiffened at the talk of Ammu's death, the reason they had set off weeks ago now a distant memory. Jamila shifted her head under Ammu's heavy palm and sighed.

'You must never speak of this to anyone,' Ammu continued. 'Listen to my warning, you *must* shelter your children from your sorrow. Don't think of yesterday when you held your husband's love with certainty. Understand that families built over a lifetime can be lost in seconds at times like this, and your heartbreak, however great it is, is a small price to pay to protect your home.'

Outside, the night was dark and misty. No stars listened in on Ammu's words and the moon hid shyly behind a cloud. Bile rose from Ammu's empty stomach and rested at the pit of her throat. Her daughters' spirits had moved to the tips of their fingers and toes, ready to bleed out into the netherworld if she did not rein them back in. They lay before her with beatless hearts. Lightless eyes. Wordless mouths. They had no strength to oppose her and none to struggle for themselves, as if they had just come out fresh from her womb. Ammu knew that if she did not persuade them to live, she would watch her daughters die.

Death. Heaven or hell. Salvation or blasphemy. It didn't scare her. If she were to fall into the pit of hell so her daughters could live and rise to the heavens, she would. And maybe one day, on that faraway plane, they would ask to see her again from their high place.

'We're not well, Ammu,' Lucky whispered. She was tired of crying and running. It felt as though she had never been right about a single thing in her life, and she craved the safety of Waleed's comfort and direction. Ammu's firm commands threatened to condemn her to a life of loneliness. And she had already lived too much of her life alone.

'Waleed has a right to know,' she begged. 'And so does Rahat.'

A warm, wordless river dripped over Ammu's nose and down her chin. She wiped her cheek on her shoulders before it could spill onto her daughters' faces. Her daughters were still young enough to believe love was enough to save them, raise them from the depths of a renewing despair, spare them from another's hapless flaws. And she loathed her part in stripping them of that last piece of innocence, again.

'Man is fragile, Lucky. He cannot even bear to hear what a woman can endure. It destroys him. And when he does hear it, his sadness, his fears, it all turns to anger, because he can't put his feelings into words like you can. He takes his anger out on you, because you remind him of his powerlessness. And when he wants to rid himself of feelings he doesn't understand, he can rid himself of you. Man takes the easy way out when it comes to his heart.'

Ammu's voice was a distant whisper, wisdom gathered from a time of similar consideration. 'Who else is a woman left with but herself? You've agreed to share your life with him, moyna, not your secrets. God alone is worthy of that.'

Waleed's gentle words, his careful handwriting, flashed before her. *I'm tired, so tired, my love, I lay sleeplessly at night missing you,* he wrote. *Then I remind myself that soon we'll meet joyously in the dream we've worked so hard for. And I find that I can go on just a little longer. For us, I kindle our dream, again and again. So come dream with me.* Was it possible that her husband could reject her?

'We said we would be honest with each other. What if Waleed is different? He is a good man, a strong man. His compassion would halve the agonies of my heart.'

Ammu was silent for a moment. When Lucky turned to look up at her, Ammu reached forward and gently pushed her face away. Her palm trembled over Lucky's eyelids, and Lucky gritted her teeth so her body would not quiver back. When she was sure Lucky would stay in place, she pulled back her hand.

'You've been blessed with a husband who will negotiate a life with you. Don't push him beyond what he can bear. He may be good enough to never despise you, but he may not be strong enough to love you past it.'

Lucky gulped in disbelief. 'He can. He should.'

Ammu sighed. 'But will he? A man's shoulders are built broader, and a woman's heart is built deeper, but worn shoulders can't recover as quickly as a worn heart.'

'I won't tell him everything, just some things, small things, nothing that will place too much weight on his shoulders.'

'My heart, don't tell a person something they'll never forget if you don't want them to remember it each day. Once you speak your story it's no longer yours, and you can't ask another to handle it like you would with your hands. One tortured memory, one tortured word, is enough for the enemy to succeed in destroying everything. A nation. A marriage. A family.'

Jamila watched them argue. Lucky couldn't tell what thoughts lay behind her sister's empty eyes, but her silence suggested she would accept what Ammu asked of her. And unlike Lucky, Jamila had always kept secrets.

'Promise me you'll take this to your graves,' Ammu begged. 'This stays between us until the next life, or I'll ask for retribution fit for a broken promise.'

A promise was a contract signed before God, they all knew that. And a mother's dying wish was the greatest of them all. If paradise lay at a mother's feet, so did hell, and Lucky could only imagine what would happen if such a pact were broken.

Jamila spoke the words first.

'I promise.'

Outside, the night was a fresh black, not yet turned blue. The birds slept in their nests. No one was awake to witness the oath being sworn in Ammu's room.

The room was silent as they waited for Lucky. She sat with the promise pointed at her like a poisoned arrow, writhing restlessly until it pricked her back and melted a small crater in her skin. As her body yielded to the toxin, her heartbeat slowed around a secret that demanded she be forever suspended between honour and honesty, loyalty and love.

Lucky thought of Rahat waiting for Jamila somewhere with real gold earrings. Of their howling laughter into the night as they re-enacted his proposal, tears spilling from their eyes. Jamila's words in the bushes, begging her to turn back.

'I promise,' Lucky vowed.

Pushing them both upright, Ammu kissed her daughters with quivering lips. She removed four of her six wedding bangles, thin rings of gold etched with flower buds. Abbu had the set made for her, a secret reference to the nights when he had hidden between the jasmine vines under her window to check on her injuries. Now, Ammu placed a bangle on each of Lucky and Jamila's wrists.

Under twilight, three pairs of golden bangles shone between three women, binding them together.

'A reminder to honour our promise.'

Jamila slept on the floor like she did the night they became sisters. Lucky and Ammu lay next to each other on the bed above her. Lucky had tried to pull Jamila between them, but Jamila pushed her away until she gave up. Ammu locked her arms around Lucky, whose neck cramped from peering down at her sister all night.

'I'm scared Jamila no longer loves me,' Lucky whispered. Fear gripped her at the thought of having to endure another loss.

'You were impatient,' Ammu said. 'You should have turned back home in the face of danger. See, I'm still alive and the war is over, but you're forever changed.'

'I made a terrible mistake.'

'Jamila too should never have left to go to you.'

Lucky remembered the Shaytan's nodding head in the water, testifying amongst the mukti joddhas. His conceited conviction until the end. Merciless but meticulous. Sinful but sure. 'The soldiers believed they were doing good,' she said. 'They still believe it and think of us as a damned people, cutting a Muslim nation in half. They had their plan, and some were patient, others hasty to reach their goal. How can we know when patience is best and when we should resist? I've never been able to understand it.'

'Patience doesn't mean doing nothing, Lucky. Act, but don't expect ease to accompany it. And when misfortune strikes, slow down. The devil makes us walk in haste, whispering false promises and conspiring to trip us up while we rush towards them. He sets traps to make us fall today so we can't run to the place of tomorrow.'

The weight of Lucky's guilt smothered her lungs. Ammu felt the tension in her daughter's back and tightened her arms.

'Waleed will be back soon,' Lucky choked. 'I lie here planning to betray him, to deny him a part of myself to the grave.'

Ammu was quiet. Dark, grey clouds gathered in her throat in the heavy, stifling way that a mother's wisdom presented itself. She gulped them down.

'Forgive yourself for what you did to survive. And prepare yourself, moyna, for the life you must protect.'

Rahat returned first, only a week after them. No one had seen him since he left to join the Mukti Bahini towards the end of the war. He appeared at Ammu's door one night with a cast on one leg, mumbling frantically, his eyes bulging, thick brows raised high on his temple unable to come down. His fingernails, black like a crow's claw, gripped the door frame, scratching the paint. A cornered animal dressed like a man. A distant look lay in his sunken face that Lucky knew would never go away. He looked right through them as he limped into the house, shoving back chairs and tables. Only when he saw Jamila did his demeanour soften.

Ammu rushed the marriage. She didn't ask Jamila what she wanted, deciding on her own that they needed to celebrate quickly. So others didn't find out. Because a woman needs protection. Because a child, if there was a child, needs two parents. She hardly let Jamila and Rahat speak to each other before the wedding day, when lovers who had become strangers would be lovers once again. Neither seemed to mind, lost in their own grievances over a future that was forever changed.

In the days before the wedding, Ammu and Lucky kept watch over Jamila so she didn't wander alone up to the rooftop. Twice they found her there, eyes closed, face raised to the sun, listening to the cuckoos sing, humming an unfamiliar tune and swaying to its beat. When they asked her what she was doing, she only looked at them and raised her hand to stroke Lucky's hair. To smooth down its jagged cut, kiss it back to its proper place. Redressed and respectable.

The night before the wedding, alarmed by Jamila's silence, Ammu sat her down and held her by the sides of her face to check for traces of wildness.

'Listen to me, my daughter. Don't fear sadness, be brave enough to look to it, let it simmer in your stomach and then retch it up quickly so you can continue on better than before.'

When Jamila didn't respond, Ammu sharpened her eyes and squeezed Jamila's cheeks like she had done when the sisters were children. 'Understood?'

'Yes.'

But Lucky was unsure if Jamila heard her.

It rained on the day. Lucky would look back and understand it as an omen urging them to turn back. Two neighbours and the imam attended. They left their muddy shoes at the door and spread their wet feet across the house in a hurry, having only been invited that morning.

'Remember, only the skies and the earth obey God's laws, people do not,' Ammu warned Jamila before the ceremony. 'Keep your promise.'

Draped in Ammu's red and gold wedding saree, Jamila sat through the imam's recitation with empty eyes. Ammu pulled the saree low over Jamila's face in case the guests saw something that would stop the proceedings. A shiver. A shadow. A wild bird clawing its way out of its cage. Lucky gripped her sister's hand the entire afternoon, worried Jamila would reach across to stroke her hair during the ceremony. If her heart feared they were making a mistake, the force of Ammu's firm hand on her back reminded Lucky that this was the best thing for them all.

Without looking at her husband, Jamila barely whispered 'qobul'.

Waleed arrived a week after Rahat. First, he went to see his mother and Rayan, then he came to see Lucky and Ammu. When Lucky saw him, only one thought crossed her mind. *I dreamt, just like you asked.* He hugged her tightly, and the stones that wound tightly around her lungs tumbled down into her stomach and dissolved.

She hardly spoke to him after that first night of desperate affection. In the morning, while he played with her hair, telling her of his time in London and asking her about distant ruined towns, she remained still and quiet. But he never protested her distant touch, nor did he notice her absent heart.

Ammu paid close attention to Lucky's interactions with Waleed. One day she took Lucky aside and shook her by the shoulders.

'Your fear is the last piece of evidence that it happened, you must rid yourself of this too,' she commanded.

In her last weeks, Ammu couldn't make a sound. A warning. A chastisement. A peep. When Ammu could no longer eat solids, Lucky chewed rice and bean curry and fed her from her own mouth. When Ammu could no longer leave the bed, Lucky wiped her down with a wet gamchha and changed the sheets when they were soiled.

When Lucky told her she had missed her menses, Ammu didn't turn to face her. No warning. No chastisement. No peep. Instead, she gripped Lucky's hand and squeezed it while gazing out of the window with unseeing eyes.

Sometimes, when her mind returned to her, she turned her head and gave Lucky a look.

When they looked at each other like that, Waleed left to give the women space.

A sick house is often a silent one.

19. BRIDE GIFTS

Rahat built Jamila the biggest house in the neighbourhood. While others struggled to grow produce after the war, the soil made rotten with a callous concoction of phosphorus fallout, the trees made limp with the weight of a chemical rain, the fish stall thrived. Like a madman, he spent his days obsessing over the design and the nights painting the walls. Yellow, then green, then back to yellow again. He vowed to give his bride the home of her dreams and himself a place to rest and forget all the things he had done. He planted jasmines by the veranda to stifle his senses, carved the floor with paisleys so the ridges would dig into his bare feet and chase the waking nightmares away, had the maids leave bread in the four corners of the house so birds would squawk night and day and drown out the phantom sounds of gunfire. Busy constructing a house to support the fortress of his mind, he didn't notice at first that his wife cared little for his efforts. Jamila had no objections and no suggestions. Yellow or green.

It wasn't long before the couple learnt that their demons had entered with them in matrimony. They hovered beneath the skin of shrouded words. Mirrored the mundane the couple tried to make heartfelt, half-heartedly. It was a deep-sounding warning which sat speechless between them while they both craved consolation from the other. Yes, vicious and veiled, the demons danced fervently.

Joy was born the year they were married.

'Not long ago I didn't want to live, and now I'll find it difficult to die,' Jamila wept as her belly grew.

'It's a blessing, a new start,' Lucky promised her. 'A baby to love, who will love you back. This is a good thing.'

Jamila was unconvinced. Her body was distorting into frightening shapes that crawled out of her to stretch for air, unlocking her organs from their resting place and raising them to her chest to breathe in with deeper, hallowed breaths, because it knew, that merciless mass inside of her, that she would have pinched her nose and stopped inhaling altogether if she were alone. It knew about the restlessness. The watchers. The whispers. The whisperer. It knew that she was not good, only waiting. She felt it wave at her from inside.

'He's already such a pleasant boy,' she began, half appealing to, half placating her sister. 'He sits inside me and causes no problems... And yet, I can't begin to love him.'

'It's a boy?'

Jamila nodded. 'I just know.'

'Alhamdulillah,' Lucky said carefully. These days, Jamila's sullen moods and cynicism upset everyone, and when they pointed it out to her, she stopped talking to them. 'And about love,' she continued, 'that comes after you give birth. It can take a little longer for some women, but all mothers love their children.'

'We aren't all the same,' Jamila murmured.

Joy came a month early. Rahat arrived home to find Jamila on the kitchen floor staring at the screeching, bloody mass positioned perfectly between her legs, still tied to her by their cord. When he lifted the baby up, she swung at them both and wailed.

The boy unsettled her. His scrunched face, stung a puffy radish red, always contorted as if listening with ill-willed absorption, collecting her secrets beneath his sheer skin, her absentminded confessions pounding visibly through his veins, desperate to expose her. His delicate fingers which stretched toward something just out of reach. His sudden smile at something she could not see. She knew he knew things. Saw things. She left him crying in different rooms, let her milk dry up and told no one about it, shook him sometimes just to see what would happen, if any secrets would spill out. One evening, Rahat returned home to see his son's mouth deftly wrapped into silence with a pashmina, his tiny nose still free, his eyes bewildered. Afraid for them both, he called on Lucky, whose own bump was now heavy, to come and stay with them.

'Rahat thinks I'm a bad mother,' Jamila explained when Lucky arrived at their doorstep. 'He follows the boy into every room and watches me like a warden. I don't know what he thinks I'll do to him.'

'He cares for you both.'

'He's afraid of me.'

When Lucky paused, Jamila's chest caved in with a sombre satisfaction. She walked to her son's basket and tapped his sleeping face to rouse him for the guest. Smack, smack, smack. Then, just as suddenly, she pushed away from him, humiliated that he would not wake easily at the force of her fingertips.

'You said I would feel like a mother the moment I saw him. I don't.'

'A mother's love isn't so simple, Jamila. A part of you is now outside you in your son, and you need to fill the empty part of yourself back up. Give yourself some time.' She spoke delicately, but Jamila was not reassured. In fact, she seemed even more doubtful.

'The boy is generous,' Jamila said, tapping at her full breasts. 'He still searches for me no matter how many times I turn away from him. He loves me, so I have no choice but to love him back, but when I turn my back to him,' she made a waving motion with her hands, 'it vanishes.'

'Then keep facing him,' Lucky insisted. 'Watch, his face will grow into yours, and your love for him will deepen.'

'And what if his face grows into another's?'

'You will love him then too,' Lucky whispered, forcing back the quiver in her voice.

The sisters stared at each other, daring the other to lift up what lay unspoken between them. In that deep, pulsing silence, Jamila realised her sister was too afraid to hear a truth she did not want to believe. She closed her eyes and leaned back in her chair.

'It's frightening to be loved so much,' she conceded. 'He looks at me like I would never pinch his nose until he turned purple or bite his fingers until he cried. He looks at me with such want, despite everything, and he wants no one else but me.'

'His little heart is a shadow of yours.'

'What if my heart is the shadow and his is red and beating?' Jamila murmured to herself.

When Jamila was distant with Rahat during her pregnancy, Lucky told him she needed space to manage her morning sickness. When she pushed away his care after Joy was born, Lucky pacified Rahat with stories of baby blues. Now, a year after Joy had joined their small family, Rahat understood that his wife's heart was a rock in the ocean that stood stubborn against the current. At night he found her standing in the rain with her head tilted upward to see how many droplets she could gather in the hollows of her eyes. During the day she wandered by the waterside, watching the waves turn to rain and back.

When the rivers and lakes across town overflowed after a devastating monsoon rain, Jamila was the first to see the bones. They began to appear on the banks, relics from the war. A thigh bone pierced though a broken boat. A rib held up a dirty shirt on the shore like an old flag. A skull detached from a small skeleton drifted between the mouths of stray dogs. Bits of bone lodged into the mud like seashells that made clanging sounds under the riverbed. Families still looking for loved ones stopped once they saw the awful gifts the water washed up. Jamila stared wistfully at the remnants of people floating by, her bangles jangling against her wrists like a windchime. With her appetite diminished she had become skeletal. All hard corners and stone. And, in her mind, brethren to the water people. The men in the neighbourhood thought she was possessed. But the women kept quiet, seeing in the fish seller's wife something familiar, something they knew to keep hidden in themselves, but that she could not hide.

'This can happen to women after they have children,' Lucky comforted Rahat one evening as mother and son napped. She had come to check in on them, leaving her own sons, including her youngest, just under a year old, with Waleed and her mother-in-law.

'I've taken her to every doctor, every healer, she refuses to see the imams...' Rahat moaned through his fingers. 'Sometimes she looks at Joy in a way that scares me. She wanders out of the house and leaves him here by himself, and I come home to find him crying and hungry. She locks the maid out by mistake. The neighbours have heard her talking to herself as if she's talking to someone else... I'm afraid to leave her alone with Joy, I don't know what she might do to him.'

Lucky might have pitied him more, but instead she felt angry. He was impatient, like all men were when it came to changing something in a woman. What was a year or two of difficulty when marriage was for a lifetime? She wrung her hands to calm herself before speaking again.

'Jamila's getting better, we can both see that. She's breast-feeding Joy now and plays with him sometimes. It's only a matter of time before she's back to herself.'

Rahat was too tired to argue with her. Dark circles burrowed deep into his sockets. 'I was thinking of bringing someone new in to look after Joy. He needs a mother, not a maid, and Jamila...'

Lucky didn't let him finish. She stood up to make her way to the bedroom as they heard the baby begin to whimper, but not before turning back to Rahat. 'I'll come by more often, and I'll take her to more doctors who help with these things. Jamila is the only mother Joy needs.'

The Old Man was considered by most to be either a magician or a madman. As a young man, he had opened a mosque in his tiny village so even the homeless and orphan children could attend communal prayers without travelling for miles. The day the mosque opened, the villagers felt a presence with them. Something brushed against them when they went to prostrate. Whispered verses were heard following the imam's recitation. The cleaner arrived early in the morning to find the floors already swept, prayer mats straightened to the southwest, the Holy Book stacked neatly and the room smelling of a sweet incense. When news travelled about these happenings, the Old Man was hailed as a friend of God, who had brought both people and djinns together for worship.

The story goes, not long after the last of the Old Man's eight children was born, a female djinn fell in love with him and asked him to marry her. He refused, so in a jealous rage the djinn took the sight from his eyes and pronounced that he would die if he were ever touched by another woman again. Blind and fearful for his life, the Old Man left his wife and five daughters in the village and moved across the river, where his sons built him a small house with only one dirt road leading up to it, too narrow for even a rickshaw to pass. For years his sons took care of him, but one by one, each of them married and left with their wives. And so, the Old Man lived alone in his house with one male servant, the war passing him by as if he were a forgotten curio of the forest.

Some people believed that after the curse was laid, the good djinns who prayed with them in the mosque had taken pity on the Old Man and endowed him with gifts in place of his sight. He could predict a person's future, tell what ailment they had when they walked into the room, cast off the evil eye. Others alleged that the female djinn had never left him and his powers were from the devil. Still, after the war, women made pilgrimage to his remote home in search of a cure for the problem growing inside them or advice on how to make their husbands love them again. Behind a curtain, out of reach and concealed from their view, he became their doctor of choice.

Lucky and Jamila stood in the middle of a bridge before the path to the Old Man's house, their way eclipsed by darkness. The electricity had given out in the villages. Starlight seeped through webbed leaves and a creature darker than the night hopped between the branches. Lucky chose not to dwell on its dance. Holding Jamila's hand, she dimly made out the moving darkness of the flowing river below, the still darkness of the riverbanks, the grey darkness of the bridge planks ahead of her. She slid her feet forward. A slow vibration rose from the soles of her feet to her head, swaying her. As if someone were shaking her very soul and telling her to turn back and run.

Jamila could feel her sister's hand tremble. 'We don't have to go,' she said behind her.

'We're almost here,' Lucky reassured her.

The tree in front of them disappeared, and they started to make out a tall, lean figure, faceless and featureless, coming towards them, a faint light emanating from its centre.

A painful coldness worked its way from the tip of Lucky's nose to the back of her head. Sweat that had gathered in her brows grew icy against the unnatural chill of her skin. As the light came closer, her heart pounded against the stifling summer night until the air itself grew afraid. Folklore and fear shaped the possibility of a horrible ending.

The figure came to a halt, hovering between the shadows of two embracing trees.

'Is anybody there?'

A male voice. Young and concerned.

'Yes!' Lucky yelled, relieved it was a human. 'We're in the middle of the bridge, we crossed just as the current went out.'

A dark, skinny man with thick, curly hair appeared at the end of the bridge. As he raised his lamp, they saw an angular face, ashen and unimpressed, its gaunt, work-hardened features stretched tight over high cheekbones. He wore a too-big white vest made cream with age and a lungi that was pulled and tied back around his waist like a pair of shorts. A chequered green and red gamchha hung around his neck.

'Follow me,' he said, scanning Lucky and Jamila. 'It's dangerous for women to walk alone in the dark.'

Around the Old Man's bed, pink embroidered curtains hung like a mosquito net. The hand-stitched flowers had faded into an off-pink colour and the thread had frayed in parts, worn from decades of washing. Lucky wondered how many nights it would take her to sew the seams back in.

The two sisters shifted on the creaky bamboo stools that Farman, the skinny man, laid out for them. Sharp bits of wood that had unwound from their bind dug into their legs.

'Which of your Lord's favours would you deny?' the Old Man recited behind the curtain.

Farman stood in the corner of the room waving a palm-leaf hand fan at a steady speed. His arms were dotted with dark brown splotches, evidence of recovered bite marks. Some were scabbed over, some were scratched raw, the pink of his flesh, framed with white edges, obscene against his dark skin. Lucky wondered if on the other side of the curtain the Old Man was also bitten half to death.

'Do you know what the soul is?'

The Old Man's breath moved behind a spot of yellow paisley whose tip bloomed into the cross-stitched midday sun. Lucky glanced at Farman, who stared back with unnerving intensity. Beside her, Jamila pressed a mosquito dead against her wrist.

'I don't.'

'That's right,' he said, pleased with Lucky's reply. 'We were given little knowledge of the soul. It's not our place to understand it.'

Silence stifled them once more. The women watched a cockroach scuttle urgently across the floor. Before it could dive under the bed, Farman stomped on it with his bare foot and dragged its carcass into a corner with his heel. Placing the fan on a stool, he made his way out the room, dribbling a shiny trail of cockroach sap behind him. The light disappeared with him, leaving the sisters as blind to their surroundings as the Old Man behind the curtain.

'Do you know what we're made of?'

Lucky racked her brain for a suitable answer to the Old Man's question, but it seemed he wasn't expecting her to have one.

'We're made of days,' he continued without her input. 'Days seen and unseen. There are days we see passing in the changing colours of falling leaves, other days we don't see flying by like minutes. The clock is an indifferent adversary, it doesn't warn the soul that death is approaching... But first, tell me why you are here.'

Lucky's teeth began to chatter. 'My sister's mind wanders...' she began. 'She forgets herself and now risks losing her husband and son. We would be grateful if you could give her something to heal quickly.'

She looked at Jamila, who looked straight ahead. Before they left, Lucky had made her promise she would not oppose whatever cure the Old Man gave her.

'She was taken during the war,' the Old Man said. It was a statement delivered with such conviction it would have felt sinful to rebut it.

A shiver took hold of Lucky's fingers. 'Yes.'

'As were you.'

Lucky paused. 'Yes.'

'But you've come for your sister alone and not for yourself too?'

'That's right.'

The Old Man moved closer to them until they saw the veil quake beneath his breath. Lucky counted the peaks until he spoke again. One. Two. Three.

'I've met many women like your sister. And I know that her sorrows will swallow her whole if she fails to look inside herself. You must speak to your soul, bend it to your will, make it serve you. Heaven lies before those who account for their soul and its every movement, not those who let it wither away.'

A large snout moth marched up Jamila's shalwar, its weight thumping against her leg in a slow, swinging rhythm. She held her breath as she watched its struggle.

Lucky's mouth tightened. 'She's the mother of a baby boy. She must get well quickly.'

'To heal quickly, you must forgive quickly.'

The Old Man's reply was quick and short, as if the answer were obvious. Worse, easy. Impatience formed on Lucky's tongue.

'God doesn't demand we forgive others.'

'Yet it would be better for you to do so.'

'The heart doesn't always work that way.'

The Old Man tutted behind the curtain. His disapproval lay heavy between them. Lucky gritted her teeth at his quick summations devoid of compassion and mercy. Like the healers before him, he prescribed otherworldly efforts, forgetting that the women also had human hearts.

'People come to me in search of a fool's cure, a potion to drink, a spell to recite, a taweez to tie around their arm, trivial things that only need an exchange of money on their part. These things are nothing to the Almighty. Life is a trial, who told you that you alone would escape its horrors? We were born to struggle! You must silence your mind, all its blames and sorrows, and grab your soul until it stands up straight before you. How does it sound when it speaks? If you listen, you'll learn quickly that it yearns to forgive and find peace.'

In the narrow beam of moonlight spilling across the floor, grey moth wings shone luminous white and fluttered uneasily against the heaving, humid air.

'And if I can't hear it?' Jamila asked, finally casting the moth from her shalwar. 'My soul.'

'Talk to it the way it can hear you, like you talk to people the way they can listen. Leave shame behind, and return your pain and fear back to God. You do yourself no good holding on to it, so let it go. It's not a fair judgement of the world, or even of man.'

'It's been fair so far,' Jamila said.

The Old Man made a throaty noise of disagreement. 'Man doesn't have a heaven or hell to put you in, he can only conjure up unworthy imitations.'

Jamila paused, taken aback by the Old Man's assuredness. *There is a way,* she thought. She had done it before. If only she could remember it. She began to speak only to stop, again and again, until her voice fluttered with the intonation of the morning wind. The Old Man waited patiently for her to gather her thoughts.

'The enemy is gone,' she said finally. 'He left no visible mark on me and when I look down, I see nothing, as if he never came. But I burn inside and when I close my eyes, I see him. At night I hear his voice. Then, the smell. Until I can feel his fingers again. I sit here with no enemy to run from but myself. The soul you speak of has already spilled out of me.'

'Jamila...' Lucky began, but the Old Man cut her off.

'You believe a soul can leave you while you live?' he asked, intrigued.

Mosquitoes swarmed Jamila's ankles, biting with impunity, but she paid them no mind. 'It already has.'

A molten heat stung Lucky's lashes as she listened to the Old Man and Jamila. One made sombre with wisdom, the other with tragedy. Between them she was driftwood, alone, hopeless dead weight and poisonous if kindled. As the Old Man resumed, she placed her hands over her stomach to stop her body from heaving.

'How long do you sit in the darkness, my daughter?' He leaned in so that his forehead pushed into the curtain like an uneven brick on a wall. 'I mean the darkness of your mind. Do you sit in it, or can you get up and move in it? Run in it, slow down, turn back?'

'I don't dance in the dark.'

'And does it speak?'

'I don't talk to it either.'

The Old Man hummed in understanding. 'Be a visitor then but don't sit for tea. Once you've exchanged pleasantries and heard a confession or two, get up and leave, promising to return another day. And every morning as the sun rises, spare it a little time. You'll soon heal with it, and even if you do nothing, time will dampen its sting.'

Jamila pulled at her empty earlobes, suddenly afraid. She had stopped wearing earrings after her wedding night, finding her lobes so thin they strained at the slightest weight.

'I can't. The devil watches me wherever I go.'

'Then let him watch helplessly.'

Birds began to twitter, and Jamila shook Lucky's hand, signalling she wanted to leave. They pressed some taka into Farman's hand and took two cartons of juice he offered for their journey back. They left with no potion, no spell and no taweez but heads full of questions and solemn hearts. Lucky could see Jamila ruminating over the Old Man's words. The journey had been worthwhile.

When they had crossed the bridge, Jamila turned towards her sister. Beneath Lucky's hopeful smile, she saw an anguished plea of tired, quiet desperation.

'I'll try my best to get better,' Jamila promised. 'Don't worry so much. And for God's sake, go back to your sons, they're too young to be away from you for so long. Thank you for bringing me here, Boro Apa... I have a lot to think about now.'

Not long after they visited the Old Man, Rahat married again. He had long accepted that his first wife's madness and her barrenness after Joy had no cure. Jamila was getting worse and Joy older, and he could no longer neglect his son's right to have a mother. Though his first wife was unusual, the neighbours thought the fish seller too quick to seek a solution in another woman, and knew that he, like many others before him, could only have done this to an orphan girl with no one to vouch for her.

Jamila learnt then what was the paradox of her womb. That there was only one greater difficulty for a woman than birthing a child, and that was being unable to birth a child. And that both lives would condemn her to the same friendless fate.

A second house for the second wife was built on the other side of Rahat's land, where he moved in with Joy. It was more beautiful than Jamila's, but without the architectural precisions designed to dampen his wandering mind. A house that echoed to announce his footsteps. A silent place with no birdsong. Each morning and evening, Rahat visited Jamila to make sure she ate and bathed. But after his second wife gave birth, visits became less frequent, and he employed maids to take on his old tasks.

They say she wandered out before dawn to the lake between the two houses and drowned alone in the dark.

The following week, children jumped into the lake and mothers washed their clothes at the water's edge. Men ran wet hands over their forearms and feet at the bottom of its steps to make wuzu, whispering their zikr, before heading to the mosque. No one worried that a hand might grab them by the wrist and drag them to the lake bottom. Curiously, men who launched their nets to find dinner between the leaves and snakes never did catch any fish in the lake again after that night. When they bobbed in the middle of the water stretching out their nets, the fishermen felt a silence tighten around them. Deep and despairing, but without struggle.

Those who knew Jamila and Rahat dared not speculate why the fish went missing, fearing something would follow them home if they did. Others whispered of madness and magic, of a foolish husband who led the neighbourhood to ruin. Of a ghost of a wispy woman who sat on the bottom step of the staircase leading down to the water, staring into its rushing blackness, empty-eyed. They saw him cry at the lake at night for years afterwards, howling, pleading, flinging himself into the water. But instead of pitying him, the people cursed him for cursing them all. The poorest starved from the lack of fish. Kept up by their wailing children, desperate parents prayed in the last hours of the night for the wispy woman to drag him down to her and spare the rest of them.

At some point, people forgot her name. The mango seller and the hog plum man died, and the people who replaced them were not told the love story of the fish seller and the silent beauty, of how he betrayed her once she was his. Slowly, life turned to fable. Fable to tales of terror. With time came courage, which dared children to tease one another at the water's edge in hopes of conjuring the witch who had cursed the fish out of the lake after being jilted by her foolish lover.

Joy, still a toddler at the time, grew up unaffected by his mother's absence, never knowing he had missed out on the love of a quiet woman who loved more deeply than anyone he would ever know. Had his father only waited for her, had his mother waited for herself, their son might have known a rare and beautiful heart.

For Lucky, Jamila's death was a cold, howling wind that settled along her spine and bent her over so her head remained forever bowed. Before the burial, she slipped Ammu's bangles off Jamila's wrists and onto her own, their weight warm against her skin. When she visited the grave, she only ever said a few words.

'Sabr, sister. Just wait a little longer.'

20. WARNING TALES

Djinns loved mishti. It was common knowledge that they walked the streets as cats, dogs and snakes to gnaw on discarded fish bones. Got angry at you if you stepped on their toes, even if they were invisible. Children made sure not to throw rocks at animals after dusk in case they were cursed forever. Adults ran from venom-less snakes. No one made eye contact with dogs at night. Distressed barks were ignored. But more than anything else, everyone knew djinns were fond of mishti. It was why young, unmarried girls were not to buy any alone after Maghrib and children always needed a chaperone to the sweet shop. Something about melted sugar and flour made djinns' mouths water and turned them either maddeningly sociable or mercilessly cruel to humans. Mishti store owners swore djinns came to their shops late at night in human form. It was common to pack an order and look up to see no one there, money and sweets left on the counter.

'But why do they leave the mishti?' Jamila asked. 'How do they eat it?'

Still in their school uniforms, noses pressed on the decorative wrought-iron grille of the living room window, the girls were peeping into the mishti shop across the road in search of djinns. With only their foreheads and eyes visible, they perched their fingertips on the windowsill, ready to duck out of sight in case a djinn decided to look back at them. If a djinn remembered your face, you were done for. Bad dreams, bad luck, bad grades, bad marriage or no marriage at all, a life of possession and children walking on their hands. Not to mention a very expensive exorcism.

'They suck the soul out of the laddu through their djinn mouths in our world while they sit at the dinner table of their world,' Lucky explained. 'They don't need to use their fingers.'

A man with a limp and a walking stick approached the mishti stall. The girls held their breath.

'Does the soul of a laddu taste the same as the laddu?'

'Of course.'

'What if it's burnt?'

'They'll curse the cook forever.'

Jamila looked at Lucky with worry. 'I see.'

'Did he pay yet?' Lucky asked.

'No.'

'Maybe he'll disappear.'

'Are we sure it's him?'

'His legs are too long for a man.'

'His legs are broken.'

'They fly so much it's hard for them to walk as humans.'

Djinns lived in clans and each clan was led by a king djinn. They lived in bamboo gardens, on treetops and by lakes, in bathrooms, under bridges, in corners and cracks and behind every child's shadow, but when they got peckish, always around dusk, they strolled into the human realm, waited in line and, after much deliberation, picked their favourite mishti, just like humans did. Everyone learnt this when they were children—everyone except Haroon Alom.

Haroon had been the neighbourhood mishti thief since he first snatched a kola pitha from Waleed's hands in kindergarten. Now in his thirties, he was so skinny he still looked to be in his teens, growing taller without ever putting on a pound of flesh, no matter how much mishti he stole. He never stood in line but hovered around the sides of the stall, slinking behind boys who eyed him with suspicion and women who thwacked him when he got too close, in wait for the perfect moment to pinch a chandrapuli, barfi or jilapi. From all his sneaking around, he never heard about the mishti-loving djinns beyond a few snatches of stories whispered by children. So, it made sense when, one day, as he made a grab for a gulab jamun at the same time as a djinn, he became possessed.

'Lord, forgive me!' his mother shouted as she ran outside. 'I'll make sure he never steals so much as a peanut again, just rid him of that devil before he marries her!' Roused by her wailing grief and the terror in her eyes, the townspeople tied her thieving son to a chair and called for an imam.

'Did you hear the gulab jamun thief is marrying the birangona girl without his mother's permission?' Waleed said, walking into the house. He placed his bag on the table and slid out of his work shoes. 'His mother's telling everyone he's possessed!'

Asim giggled at the funny new word, 'possessed'. Lucky squeezed his fat cheeks until his lips disappeared, afraid he would grow up to laugh at misfortune like his father did. Her husband was the type to joke about a tragedy before tackling it. It was a flaw Lucky had recently begun to notice. His nerves that turned to laughter. Its callousness. And it bothered her.

'She's collecting money to pay the imam,' Waleed went on, jiggling his eyebrows at Asim. 'He's prescribed spreading oil on a plate to look into the future—five thousand taka, apparently! I might donate, maybe their djinns can tell me if my boss will pay me on time this month.'

Lucky shot her husband a warning look. It worried her that he mocked the imams. His wisecracks came dangerously close to questioning the machinations of God, and she feared that his careless tongue would invite tribulations to befall them.

'Foolish woman, if she didn't mention it no one would know,' her mother-in-law muttered. 'They could have locked that girl in the house for the next sixty years.'

The thief's wife-to-be was a pleasant young woman with a serene smile. Though she was well-mannered and cheated no one, when she walked past, people whispered, *Khane-laga*. The Khans came to that woman. Still, her moon-faced radiance captivated young men, and they fancied themselves the hero who would rescue her from disgrace. They followed her from college and bumped into her in odd places, gifted her the sweets their mothers had packed for them in their lunch boxes. Some went so far as asking their parents to make an offer of marriage, and it took weeks of beatings and threats of disownment by mothers, fathers and dying grandmothers to put a stop to their ideas.

'He's marrying the girl for benefits,' Lucky's mother-in-law added, moving from speculation to accusation in a matter of moments. 'Or his mother would have cut him into little pieces for losing their fortune a long time ago.'

'If that's true he should think again,' Waleed said. 'They've hardly paid anyone, the money disappears before it reaches the girls. I doubt anyone in the government will see that it ever does.'

The president had been assassinated by military defectors a few years ago, on the first anniversary of Jamila's death. Lucky remembered hearing the news more clearly than the births of her own children. A part of her grieved him for honouring the women in the war, while another part resented the grand promises he had made to them that never came to pass.

Lucky's mother-in-law tutted. 'No one ensures a woman is well looked after when she becomes a stain on the family's reputation.'

A bowl of sliced watermelons lay on the table where Rayan, Asim and Minna did their homework. Lucky mended their school shirts while they worked, keeping her ears perked for the signs of an impending scuffle. After years of muttered complaints and arguments, the family had entered a comfortable compromise: her mother-in-law and Shaheena were in charge of the cooking, while Lucky was sovereign over the children's education. Gone were those days where she was as measured as the food she cooked, a perfect mix of half-smiles, servitude, silence, shame and embarrassment, with a generous helping of gratitude. The war had changed everything. Everyone had seen the educated commit heinous crimes and the illiterate save lives. School was no longer a measure against madness or immorality. So it was a mother's job to reach into her children's minds and hearts and shape them into humans, reminding them that just as they had a soul, so did others.

Asim scribbled on his sister's page and the two began to squabble. Lucky watched them from across the table. Asim's eyes that hinted hazel under sunlight were so like Waleed's in their sharpness, his fair and thin, gangly limbs the closest in complexion and physique to her husband. But unlike Waleed, there was something unsettling in the way Asim regarded others, how he needed to test them to see if they loved him. It distanced him from the warmth usually afforded by others to a boy of his age. His mind was full of fiendish questions, which he put to people with the honesty of a child but the wisdom of an old man. He would ask a man why he had a second wife, the second wife why she loved her son more than her daughter, the daughter why she hated her stepsister, the stepsister if she was too ugly to marry rich. It terrified them all.

Asim looked up at her from his workbook. Face blank, mouth straight, he dropped his pencil, slid from his chair and disappeared beneath the table. He moved with a quiet intensity, as though he could see into her thoughts and note each of her suspicions, planning a counterattack to weaken her defences. She remembered quiet moments with him as a baby, his piercing gaze, even then, measuring the world around him, in accordance with her doubts.

'Back to work,' she insisted, tapping his nose. He waited, refusing to blink, so he could see all of her. Only when she smiled back at him, with a smile that creased around her eyes, holding its practised warmth for him to recognise and repay, did he pull back, vanish under the table and reappear on the other side.

Once the children fell asleep, Lucky made her way to the kitchen to make chaa. These days she could only sleep once she had a warm drink in her or she would wake at night shivering. Her mother-in-law was already sitting with a steaming cup and hard biscuits. A potato with an incense stick sticking out of it sat on the floor, its smoky fingers spreading wide into the corners of the room, swatting away mosquitoes that dared consider her prey. The smell made Lucky nauseous.

'The neighbour came by with mishti and a wedding invitation. His youngest niece is getting married.'

'It'll be nice to see everyone.'

'Of course. It's been a long time.'

Her tone made Lucky weary. It was the same one she used to entice people into gossip. Lucky stirred her tea faster. The chair behind her scraped across the floor and her mother-in-law gestured for her to sit down with an offer of biscuits.

'Only one,' she yielded, taking a cake rusk.

'Have you ever seen a djinn, ma?'

Lucky paused, wondering where this was going. Like most old ladies, her mother-in-law began her stories with a riddle, with an unspoken promise to answer it later. 'No,' she replied.

Her mother-in-law nodded. 'In my generation every house was haunted,' she began, 'even if it had been lived in a single day. It doesn't take much to trap a ghost inside. Floors are built on top of hundreds of years of horror, walls collect memories of strange things. It leaves a damp kind of smell, one that no new coat of paint or expensive rug can cover.

'The family who sent this invitation have another daughter. She went missing during the war. Dead, they concluded after some time, and her parents learnt to forget her. Two years ago, she returned a married woman with a big boy Asim's age! Everyone had questions. What happened? Did the girl forget where she lived? The country wasn't so torn that she wouldn't recognise her own village. Who was that old man she had married? How old was the boy?'

Lucky bit into the crunchy biscuit, careful to keep a straight face in front of her mother-in-law, who was always eager to provoke a reaction she could judge you for.

'Well, it was discovered that someone saw the father and brother visit one of those rehabilitation centres years ago,' her mother-in-law continued. 'They left her there, poor thing. Even a parent's love has its limits, may you never be so unfortunate to find out. Maybe he believed it was best she remained there. They'd call her a witch in that shabby little village they're from, and they'd never be able to show their faces again! After all, you can't condemn all your children just for one.'

Lucky's mother-in-law paused, taking a loud sip from her cup. Clearing her throat, she broke a biscuit in half and tapped the stray crumbs onto a plate. Lucky pulled another cake rusk out of the packet.

'The husband was given a government job to marry her. Her family deny it, but no one believes them.'

'Is he a good man?'

'Of course not.'

'How do we know that?'

'We don't know anything about him, that's how we know.'

Her mother-in-law furrowed her brows in displeasure. Asking the wrong questions made her impatient, and with Lucky, who she had come to realise was hopeless with idle chat, she learned to add only the details she liked most, like how fat a person was, how poor their father had become, if they prayed or not. Brushing stray crumbs from her lip, she leaned in to whisper.

'They built a second floor on their house not long after the war. It was a wonder where they got the money from. Well? Haa... they took payments for the girl! Built the second floor with the money she was given by the government, even though they didn't take her back.'

Lucky swirled the remains of tea in her cup, her face distorted in the liquid. Bits of biscuit floated from the bottom where she had dipped it, piercing her eyes and mouth so that a dejected ghoul looked back at her.

'That's not the worst of it, the unfortunate girl. Her husband's old and as black as a factory floor, and jumpy too. No one knows who he is or where he's from. People have suspicions about his allegiance during the war. The man walks around with a Mukti Bahini certificate in his back pocket! Rumours say he was a razakar who fled his district to start afresh in a new one and uses the girl for protection.'

'Is it true?'

'He has the eyes of a traitor, you can tell these things. Now, wouldn't that be a story? The girl married a man who may have sent her to hell in the first place.'

'Then she should leave him.'

'And go where?' her mother-in-law countered, waking the foxes from their slumber under the window. 'The only thing worse than a witch or a whore in those backwater villages is a divorced woman.'

Sunken eyes appeared before Lucky, holding rainwater in their hollowed depths. Balancing a rising river in its concave sockets, the vision tilted its head back so its face could appeal to the heavens with its cries, even if its empty eyes could not.

'Madness isn't better than divorce.'

Her mother-in-law tutted loudly. 'Madness is better than poverty and death! Only the young have the kind of arrogance to believe those things are small. Madness for a time is a rite of passage for every married woman, and she must push through it to find peace. You think leaving is any easier? She has a son. That traitor will take him from her if she tries to leave. Now listen, the women before you endured their share of madness, just like this girl will, so it won't follow behind her son's every step like cow dung under his shoes.'

Lucky bristled. A promise made by a broken bridge, surrounded by dark creatures and the brightest stars, sounded in her ears. And before her eyes swam the feigned smile behind it.

'Birangona or not, a woman shouldn't be so sacrificing that she destroys herself for the good opinion of others.'

Her mother-in-law hadn't expected her backtalk. The cup rattled in her hand indignantly and a few drops of tea fell over its side.

'Destroy herself? By marrying that man she is saving herself! Goodness, when did the young become so enamoured of love? In my day we never put much faith in the affections of men in the first place. Didn't you see how in their excitement to become martyrs the men of this nation rushed off to war, leaving their widowed mothers, pregnant wives, virgin daughters alone without protection? So much for men's affection.'

Lucky shook her head. 'That was different, they left so we could all win.'

'You'll learn one day that things are not so different as you might think. Who did all those mukti joddhas return from their fighting to find? Murdered parents, sisters ruined beyond a hope of a happy life. To this day, they reap the miserable rewards of their actions, the men who began the war and the men who ended it.' Her mother-in-law sighed. Like all the other women Lucky had ever met, it seemed as though she knew something that Lucky did not. 'We old women with our old ideas that you young women laugh at, we knew our protection lay with ourselves, the men came second. Care for our children, guard our gold, hide the extra taka, whisper our grief only to our sisters, let him do what he wants as long as we get what we want. Somewhere between the love songs and the exchanging of jasmine garlands, women have forgotten this.'

Lucky got up to wash the cups, afraid her mother-in-law, with her owlish stare, would see her rising anger. Three. Two. One. A scolding whisper reminded her to count down. *Stop thinking terrible things,* it said.

'I'm not finished,' her mother-in-law said, the hardness in her voice demanding Lucky sit back down. 'The father became senile, forgot all he did to his daughter, and now she's his carer.

He curses her, hits her, accuses her of trying to set the house on fire with him inside! Yet she remains there, cleaning his shit like a dutiful daughter, and nurtures the man who abandoned her. That's what life can do. Humble you in front of your greatest enemy.'

Her fingers felt wet. Sticky red. Wiped from a pair of tearing piercings, stretched so low that only a hairline's width of skin held the wearer's earlobes together. A mother's lullaby made eulogy began to play in the distance.

'So should there never be any justice for this woman? Shouldn't someone help her? What about her brothers? Men are so forgiving of each other's crimes against women, ready to rally to their friend's aid as soon as he declares himself reformed.'

Her mother-in-law scoffed. 'You walk a dangerous path if you seek justice in this world. You'll only end up doing more harm than has been done to you and becoming who you despised. Justice, my daughter, does not belong to the living.'

'Then who does it belong to?'

'The resurrected.'

Lucky felt a woman's fingers brush her hair and another laugh beside her, shaking the ground as the thump, thump, thump of ants marched on. She heard the wailing pleas of a little girl snatched from her grasp and the terrified screams of a little boy who called for her, *Lucky-ma!*

'I should go to bed,' she said. 'Asim has to wake early tomorrow.'

Her mother-in-law ignored her request to leave. Sensing she had upset Lucky, she wanted to make amends.

'There are other kinds of wins in this world. Justice in the small things. Someone takes your rickshaw, he steps in a muddy puddle later in the day. We should take comfort in those wins and not seek much beyond it.'

'And what about Rayan's Abba?' Lucky asked. Suddenly, she wanted to hurt someone back. Injure instead of heal. Mutilate everything she protected.

Her mother-in-law raised her eyebrow, offended that her son had come up in such distasteful conversation. 'What about him? He gives you everything you want. You were never humiliated. You were not beaten.'

'He wasn't here during the war.'

'He had been gone for two years already.'

'He left me with a new-born when he knew how dangerous it was becoming. He sent letters warning us to be careful but didn't return to protect us.'

Her mother-in-law paused, noting the defiance in Lucky's face, its morbid challenge which had no winners. 'That was a mistake, but there's no use thinking of that time now,' she said. 'Remember that you were blessed in other ways. You had me by your side, and that's no small thing.' Fear melted into the space between Lucky's throat, nose and eyes as her mother-in-law's words began to take on a double meaning. 'You know what they say, better to listen to a wise enemy than to take advice from a foolish friend. Sometimes only an enemy is standing far enough away from you to see you're heading down the wrong path. My son may not have fought in the war, but he is a great father. And it may have turned out better for you that he didn't, that it was us women around in those days. Because as we know from people like that girl and her father, no woman lives with her head held high after being called a heroine.'

A promise between the dead and the living lay between them. Its hallowed breaths chimed down Lucky's wrists as she put her cup down.

'Allahu alam,' she praised. God knows best. Her mother-in-law took her cup and tapped her knee in approval, leaving a trail of crumbs behind her.

21. THE WHITE THREAD OF DAWN

On a day when rice stocks were low and the stalls were still bereft of beans, on her way back home from the bazaar, Lucky saw Mohini crouching in an alleyway behind a rusty tin house.

Face half hidden behind her purdah, she spoke in low tones to a man whose chest heaved with haughtiness. Mohini froze as she locked eyes with Lucky. Her fingers fell limp as the man placed rolls of taka into her hand. Her gaze moved down to Rayan, who held Lucky's hand, and then to the new-born wrapped around Lucky's chest.

When their eyes met again, both women looked away, hastening to their destinations.

That night, Lucky dreamt of ants swarming over her. They came from her front, her back, her right and left. Until she was a mountaintop, high and blind to everything below.

The ants crawled to the corners of her body, their weight on her limbs making her collapse. Pinned to the ground, her body began to speak. Separately. Each limb with a voice she recognised as her own throughout the ages.

'You didn't push away with all your strength,' her hands said.

'You didn't kick with all your might,' her feet said.

'You didn't scream as loud as you could have,' her throat said.

'You didn't protest as hard as you should have,' her tongue said.

'You didn't shed as many tears as the others,' her eyes said.

Lucky woke in terror, her frantic heartbeat hammering with the beat of her own slapping hands over her body as she moved to cast off the phantom ants. When she was sure there was nothing on her, she turned to face the women in the corner of her room. Sitting knitted together in curved shapes, like the skins of green beans once the beans had been pulled out. Empty-eyed. Singing their wordless songs that came from the gut. A prayer. The Quran. The Vedas. A lullaby sung to the children.

When she hurried to light the lamp, they cried, 'Don't speak to them, you'll die sooner if you do!'

Pushing her heart back in place with the palms of her hands, she looked over at Waleed, who slept peacefully by her side. A glass of Zamzam water was prepared on her bedside table. She finished it with large gulps and recited a protection prayer, blowing the words over her skin. Closing her eyes, she imagined the thick, black letters slipping down her bare limbs, over her breasts and her still bloated but birthed belly, washing away her fears and doubts, like hot water on a dirty plate. Once it fell from her toes, she gently pushed the covers off and walked to the bathroom on her forefoot, locking the door behind her. In the dark, she scrubbed her skin raw. Bloodshot patches of pink pulled from her bones. Layers of flesh tore until she thought she could see the taut muscles inside. The burn made her grit her teeth, but she did not stop. Zikr wetted her tongue as she scrubbed to silence the talking limbs that taunted her in her dreams.

Astaghfirullah al-azeem allazi la ilaha illa huwa-l-hayyu-l-qayyum wa atubu ilayh.

Astaghfirullah al-azeem allazi la ilaha illa huwa-l-hayyu-l-qayyum wa atubu ilayh.

Astaghfirullah al-azeem allazi la ilaha illa huwa-l-hayyu-l-qayyum wa atubu ilayh.

In a trance-like state, equal parts fever and religious fervour, her thoughts drifted to the Singing Spinster who always stood in the corner of the bazaar. Each day, the police tried to remove her with force, but the Singing Spinster hit them with her stick until the people gathered around her and heckled them to leave. She waited at the edge of the market, near the courgettes and cauliflowers, where shoppers passed through to exit or loitered to smoke with old friends, and told her story to those who walked by. It angered people. Why was she still here? Bringing up old news. Bad news. Mothers pulled their children along quickly, men muttered about shame, thieves swore and she swore back at them. And yet, every day when she began her tale, there were some who stopped to listen or stood next to her and cried out in agreement. Others placed money at her feet quietly and rushed away before she could give thanks, out of respect.

Before leaving the bazaar, Lucky would linger behind the congregation that assembled around the Singing Spinster to listen to what she had endured at the hands of officers and her own countrymen. Her courage was furious, destructive. It darkened the sunny day and made people take a fearful step back. Then, when the wind blew warm and loose jasmine flowers littered the ground, and the Singing Spinster had simmered long enough under the summer rays, she would sing a sad song that brought tears to the eyes of even those policemen and traders who wanted her gone from the marketplace. The haunting melody struck the heart of an evil truth, and in Lucky it brought forth a frightful solace. Sometimes their eyes met, and Lucky felt a gaze of understanding reach towards her like a soft outstretched hand. Lost behind the crowd, she held its tender admission against her chest before whispering her thanks and returning home.

The Singing Spinster's song had a habit of following her home uninvited. It whispered in her ear when she picked up her new-born, breathing in his soft skin and even softer, happy smell. Only after she had kissed him a dozen times and heard him convulse with squeals at her affectionate attacks did the song flutter away like morning mist into the sky, screeching as it went, promising to come back. Some nights, Lucky woke in a burning sweat from a dream that she was being choked by the Singing Spinster, and when she recited her prayers and willed herself back to sleep, she returned right back to the moment that her fingers closed around her throat.

Behind the bathroom door, Lucky heard her baby wail. Rushing to dry herself, she ran out to pick him up before he woke Waleed.

In the last third of the night, while her husband slept and her mother-in-law and Rayan slept in the adjoining room, Lucky sat at the kitchen table trying to breastfeed her baby under the buzzing lantern light.

Asim's head faced towards the room's corner, his eyes set at an angle she could not see. She stroked the edges of his small pink mouth. Up. Down. Around. Still, he didn't turn. Her heavy breast ached with disappointment. He cooed towards the darkness.

She tapped his lips. Softly. Then harder. Adding more and more pressure with each tap, until her little finger made smacking sounds. Smack, smack, smack.

Finally, his large, dark eyes met hers, unblinking, with a stillness that seemed mature. Experienced. Knowing.

He gripped her blouse in one fist and pulled at her long plait with another. Slowly, his small pink lips opened. She turned his head, and he latched on. His gummy mouth sucked with force. Wincing, she closed her eyes, succumbing to a drowsy fog as he drained her.

Go away, O black clouds, my moyna will have his bath now, Lucky hummed. *Go away, O disease and harms, I have charmed my house against you...*

After patting him to sleep and placing him in the middle of their bed, out of reach of her husband's flailing arms, she slipped out of the house with a prayer mat and climbed the winding stairs to the open rooftop. Ammu's words hurried her footsteps. *There is no better place to cry than in prayer.*

With her head knelt in tahajjud, she cried in the dark. Her tears dripped down her shaky palms. Her chest rattled. Her stomach shuddered as her tongue twirled silently with weighted words, her throat too taut to speak aloud.

The autumnal breeze lifted her hair out from under her scarf and floating strands pricked her wet cheeks. No birds or crickets sang their song. The night bared its silence for her confession.

She sought refuge from a heart encased with a crushing secret. From its blackened layers that wrapped around her, a burden borne by one, two, three women.

She sought refuge from her husband's trusting eyes, from her baby's strange eyes, from his unfamiliar smile and pointed ears she did not recognise, from his long, pale fingers and toes that slanted downward, from his touch that burned, and her touch that quivered.

From how she saved herself and continued to save herself.

For the twirling clot that grew steadily in her stomach, she asked that it bring her joy. Complete her family. But not a girl. Never a girl. She didn't know how to protect one.

Then.

Three.

Two.

One.

A faint white thread appeared in the sky, casting its light on the ground. Slowly treetops returned to their gusty green, crickets conducted their chorus, cuckoos sang their songs, and the town awakened from its slumber.

The thread grew more radiant each second, cutting her hands, joined in prayer, in half. It warmed where it stretched. Bright on her brown skin.

An enchanting, dazzling light.

Its rising rays beamed down on her. A golden smile. Shimmering on each criss-crossed crease on her palm. Erasing every wayward line. Washing away that tainted touch seared beneath her skin, palms long since weighed down by what she had endured.

The light pushed past night watchmen making their way home. Past rickshaw drivers preparing for the school run. Past closed-eyed mothers pulling children through front doors. Past market vendors arranging their produce. Past strolling fishermen eager to cast their nets. Past farmers trudging through paddy fields. Past the green and red flags waving in the wind, rejoicing at a land they called their own. Until the town was bathed in light and blared with life, and the smell of jasmines rose in the air, seduced by the persuasions of the warm sun-baked winds, the same as those that filled her hands when she was a child.

The shackles of a darker time cut loose by the white thread of dawn.

AUTHOR'S NOTE

The last line of this novel came to me first. It was inspired by a powerful and devastating photograph, taken by Naibuddin Ahmed, of a college girl freed by the Mukti Bahini from a Pakistan Army camp. I looked to her for years. Her long hair, her saree covering her head partway. Her fisted hands held before her in defence, the bangles on her wrists, which spoke more of her experiences than they should have.

Almost ten years ago, while I was searching for both primary and secondary sources for my undergraduate English Literature dissertation on the birangona women—women who were raped by the Pakistan Army during the Bangladesh Liberation War of 1971—and found only snippets of fictional mentions in novels, sparse translations that I could hardly use, and a handful of academic papers, I became aggrieved. In my disillusionment that so little of my country's history and its women had been recorded and translated to the world, my thesis became a source of sorrow and existential contemplation rather than academic enquiry and collation. I put off writing it for years. Then, one afternoon, as if my subconscious were gifting me with what my research could not, a scene of two sisters running through the bushes, away from enemy soldiers, flashed before my mind and remained with me all through the following decade. It was lucid and green and full of a haunting emotion. It followed me, reminding me of its importance. Its terror. Its humanity. Its love for the other.

Initially, I thought I needed to do a PhD on the women of the war, so I could make accessible to the world what felt vital to me and the history of my people. But I quickly realised academia wasn't the medium I needed. It didn't have the heart and soul, the words for love and life that I knew of my people and our homes. I wanted to read about families, women, sisterhood, friendship, about loss, love, renewal and redemption—about humanity. As time went on and the scene grew more vivid, I found in Toni Morrison's words the only true option I had: 'If there's a book that you want to read, but it hasn't been written yet, then you must write it.' Though I had no fiction-writing ability, I felt this story. So, I submitted the first piece of creative writing I had ever written to competitions in hopes of making the story exist. And nine months later, mirroring the length of the war itself, I was given a chance to write something new.

Many parts of the women's stories in this novel have been inspired by testimonies and histories collected by academics and social workers in Bangladesh and beyond, some directly after the war, from the rehabilitation centres created in 1972, and some through interviews many decades later. These include Dr Nilima Ibrahim's *War Heroines Speak*, the first chronicle of the unheard voices of the women taken during the war; the collection of testimonials in *Rising from the Ashes: Women's Narratives of 1971*, edited by Shaheen Akhtar; Akhtar's *The Search*, the only novel in translation that I found centring the women; Leesa Gazi's documentary *Rising Silence*; Yasmin Saikia's volume *Women, War and the Making of Bangladesh: Remembering 1971*; and Nayanika Mookherjee's *The Spectral Wound* and graphic novel with Najmun Nahar Keya, *Birangona: Towards Ethical Testimonies of Sexual Violence during Conflict*. Through it all, my wonderful mother laboriously translated works for me which I could not access otherwise. I also took inspiration from stories told to me by those who had been young women and men during that time, and those whose families had passed down their memories, which they kept safe.

The development of this novel has been a collaborative process with my phenomenal editor, Farhaana Arefin, who helped organise and refine my scattered ideas and bolstered encouragement when I grew afraid at my own limitations to do this story justice. I didn't allow anyone else to read this novel until we were well into the final touches of the publication process. I couldn't risk the dilution of my intention and vision, and what I had learnt to be truth, by the differing sensibilities and values of others. I didn't want anyone to ask me why I would even write a novel like this while ignoring the accompanying question: why hadn't they read anything like this before? So, any flaws you may find in this novel are entirely my own.

The testimonies of these women are neither a unique nor an exclusive experience. Across the world, in almost every war and conflict, women are raped en masse as a strategy of military domination. From Bangladesh to Rwanda to Bosnia and beyond, women have not been able to escape the depraved machinations of war, though they are silenced afterwards by enemy and ally alike, and the horrors they faced go unrecognised.

Hundreds of thousands of women were raped during the Bangladesh Liberation War of 1971. Though the women were given the title of 'birangona', literally meaning 'brave woman', signifying 'war heroine', by the new government shortly after the war, only few had access to the rehabilitation centres which offered treatment—including abortions and international adoption programmes for their babies—or received any money or vocational training that was promised through government schemes to help them restart their lives. Mostly, they were forgotten and shunned by society, and to this day little has been done to afford them recognition or provide them with social, economic or psychological support.

At the moment I write this, Bangladesh is at a crossroads. The student revolution of July 2024 has ousted an authoritarian dictatorship and the country sits in an interim period, distrustful of power and hopeful for renewal. Time and again, the repressive former regime conjured memories of the Liberation War and its heroes and villains for political ends, casting accusatory fingers against its opponents to brand them traitorous and evil. Simplistic narratives from an officially backed representation of the war were used to submerge and forget memories of its brutalised women while chastising a majority population never implicated in the war, inscribing onto that complex and contentious site further violence and power. Under the numerous governments that have come and gone since 1971, the women themselves have remained marginalised—taboo tales within a skewed official narrative that commemorates leaders, campaigns and combat strategies in national history and museums while leaving the women out of public collective memory.

By privileging the voices of these women, I hope to enter conversation with those who value sharing space with multiple narratives of war and its people—narratives where women are acknowledged beyond a few lines of prose or the footnotes and appendices of history books. I hope to earnestly explore the deep pain of these unfamiliar heroes, the violence they suffered without ever having their needs met by confidants or by governments. Against societal systems designed to supress and hide their memories, I hope to finally turn the narrative back to their humanity, resilience and heart. To stories of women, nation and history filled with endurance, goodness and compassion. Their lives represented not just as victim, casualty, cipher or estimation, but as fighter, activist, carer, mother, daughter, sister, woman, girl, flesh and blood and human soul. Friends and lovers. Dreamers and thinkers. Architects of family and community.

ACKNOWLEDGEMENTS

I am immeasurably grateful to my publisher, Hajar Press, and MFest, who hosted the Short Story Competition in 2021 and gave this story the perfect home to become something more.

My deepest thanks to my brilliant editor, Farhaana Arefin, without whose endless kindness, patience and compassionate insight this novel would not be what it is today. Her collaboration, conversations and belief in this work have been invaluable.

Brekhna Aftab, Jade Chao and Shibanee Sivanayagam, who helped send this book out to the world. Han Gunji Stephens, the cover designer, for this beautiful piece of art.

Syed Manzoorul Islam, great-grand-uncle, whose gift and guidance guaranteed a win! Saira and Jahara Kamaly, cousin confidants, whose trust and support I am beyond lucky to have. Hanna-Johara Dokal, beloved friend, who told me about the competition and made sure I entered, and whose encouragement has sustained me until now. KQ, QS, SM, NR, FH, KM, MB, whose light and friendship were what I needed.

To my joyful and generous family in Bangladesh, the UK and across the world who never stopped asking when the novel would be out, here it is!

To my wise and wonderful parents who created space for me to dream, thank you.

To those beautiful women who shared their stories with me, I am honoured.

To the Giver of Gifts, alhamdulillah.